A WILDERNESS OF MIRRORS

Fisher had landed at Heathrow two days later and Hallam had met him. He used one of the security offices at the airport to brief him. The photograph, the description of the girl and the date of the planned trip to see her father. He could even give her father's address in East Berlin and a rough description of him.

Fisher had listened without questions until Hallam had finished. He asked only two questions.

'How soon shall I know her actual travel arrangements?'

'I'm not sure. Probably some time in the next week.'

'And what sort of outcry will there be when she disappears?'

'In public, nothing. But the KGB and the East Germans will be mounting a full-scale search for her as soon as she doesn't turn up at her father's place.'

'There's a flight back to Hamburg in an hour's time. Do you need me any more?'

'No. Get your seat booked and we'll go and have a meal and a drink in the restaurant.'

'I don't need it.' Fisher stood up. 'I'll wait for you to contact me. See you.'

A Wilderness
of Mirrors

Ted Allbeury

NEW ENGLISH LIBRARY
Hodder and Stoughton

First published in Great Britain in 1988 by New English Library hardbacks

First New English Library paperback edition 1989

British Library C.I.P.

Allbeury, Ted, *1917–*
A wilderness of mirrors.
I. Title
823'.914   [F]

ISBN 0-450-50814-5

Printed and bound in Great Britain for Hodder and Stoughton paperbacks, a division of Hodder and Stoughton Ltd., Mill Road, Dunton Green, Sevenoaks, Kent TN13 2YA (Editorial Office: 47 Bedford Square, London WC1B 3DP) by Cox & Wyman., Reading.

In the first few months after the German surrender, I was occupied with tracing, arresting and interrogating people who were suspected of having been involved in war crimes. Suspects wanted by 21 Army Group, the security services, or for trial at Nuremberg. The list was enormous and the deep interrogation camps were bursting at the seams.

So without anybody's permission or agreement I decided to institute my own criteria for arrests. After careful interrogation, did I really feel that the man or woman deserved to go in the bag? If I thought not, they were put on parole and left to get on with their lives.

A Wilderness of Mirrors is about an SIS officer who is efficient, loyal and patriotic, who is ordered by London to carry out the kidnapping of a girl from the other side of the Wall. When the operation collapses and he finds out what his superiors expect him to do with the girl, he decides that their solution is unfair and unjust. As I did, way back, he decides to make his own rules for the game. And that decision is to affect the rest of his life as his unauthorised involvement becomes more and more complex.

The story is set in Berlin, the Soviet Union, the United States and Britain, and it is essentially the story of what can happen when a good man decides to ignore the rules of the game.

Acknowledgements

The extract from a poem on page 135 is by Alexander Galich, published by André Deutsch and Doubleday & Company Inc. © 1976 and Coronet © 1977.

We are at the stake,
And bay'd about with many enemies;
And some that smile have in their hearts, I fear,
Millions of mischiefs.

Shakespeare: *Julius Caesar*

CHAPTER 1

The Washington to London Concorde flight was only half full and Thornton put his bag on the vacant seat beside him. He wondered why Facilities at the embassy had booked him a Concorde flight. He was at least a grade too low to warrant that luxury. Maybe it was to soften him up for when he filed his report. There was an annual security check on the embassy and its staff. It checked for all the routine things. Document security, code security, radio security, bugs and procedures. And whoever did it was loathed from the moment he arrived. But at least for one week in the year the embassy was very security-conscious.

But SIS had taken to sending somebody across unannounced once in a while. Somebody who was ostensibly Foreign Office with some spurious low-key assignment as his cover. And that assignment was to look at people, not routines or hardware. Which was what he'd been doing for the last month. Looking at people. Like a lioness watching a herd of grazing gazelle after making a kill. No danger to anyone. Asking no leading questions, just listening and observing. But while you were listening you looked at their eyes and their hands and their feet. Those silent tellers of tales that so often said much more than the words.

Despite his years in SIS it still amazed him. The antics that people got up to. And these weren't the odd-balls of the complex, shifting world of espionage, but diplomats. They weren't even foreigners. They were true-blue Brits. Or at least they were supposed to be. But there they were, all of them looking so normal on the outside, but inside, the turmoil of the minds that drove them to risk careers and even lives for the gratification of some hidden desire. Sex, money, power, recognition, and sometimes, even, love. The more formal their jobs and the more senior their status the more surprising their weaknesses. But fashions in sin, and its acceptability to

9

authority, had moved on from the old days. There were even official classifications now for homosexuality. Classifications that ranged from instant dismissal, through the need for warnings, to what seemed to be almost tacit approval. Fiscal dishonesty too had its own league-tables of tolerance. Transvestism no longer called for more than a reference in a 'P' file. Ambition when it was too overt or ruthless could be dealt with easily enough by inferior postings and pointed passing-over for promotion. But, thank God, SIS's remit covered only the discovery not the retribution, unless there was an obvious top-level security risk involved. And even then it could be legitimately fobbed off onto MI5.

He leaned back in his seat and closed his eyes. He'd called the flat before he left but there had been no reply. Maybe she'd been too busy to move in yet. Or maybe she'd decided that her place was better for them both. Dear Penny Lambert, instant decision-maker and instant changer-of-mind. He tried not to think that maybe she had eventually decided that twelve years difference in age really was too much. He had mentioned it several times but she had just frowned, waving her arm dismissively as she went on talking about the iniquities of agents and stage-managers. But she had never actually *said* that it didn't matter.

Thornton looked at his watch to recall what day it was. It was Thursday. One of the first things he must do was phone Elaine about having Jamie on Saturday. Maybe for once she'd do the decent thing and let him have him on Sunday as well as he'd been away for five weekends. Not that Elaine had ever been one for doing the decent thing.

He wondered how she got on with Arthur Padstow. Did she still get up to the same old games or was she having to toe the line? Arthur Padstow, merchant banker and investment advisor, hadn't made his quick pile by being a soft touch. And Elaine hadn't been the first by a long way. The others that he knew of from gossip and the newspapers had been out of the same mould. Cool, Swedish-type blondes with long legs and all the trimmings. When she had told him that she was marrying Padstow he'd checked his personal file. A perk that was frowned on by one and all, but a universally indulged privilege all the same.

There was nothing of any great interest on the file. Suspicions of moving funds out of the UK when that wasn't legal. Some queries about a tangle of holding companies in tax havens. The kind of stuff that few people could understand and that usually ended up in the back pages of *Private Eye*. He guessed that anyone who understood it knew about it already. There were a couple of cuttings from copies of *Private Eye* referring to Padstow's 'Ugandan' discussions with an heiress, a rich Arab's divorced wife and a gossip-column girl, with the hint that those relationships might have stopped him from getting the knighthood he so obviously and desperately wanted.

When they landed at Heathrow Thornton waited for his two bags to come round the carousel. The service for Concorde passengers had priority and a few minutes later he walked across to Immigration. The man at the desk obviously recognised the coded passport number and smiled and nodded as he handed it back. He picked up his bags, found a trolley and headed through the green customs area. Outside the terminal building he instinctively let the first two taxis go and got into the third, giving Queensway as his destination. He paid off the driver a couple of streets before his own.

The sun was still shining but the lights were already on in Queensway. It reminded him of some of the streets in Lower East Side below Houston Street, east of the Bowery. Queensway was brash and garish; it stank of curry and chips but it was warm and alive. Queensway had character. Not necessarily good character but it was full of vitality, a village where the inhabitants belonged.

At the top of the stairs he put down his bags and fumbled for his keys. As he pushed open the door and reached for his bags he saw her standing there, smiling. He'd tried not to expect her to be there. It didn't pay to count on people doing what you wanted them to do. For a moment he was lost for words. Some girls would have been hurt or offended at the lack of response but Penny Lambert knew her man too well to feel anything other than pleasure at seeing him back, and a fleeting moment of anger at the people who had left him so insecure.

She laughed softly. 'Don't just stand there gawping. Come on in, you eejit.' And then her arms went round him and she kissed him. Not passionately. More like a mother welcoming her child home from school.

'What was Concorde like?'

'It's lovely to see you, Penny.' He paused. 'How did you know I was on Concorde?'

'Some chap rang from your office. He told me. Wants you to phone him . . .' she laughed, '. . . at your earliest convenience . . . I told him that that was the one next to the pub.'

He smiled and looked around the room. 'It's nice to be back, honey.'

'Honey . . . sounds interesting. Who was the lucky lady who taught you that?'

'You've painted all the walls.' He laughed. 'White.'

'Yes. I thought you were right after all. Cheaper than Laura Ashley wallpaper anyway. Sit down and I'll make you some tea.'

There was no door to the tiny kitchen and she stood leaning against the opening as she waited for the water to boil. He turned to look at her.

'Tell me what you've been doing while I was away.'

'Oh, a couple of long weekends with Robert Redford. Parties most nights.' She grinned. 'Nothing special.'

'I meant work.'

'Oh, work. Well, *Good Time Girl* folded after three weeks. I got a TV commercial for a toilet soap. Two voice-overs – one for a building society – all Manchester and sincerity.' She shrugged. 'I've had two auditions for a new musical called *Roses All the Way*. I auditioned for the principal juvenile but I suspect they'll only offer me chorus and understudy.'

'Who was the guy who phoned?'

'I think he said his name was Alan. The number's on the card on the mantelpiece.'

Thornton looked at the scrawl on the card. The number was the duty officer's number at Century House.

When they were drinking their tea he said quietly, 'Are you staying, Penny?'

'Of course I am.'

'I'm glad.'

She watched him as he sipped his tea. He wasn't handsome but he was definitely attractive. The big brown spaniel's eyes

12

belied the strong jaw and the muscles at each side of his determined mouth. But the real strength was an inner strength that sometimes bordered on aloofness. She often wondered if it was the desperately unhappy childhood or his job that had made him like that. She had come to accept that despite all that closed-in defensiveness he genuinely cared about her and their relationship. Perhaps one day she might penetrate that protective fortress but until then she was happy to be friend, mother and lover.

He put down his cup. 'I'd better phone the office.'

He dialled the number, and it gave only two rings before it was answered.

'Can I help you?'

'It's Thornton. I got a message to ring somebody named Alan. D'you know who he is?'

'Is that first-name or surname?'

'I've no idea.'

'Let me check the list. I won't be a moment.'

Thornton heard the rustle of pages being turned and then, 'Mr Thornton?'

'Yes.'

'There's a message here for you. It's not Alan, it's Mr Hallam. He'd like you to contact him as soon as possible.'

'OK. Thanks.'

'Have you got his number?'

'Yes – thank you.'

When he hung up she said, 'Did they keep you busy in Washington?'

He nodded. 'Yes.'

'What were you doing?'

He smiled. 'Just counting the pencils and checking the carbon paper.'

It was late evening when he rang Hallam's number but there was no reply. Hallam was a department head but Thornton hadn't worked with him for a couple of years. Thornton wasn't sure what Hallam was responsible for now. He had been CIA liaison when Thornton had previously worked for him. He liked Hallam.

It was just after ten the next morning when Hallam rang.

13

'A good flight?'

'Yes, thank you, sir.'

'You're due leave aren't you?'

'Ten days.'

'Have you got anything planned?'

'No.'

'Would you be willing to postpone your leave? I've got something I'd like you to do.'

'UK or overseas, sir?'

'UK so far as I know.'

'OK. When do you want to brief me?'

'There's a small semi-official committee involved. I could get them together about two if that's convenient for you.'

'Right, sir. I'll be there.'

Hallam was waiting for him by the entrance to Century House and he took Thornton's arm, steering him towards a waiting taxi.

'I thought we'd get away from this place and I've arranged for the others to be at Ebury Street – the safe-house.'

As they climbed in the back of the taxi Hallam nodded to the driver and Thornton realised that this must be one of the SIS cabs used by the surveillance teams.

Ten minutes later they were at the safe-house and Hallam opened the street door with an old-fashioned key. Inside was another door, a metal door, and a TV monitor above it purred softly as it worked on auto-focus, moving slowly as it covered them both from head to foot. When a red light glowed Hallam pressed the button and the door opened smoothly and silently, closing with a solid 'clunk' when they had both passed over the metal grid under the carpet. The rest of the small town-house was no different in layout and style from any other small house in the street. A narrow flight of stairs and a small landing where a plain-clothes man sat on a wooden bench opposite one of the solid doors.

'Good afternoon, Rogers. Which room are they in?'

'Number seven, sir.'

Hallam turned left and opened the door facing them and Thornton followed him.

There were three men sitting in armchairs around a low

circular coffee table and the remnants of snacks and half-filled glasses. He had seen them all at various times at HQ but he only remembered Clayton's name.

Hallam waved his arm at the others. 'Mr Seymour, Professor Clayton and Mr Macleod. This is Thornton. Do sit down, Mr Thornton.'

He found himself looking at the four men as if they were suspects. Macleod with his pale, round moon face, beads of sweat on his upper lip. Pushing his glasses back up his nose again and again. Seymour with the unruly blond hair and the open schoolboy face but his hands clasped so tightly that the knuckles were white. Clayton, 'The Prof', and a genuine professor. Now in his sixties, Professor Emeritus of St Antony's College, an acknowledged expert on Soviet affairs. Lean, with a gaunt, haggard face he sat unmoving except for a vein pulsing by his left eye. And Hallam. Hallam had played lock for London Scottish and the Barbarians, and looked like it. Tall, about fifteen or sixteen stone and bald at the front. He came from a wealthy family and had been recruited into SIS from one of the merchant banks. Amiable, tough and shrewd, he had good connections throughout SIS and the Foreign Office.

Hallam sat down, leaning forward, his elbows on his thighs, his big hands hanging loosely.

'We've got a small problem, Thornton. An internal problem.' He paused. 'One of our senior field officers has gone missing. And we've no idea why. We've looked at all the usual reasons. Money problems, women, mental breakdown – even defecting – but we're all quite convinced that it's none of those.' Hallam glanced towards the window for a moment and then back at his hands. 'The four of us all know him pretty well and obviously we're very concerned. Concerned on two counts. First of all for the man himself and then, of course, there's the official aspect. You can imagine what it would be like if the press got hold of this.' Hallam shrugged slightly uncomfortably. 'We've not made it official even inside SIS as yet. He's been posted as on accumulated long leave.' Hallam paused and looked directly at Thornton. 'We'd like you to find him.'

'Who is he?'

'David Fisher. Do you know him?'

'I think he gave a talk to a refresher course I was on. He'd just come from Berlin.'

'That sounds possible. Is that the only time you met him?'

'Yes. But I've heard his name mentioned from time to time. Or seen it in summaries.'

Macleod said softly, 'When you say you heard his name mentioned, in what context was it mentioned?'

'Promotion I think. Something routine.' Thornton turned back to Hallam. 'How do you want me to tackle this, sir? Can I choose my own team?'

'I'm afraid there won't be any team. It will have to be a solo effort – at least in the beginning – if you make some progress we can think again.'

'Wouldn't it be easier to pass it to Five or Special Branch?'

Thornton noticed Hallam's raised eyebrows and realised that his question was tactless. If Hallam wanted it this way it was not because he hadn't been aware of the alternatives.

'I don't think so. First of all he may not be in the UK and secondly . . .' he shrugged, '. . . we don't particularly want to advertise to all and sundry that one of our senior men has disappeared.' He paused. 'Even in the organisation you've got to keep up the cover that he's only on extended leave. Do you understand that?'

'Yes, sir.'

'You can call on the advice or knowledge of any of the four of us here but that is as far as you can go. Use the records. Anything you like but nothing more.'

'When do you want me to start?'

'If you're willing to postpone your leave I should like you to start right away. You can have one of the offices on the ninth floor.'

'What if I'm asked what I'm working on?'

'Refer whoever asks to me and say nothing.'

'Right, sir. Well, I'd better get moving.' Thornton stood up and when nobody responded he headed for the door. As he opened it Hallam called out, 'I'll phone through instructions about allocating you a room. See my girl when you get back to the office.'

CHAPTER 2

The main road to the coast was known locally as the LaHonda Road. It came off the freeway at Woodside then through LaHonda and on to the coast road at San Gregorio. It was seldom overcrowded with vehicles as it served no purpose other than linking the two towns on its route to the coast.

The white Cadillac turned off the main road a couple of miles before San Gregorio down a narrow metalled road and then turned left between two gateposts and along a rough track to a large ranch-style house. The Spanish-style arches and windows fitted the sandy setting with its yuccas and cacti and the bougainvillaea that billowed over and across its red-tiled roof.

The two men who got out of the car were casually but stylishly dressed and they talked animatedly as they walked to the open doors in the shade of the porch.

The tall man was the younger of the two. In his middle thirties. Tanned and well built he looked more like a lifeguard from one of the beaches than what he actually was – a neurologist. The shorter man looked more like a doctor than his companion but in fact he was fashion-buyer for a quite large department store in Los Angeles. At least that was what he had been until a few months ago. It was his fortieth birthday that day and they'd had lunch together in Palo Alto at Café Maroc.

The younger man received his monthly pay-cheque direct from CIA HQ at Langley and the older man got his from a company called Field and Jones Enterprises which was wholly owned by the CIA, and the cheque came from a bank also entirely owned by the CIA. The staff at the house were all CIA employees and the house itself was on long lease to the State Department.

The neurologist was Adam Siwicki and he had been recruited into the CIA from Johns Hopkins. He had not been keen to join until he had been told in confidence what his brief

17

would be if he made the move. He was aware from the start that his research would be both tentative and esoteric so far as the CIA was concerned. But what they offered was the neurologists' equivalent of the keys to Fort Knox. There had been continuous interest but no pressure. The funding was modest but the programme was not cash-intensive. The costs appeared in the CIA's internal budget applied to Operation Aeolus. A code-name not thought up by some deviously minded Greek scholar in CIA Accounting but what the computer happened to throw up from its list of thousands of code-names that could be used for any project.

The older man, Paul Martinez, had been making just over $34,000 a year from salary and bonus as fashion-buyer for an upmarket store. He had a flair for choosing the kind of clothes that would appeal to wealthy women of all ages. He had never married and that, combined with his obvious charm, had sometimes worried the two men who owned the store. In fact they had no cause for concern, Paul Martinez had no homosexual leanings. He just happened to be naturally charming and had decided that he had no taste for the responsibilities that went with marriage and a family.

He had always been much in demand at parties and fund-raising events as a fortune-teller. A description he detested. He neither read palms nor tarot cards nor did he peer into crystal balls. He just held the people's hands and talked about their past and present lives with remarkable accuracy. What impressed people most was that while he was talking his eyes were always closed. Never once did he look at their faces for a tell-tale reaction that might indicate if what he said was on target or not.

When he once suggested not only that a woman's husband was going to die very soon but described the circumstances and gave a detailed description of the location it had caused a minor sensation in the local press. When the woman returned home late that night she had discovered the dead body of her husband, killed as Paul Martinez had foretold and in a room that substantially resembled the location he had described.

He had been interviewed by the police a dozen times but he had nothing to tell them. He had told the woman what he had seen in his mind. He had not even known the woman's name, her circumstances or where she lived. There was no point in the police pressing him further. It had been clearly established that at the time the man had been killed Paul Martinez was nearly two hundred miles away in Pasadena with an audience of thirty or forty members of a local arts club. A small follow-up piece had appeared in the *Los Angeles Times* and it was that item that had been passed to Adam Siwicki.

A chain of three people had led discreetly to a meeting between the two. Martinez' background had already been checked out and there were no security problems there. Siwicki had told Martinez that he was interested professionally in his psychic powers and Martinez had seemed delighted to have met a scientist who didn't immediately assume that he was a fraud.

For two or three meetings it had been low-key. Social chit-chat and Siwicki telling Martinez about controlled scientific tests in several countries that had convinced the scientists concerned that psychic insight actually did occur under the most stringently controlled conditions. Slowly they arrived at a relationship that allowed Siwicki to suggest that they cooperate in the cause of psychic research.

After two months of cooperation Siwicki knew that he had found what Langley wanted. He had been authorised to take the next step and reveal that he was employed by one of the United States' intelligence organisations and Martinez would be performing a real service to his country if they could use him on more specific problems.

That was the danger point in their relationship, a test not of Siwicki's scientific skills but of his efforts to build up such confidence in him that Martinez would agree.

Martinez asked for time to think about it and after two or three inconclusive meetings Siwicki arranged one weekend to take Martinez to meet senior people at Langley. The respect shown to him and the seniority of the people who talked with him had swung the balance. They had offered to put him on the CIA's payroll and give him the status of an officer but Martinez had declined to go that far. He would do it on a temporary basis for six months and see how it worked out.

Operation Aeolus had only been mounted originally because frequent reports had come back that similar experiments were

19

taking place in Bulgaria and the Soviet Union. Nobody senior expected anything from it. It was a 'me-too' operation that at least provided some insurance for the top-brass against being accused at some future time of letting the Russians gain knowledge, however negative it might be, that the United States didn't have.

Chapter 3

Thornton was just dialling Elaine's number when Penny walked in. He put the phone back on its cradle.

'Hi. I was just going to phone Elaine about having Jamie at the weekend.'

'Good. I'll put the kettle on.'

'What happened at the theatre today?'

She grinned. 'I got it. Principal juvenile and two good songs.'

'Marvellous. Well done.'

'And full Equity rates for rehearsals.'

'Great. Congratulations. We'll eat out to celebrate.'

'OK. You do your phoning.'

He picked up the phone and dialled the number. A woman's voice with an Irish accent answered.

'The Padstow residence. Can I help you?'

'Is Elaine there? Mrs Padstow.'

'Who shall I say is calling?'

'Robert. Robert Thornton.'

'Just a moment.'

He heard the recognition of his name in the woman's voice. She'd obviously heard his name before, and he wondered what she'd been told. Then Elaine came on, using her Deborah Kerr voice.

'Elaine Padstow here.'

'It's Robert, Elaine. I was ringing to fix up about having Jamie on Saturday.'

'Good grief. You really have got a nerve.'

'I don't understand. What are you on about?'

'I don't know about "on about". I'm suggesting that when he's not seen hide nor hair of you for five or six weeks you've got a bloody nerve to come bursting in with a demand to see him.'

'It's not a demand, Elaine. It was laid down by the court. Saturday or Sunday alternate weekends.'

21

'Why the sudden interest?'

'It isn't sudden. I've been overseas. I told you that I'd be away. I told Jamie too. And I've written to him every week.'

'You call a couple of postcards writing to him?'

'Look, Elaine. I don't want to get into an argument with you. I just want to make arrangements to pick up Jamie on Saturday.'

'I'm afraid that's impossible. He's going with his father to the races.'

'Don't play silly buggers, Elaine. *I'm* his father and I want to see him on Saturday.'

'Arthur wouldn't agree. He's very fond of Jamie, you know. He couldn't bear to disappoint him.'

'Elaine, if you refuse to let me have him Saturday or Sunday then I shall get my chap to go back to the courts on the grounds that you are denying access.'

'You do that, little man.'

And she hung up the phone.

He looked around for Penny. She was standing behind him, hands on hips.

'What was that stupid bitch up to this time?'

'Says that Padstow is taking him to the races on Saturday. She calls him his father.'

She walked round him and sat in the other chair facing him. She reached out and put her hand on his knee.

'Can I give you some advice, Robbie?'

He sighed. 'I guess so.'

'The more you fight with her the more she enjoys it. It's the only hold she's got on you now. You've got the court order giving you access but you can't keep going back to court every time she plays you up and claim that she's being deliberately vindictive. She'd make it all sound terribly difficult to fit in with your trips abroad or her married life. Judges are well aware that it goes on but it's impossible to prove it.'

'So what do I do – let her get away with it?'

'Actually that is one way. If you showed no interest in Jamie she'd be on that phone in a couple of months. But that's not what I was going to suggest.'

'Tell me.'

'Let me speak to Charlie Springett.'

'Who's he?'

'The diary journalist I introduced you to. Red hair and freckles. The Fats Waller fanatic.'

'Why him?'

'The one thing that madam won't want is to cause some scandal that affects Arthur Padstow. A diary piece hinting at her spite to her former husband wouldn't go down very well with his social circle.'

'I doubt if a paper would print it. It's of no interest to the public.'

'It doesn't have to be printed. All Charlie has to do is ring up Padstow and say he's investigating a story about him and his wife trying to prevent her son seeing his father. Is it true et cetera?'

'He'd just say it was a pack of lies.'

'Of course he would but he'd read her the Riot Act to make sure it didn't happen again.'

Thornton looked at her. 'Maybe we ought to swap jobs.' He paused. 'Would Charlie do it?'

'Of course he would.'

'Let me think about it.'

'OK.' She smiled. 'Don't let them get you down, Robbie.'

He sighed and smiled. 'Let's go and eat. Celebrate your latest success.'

CHAPTER 4

When the Red Army's tanks rolled into the rubble that had been Dresden there were few of the city's inhabitants who were pleased to see them. After the bombing that had virtually destroyed the city people were only just beginning to filter back, and the authorities were trying to organise the clearing of the rubble. The advent of the Russians was just one more element of Germany's defeat. Surviving was of more importance than whether they were ruled by Nazis or the Reds. But there were small groups of people who hated the other Occupying Powers enough to find the Russians more acceptable than the British or the Americans. There were a few individuals who found the Russian occupation of their city the best thing that had ever happened, a dream come true. One of these was Ilse Laufer. A dedicated member of the KPD, the German Communist Party. In April 1945 when Koniev's columns rolled into the city Ilse Laufer was twenty-eight.

The second day after the Russians had occupied Dresden Ilse Laufer had contacted the commissar at the derelict cottage that was then the HQ of a Red Army tank unit. Her party card and credentials had been examined carefully and she had eventually been given a privileged job in the Arbeitsamt that controlled all employment in the city and its rural surroundings.

Ilse Laufer lived a simple life despite her Party connections, and almost the only privilege she ever claimed was the education of her illegitimate daughter Anna.

Anna was a conscientious student and, scholarship in hand, she was transferred for her medical training to Moscow University. She stayed in Moscow for two further years on a post-graduate course and when she eventually returned to Dresden it was as a consultant neurologist at the city's main hospital.

Anna Laufer married Ernst Jaeger, one of her mother's old friends in the Party. He was twenty years older than she was when they married. She gave birth to their daughter a few months later.

Ursula Jaeger grew up to be neither like her mother nor her father. She was a dreamer, inattentive at school but much liked, and completely uninterested in politics. To say that her parents were disappointed in her would be quite untrue. She was a mystery to them but much loved. And she was beautiful too. Music, painting, poetry and novels were her pleasures. Those things and the countryside. She had no talent for any of them but she appreciated them all. In her teens she went for long walks in the countryside. They lived outside the city. When they asked her where she had been or what she had seen she just smiled and said she'd seen the sky and the clouds.

They found her jobs that might interest her. At a publisher's, at a small art gallery, as secretary to a local orchestra. And much as they all loved her they eventually had to confess that Ushi Jaeger was a delightful young woman but they saw no future for her with them.

There was no pressing need for her to earn money. Both her mother and her father, who was a paid Party official, earned good money and had all the privileges of housing and purchasing goods that went with being respected and long-established Party members.

When her mother had been offered a special research post in the Soviet Union she had accepted immediately. The prospect of a new challenge and the recognition of her skill and experience had been irresistible.

But for Ernst Jaeger it had no appeal. He had been ill at ease on their few trips to Moscow. He didn't speak any Russian, he didn't like the food and he was too confirmed in his ways to be able to compromise. Their life as a couple was platonic rather than romantic and he had no wish to stand in the way of her career. They talked it over calmly and sensibly and the Party had helped provide a satisfactory solution. She would take the new post and he would be transferred to East Berlin where he had lived before the war. And he would be upgraded to a post that would enable him to visit his wife from time to time at the State's expense. Their daughter would go with her mother.

Anna had regretted her impetuous acceptance of the new post when she was told in Moscow that her new work would be in Novosibirsk, in Siberia. Nobody, not even loyal Party members, wanted to be sent to Siberia, that harsh, cold, snow-bound region that was the punishment for dissidents and those who had offended the Party. It would be a grim enough life for her but impossible for her daughter.

But she made no protest and during the next few days various new acquaintances in medical and scientific circles assured her that Siberia was not as disagreeable as foreigners and untravelled Muscovites might think. But she still regretted her impulsive agreement to the move to the Soviet Union and the sale of the house. It had all seemed so convenient. New job, new environment and wider fields to conquer. But now, it all seemed a poor reward for her hard work and her loyalty to the Party.

Like most people outside the Soviet Union her impression of Siberia was of snow and pine forests and a primitive existence. An area bigger than the whole of Europe that nobody ever went to voluntarily and where many of the population were inmates of the state labour camps run by the Gulag organisation.

The day they left Moscow she was deeply depressed. The flight took six hours and it was mid-afternoon when they landed at Novosibirsk. They were met by an official car and a professor from the University, a man she liked immediately. He spoke good German, smiled a lot and assured her that she and her daughter were going to be very happy in their new home.

Her new home was literally new. Twenty miles south of Novosibirsk, on the River Ob, a whole new township was being built, a separate district called Akademgorodok, Science City. Set in a forest of birches and pines Akademgorodok was equipped with the finest facilities and staffed by some of the best brains in the Soviet Union.

The house they were allotted was spacious and well-furnished, with a maid and a cook provided. When they arrived the stove was already lit and the house was warm. And a meal was waiting for them. In the privacy of her bedroom Anna Jaeger sat down and wept with relief. Relief from her fears and depression. She knew right away that all was going to go well. The future was not going to be grey and stultifying.

After a few weeks she realised how lucky she was. All the technical and support facilities she needed for her work, and a better social life than they had ever had in Dresden. With the concentration of hundreds of bright minds and lively spirits went a freedom from the bureaucracies of Moscow. There was almost a holiday atmosphere generated by people who were doing advanced work in their various sciences, almost without restriction, encouraged to explore pure science rather than the practicalities of industry. Lively people who talked and argued into the night about their pet theories, and art and literature. It was more like Paris, Berlin or London than the Soviet Union. And, as in those cities, there were imported food, clothes and household goods all available to the privileged community.

It was a year later before she had to face her first problem. And the problem was Ushi. The head of Anna's section had called her to his office. He emphasised that it wasn't a formal complaint but it had been noticed that her daughter was not employed. And that was a situation that could cause problems. Everybody who was old enough had to be employed. She pointed out that Ushi had no qualifications and her Russian was elementary. He'd smiled and said that that didn't matter. As a matter of fact there was already a job she could do. A nice undemanding job. Looking after Professor Rykov, who was disorganised and very absent-minded. Just reminding him of meetings and so on. And Rykov spoke good German. There would be no problems.

She had agreed. She had no choice. She knew that. And it had all been done in a kindly way. They wanted to make it as easy as they could.

That night she told Ushi who, to her surprise, quite liked the idea. She said that she already knew Professor Rykov. She had met him when she was walking along the edge of the woods one day. They had talked about trees and he'd explained about how they counted the medullar rings and could tell from their colour and texture and spacing what the climate was like each year of their growth. All the way back for a hundred years or more. He had told her the Latin name for the birch trees – *Betula pendula* – and he'd told her about Sylvanus the Roman god of woodlands. He'd said she should write a poem to Sylvanus because she

27

liked the woods so much. Anna Jaeger had sighed a deep sigh of relief. Nothing was going to spoil their lives. Once again it had all fitted into place. So Ursula Jaeger became the personal assistant of Professor Rykov, Head of the Department of Noetic Sciences at Akademgorodok.

Chapter 5

Thornton picked up the key to Fisher's office when he collected Fisher's 'P' file. There may be nothing in it but it was worth a look even if it only gave him some impression of the man.

Fisher's office wasn't luxurious but it was well above average in size and furnishings and Thornton stood at the door for a moment taking it in. It looked ass though it had been cleared up and tidied. The walls were panelled in mahogany and the modern furniture was Swedish-style teak and chrome. At first glance there was a rolled umbrella in the standard issue hatstand and coat-rack. He put the 'P' file on the desk then walked back to the door and put on the catch before walking over to sit in the leather chair behind the desk.

There was a side table with six chairs round it, two leather club armchairs and a low glass coffee table, an empty china vase on the window sill and a photograph on the wall facing the desk. It was a portrait of a young woman. Very pretty with long blonde hair, big luminous eyes, a neat nose and wide mouth. There was a signature across the corner that was obviously the photographer's. The photograph was black and white and had the style and lighting that made it look vintage 1950 or thereabouts.

The standard A4 buff file in front of him on the desk had no title on the cover and when Thornton opened it there was a card inside with the names, addresses and telephone numbers of the four men on the committee. He closed the file, stood up and walked slowly to the window. You could just see the river. The sun was already lifting the early morning mist. He wondered when was the last time that Fisher had looked at that view. Did he know then that he was looking out for the last time? Had he been planning it for years or months or did something happen that made him go on the spur of the moment? One thing that he needed to know was the last time Fisher had been seen, and by whom. He took a new notebook from his briefcase, and a pen from his jacket pocket, and opened the file again. It was time to get on with the job.

The full name was David Beauclerc Fisher and he was born on the 24th October, 1935. Place of birth: Hawkhurst, Kent. Father's occupation: schoolteacher. Mother: housewife. State education at a local primary school and secondary education at a grammar school for boys in Tunbridge Wells. School Certificates in English, French, History, Religious Studies and Botany. B.A. from Durham.

He had been sent on a course at St Antony's College, Oxford and he had read Russian and German, with the History of the USSR as a subsidiary subject. Seconds in both languages and a pass in the subsidiary.

In 1957 at age twenty-two he had been recruited into SIS. He had been given a Grade 2 security clearance which had never been downgraded or rescinded, and there were no amendments at the biannual checks. He appeared to have spent short periods in most Western European countries but had subsequently been stationed permanently in Germany, both the Federal Republic and West Berlin. His wife had died nearly two years ago. And it passed through Thornton's mind that maybe that had upset Fisher more than his colleagues had realised. In their kind of business a wife could be a refuge from cynicism and disgust for the human race. A wife could also be the burden that broke a man's self-confidence.

There was a series of file reference numbers relating to his assignments and most of them were classified Top Secret. There were the usual annual assessments by controllers or directors which were as unrevealing as they were intended to be. But there were no negative assessments.

Half a page of typed reference numbers indicated other relevant files and a separate page gave the dates of his promotions, courses and pay scales.

He leaned back in the chair, his eyes closed as he thought about what he was doing. One thing was obvious. Despite what Hallam and the others had said he would make no progess until he could talk to all sorts of people about Fisher. They could suggest that he'd applied for early retirement and he was doing a check on how Fisher's current work would be affected. But he would do a bit of routine checking first, just to show willing.

Penny Lambert phoned him at four o'clock. The whole cast had now been chosen and there was to be a casting party at the theatre. It started at six and he was welcome if he'd care to come. He said he'd be there about six-thirty.

He found theatre people a pleasant change from the people he met in his work. He sometimes risked his life but theatre people risked themselves every night they were working. Begging and pleading for the approval of an audience. Like Penny they had guts but they were hampered by emotions. Emotions that were always near the surface. Hearts that were always on their sleeves. The camaraderie made them seem rather like soldiers on some special mission. The theatre itself bored him, but not the people.

The party was on the stage, and there were thirty or forty people there. Sainsbury's white wine and sausages. It took him nearly five minutes of threading his way through groups of laughing chattering people before he found Penny. She was with two men. A very young man who she introduced as the ASM and an older man, an actor he had met before. She got him a drink and three warm sausages and the conversation went back to the new production and its backers.

It seemed that *Roses All the Way* was going to be better than *Cats, 42nd Street* and *My Fair Lady* combined. There were the usual wild rumours that always went with new musicals that Wayne Sleep, Andrew Lloyd Webber, Elaine Page, Cary Grant and Gene Kelly might become involved. And there was talk of wealthy backers having to take their turn with the management to grab a stake in the certain winner. And Penny was not understudying, she was playing Rosie when young, the Cockney girl who made it to Drury Lane and Broadway.

As he stood listening to the enthusiastic chatter he remembered that he hadn't checked who had last seen Fisher. And he hadn't taken the elementary step of checking for any photographs of the missing man. Instinctively he reached into his jacket pocket for his notebook and then thought better of it.

They left half an hour later. Penny slid her arm into his as they sat back in the taxi. She had the usual euphoria that came from being chosen for a part and he took her to dinner at the Ivy to celebrate again.

Hallam was in a meeting when he phoned but he returned the call ten minutes later.

'I wanted to ask who first noticed that the person was missing?'

There was a pause and then Hallam said slowly, 'It was Mr Macleod who first raised it but Professor Clayton asked about him the same day.'

'How long ago was that?'

'Let's see – nine, no, ten days ago.'

'What made them notice that he wasn't around?'

'He had a date for a chess game with Mac and I think Clayton wanted to discuss something with him.'

'And who saw him last?'

'So far as we can tell it was me. I saw him waving down a taxi outside this place about five days before Mac asked about him.'

'Who spoke to him last about his work?'

'Again that was me and it was the day before the taxi incident.'

'What was the conversation about?'

There were several seconds of silence and then Hallam said, 'You'd better come across to my office.'

'Now?'

'Yes.' Hallam paused. 'On second thoughts I'll come over to you.'

Hallam was wearing the black jacket and pin-stripe trousers that went with his Foreign Office meetings. He took a pipe from his pocket and laid it on the desk in front of him.

He shrugged. 'The internal phones are supposed to be checked automatically but you never know.' He paused. 'About Fisher. Fisher was just back from a week in Berlin. He'd been negotiating the defection of an East German. The chap was a very senior man in Section II of the East German Secret Police, the MfS, working directly under the control of the KGB. We've had contacts with him for four years and it was planned for him to come over in about two or three months' time.'

'What's the position with him now?'

'We haven't told him that Fisher is missing because contacting him is extremely difficult and complex. Well nigh impossible without Fisher being involved.'

'What did you talk about that day?'

'The details of a new identity for the German and the level of financial support that we'd give him. I raised the question of his de-briefing when he came over and Fisher wanted to do it himself. There was no problem with that but I told him that I'd prefer to put a team on it so that we could speed things up.' Hallam shrugged. 'It was just the usual discussion that goes on when defections are in process.'

'Is there a file on the German?'

'Yes.'

'Can I see it?'

'No. Not at this stage anyway. I'm sure that it's not relevant anyway. It just happens to be what we discussed that particular day. Fisher was involved in a dozen other operations.'

'Can I see it if I find that it's necessary?'

'If you can convince me that it's necessary, yes. But the German's life is at risk. Bear that in mind.'

'Was he dealing with any other defections as well?'

'Yes. But it wasn't as far advanced as the Berlin job. It was a German from Leipzig. A scientist. A mathematician.'

'What else was he concerned with?'

Hallam looked at Thornton for a few moments before answering. 'We all seem to be slipping into the past tense a bit prematurely. He was mainly concerned with line-crossing networks into East Berlin and East Germany. But those are under control and not affected at this stage by him not being around.'

'If I don't find him what happens to the two defectors?'

Hallam sighed. 'Sufficient unto the day but I fear they would have to be abandoned.'

'Would that harm them?'

'No. Not so long as we keep a tight security clamp on at this end.'

'Did Fisher seem disturbed in any way?'

'No. He was his usual self. Cool, efficient, meticulous.'

'Did he have any friends at all, either inside or outside the organisation?'

Hallam sat as if his thoughts were far away and then he said, 'I can't speak for outside but inside I'd say no, no friends. He was inclined to be a loner. At one time I believe he and Macleod were quite close. But that seemed to fade away.'

'For any particular reason?'

'I don't think so. I never heard of any reason.'

'Who could I talk to who could give me an impression of what he was like as a man? Maybe somebody who didn't even know what his work was.'

'Let me think about it. Nobody comes to mind.'

'Could I speak to your wife about him?'

Hallam looked surprised. 'My wife? Why my wife?'

'You said the other day that he and his wife sometimes visited you.'

'I see.' He paused and shrugged. 'By all means. I'll tell her you might call her. But I doubt if . . . I must go.' Hallam stood up. 'Keep me in touch.'

CHAPTER 6

The gardener pointed the way to the patio at the back of the house, and as he approached a black and white spaniel came to investigate him. A woman came out of the French windows when the dog barked, and she was nothing like what he expected. She wasn't just pretty, she was beautiful. Tall and graceful, and smiling as she said, 'You must be William's friend, Robert Thornton.'

'Yes. I hope I'm not disturbing you.'

'Not at all. Would you like an orange juice? It's the real thing.'

'I'd like one very much.'

'Let's sit at the table.' She smiled. 'We mustn't waste the sun.'

As she poured the juice from a tall glass jug he realised that she had a slight accent and he vaguely remembered that someone had once said that she was Italian.

'Now, Robert Thornton, tell me what you want to know.'

'I wanted to ask you about David Fisher.'

'Ah yes. How is he?'

'He's quite well I think. He came here several times with his wife, Mr Hallam said.'

'I think it was only once – about six months ago.'

'What sort of man was he?'

'David? Oh a nice man. Very easy to entertain. Quite a charmer I always thought, although Bill used to laugh when I said so.'

'What did you talk about with him?'

'Languages. He was a very good linguist. I am originally Italian and his Italian was fluent. I think he also spoke French and German. What did we talk about?' She looked towards the garden and then looked back at him. 'We talked about music and books and painting. At least I did. I tried to persuade him of the virtues of Vivaldi and Tartini. He himself was very much the *cinquecento* man. There's an English name for it . . .' She shook her head frowning and then said, '. . . patrician, that's the word. He should have been a *grand seigneur* with servants and an estate. He would have been another Montaigne writing away in his ivory castle about ethics and *les philosophes*.'

'You liked him?'

'Oh yes. Any woman would like him and I think most men would too.' She laughed softly. 'Of course there would be men who were jealous too.'

'Why would they be jealous?'

She shrugged, elegantly. 'Because he was different. He was not what they call a man's man. More a thinking man. And a gentle man.' She laughed. 'Even that thing that today's Englishmen so detest – a gentleman.'

'And his wife?'

She thought for several moments. 'I would say a good balance for him. Understanding. Loving. More emotional than he was. Very attractive and much younger than him. Obviously adored him. They're a good pair.' She shrugged. 'Sadly no children. I think it was some infection she once had.'

She sat with her head slightly tilted as if she was waiting for his next question.

'Did Mr Hallam tell you why I wanted to talk to you about Mr Fisher?'

'I think he said it was something to do with his pension, was it not?'

'Did Fisher ever talk about what he would do when he retired?'

'Not seriously.' She smiled. 'He did say that one day he would like to live on the Ligurian coast. At Portofino or Santa Margherita. But he may have been saying that as a joke, or to please me because it is Italy.'

Thornton smiled. 'Would *you* prefer to live in Italy?'

'What a shrewd question so soon.' She closed her eyes for a moment before she answered. 'My William always tells me that truth is the best defence. So the answer is yes. I miss the sun. I miss the happy people. I miss the family gossip. And that terrible word – I miss the culture.'

'Does your husband know this?'

'Sometimes I wonder. He likes Italy and the Italians but he's very English, my man.' She laughed. 'You must know that already. For him the rain is Twickenham and the English all wear black and white Baa-baa scarves. The good English anyway. And equally important they do not pinch pretty girls' bottoms.'

'Thank you for talking to me, Mrs Hallam. It made a duty a pleasure.'

She smiled and nodded at the rather stilted gallantry.

He called in at a flower shop in Maidenhead and sent her a bunch of roses. And jotted the cost down at the back of his notebook to put on his expenses.

As he drove back to London he felt that he had learned more about Fisher in that brief conversation than in all the office discussions. Maybe there were other outsiders who could be more use than Fisher's colleagues. The combined information was contradictory in many respects but instinct told him that Mrs Hallam's picture of the man was the least prejudiced and the most accurate. Some time it might be worthwhile checking on whether Fisher's wife was dead or alive.

There was an envelope on his desk and a message on his pad. The message said that Miss P. Lambert had phoned and would phone again. The stiff brown official envelope was from Personnel in answer to his request. It contained two photographs, both black and white, of David B. Fisher.

When he phoned Hallam he told him that he could see him straightaway but only for ten minutes.

Hallam pointed to a chair. 'I understand you've already had a chat with Gabriella. Was it useful?'

'Very. That's what made me want to see you.'

Hallam leaned back in his chair. 'What is it?'

'My present brief is too restrictive. I need to be able to talk to a lot more people. People in SIS and people outside.'

'Go on.'

'That's it. There's nothing more.'

'I can understand your frustration but people would begin to put two and two together and we can't afford to let that happen.'

'I could have some cover story that makes it seem routine.'

'Like what?'

'We could say that I'm checking opinion for a possible promotion to Regional Director. I don't need to specify the region.'

Hallam smiled. 'That could cause a lot of fluttering in the present regional dovecotes.'

'I could imply that a new region was being created.'

'Tell me. Why haven't you interviewed the other three on the sub-committee? Only me. And that only very briefly.'

'I'd rather keep them in reserve until I've learned more about Fisher from people who were less involved with him. People who are disinterested. People who saw him as just a man rather than as a field agent.'

Hallam sighed, and his eyes went to the Karsh portrait of Churchill by the door. When he looked back at Thornton he said, 'You're sure you need this? Quite sure?'

'Yes.'

'OK. But make the promotion for something less specific. I'd suggest inter-region co-ordinator. Something that doesn't exist but has a vague air of possibility.' He opened a drawer in his desk and took out a labelled key. 'There's a duplicate of the key to Fisher's flat. The address is on the label.' He hesitated. 'Don't apply for a warrant. Understand?'

'Yes, sir.'

Thornton reached for the key, glanced at the label and slipped it into his jacket pocket as he stood up to leave.

'Maybe we gave a rather low profile to this operation when we briefed you. So let me just say that, in fact, it's not quite as routine as it looks. I'd like you to bear that in mind. I'd be prepared to give you one assistant if and when you felt it was necessary.'

'Thank you, sir. I'll see how it goes.'

Fisher's flat near Turnham Green underground station was the first floor of a converted Victorian house. There were two separate entrance doors side by side. The key turned easily and Thornton walked into the narrow hallway and up two flights of steep carpeted stairs. Outside the flat door was a clay pot that held a wilted geranium. Thornton pushed a finger at the soil. It was bone dry and as hard as cement.

Inside, the flat had the silent, stuffy warmth of rooms that had not been lived in for a long time. Longer than the time since Fisher had last been seen. The twin beds in the bedroom were made and the covers were over the pillows. The bedside tables on each side were empty and clean. The fitted wardrobes and a dressing table were empty too.

In the sitting room everything was spotlessly clean except for a thin layer of dust. There were two white rectangles and two hooks on one wall, and one white oval patch on the wallpaper over the fireplace where pictures had been taken down. There was a small desk but that too was empty as was the sideboard along one wall.

It was almost as if the room had been gone over by a professional team with a brief to leave absolutely nothing. And he was conscious of a strange aura of sadness about the place. As if it had been deserted by something more than just one human being. It seemed a stupid thought but he had sensed such feelings when looking over a room where a murder had been committed or someone had killed themselves.

He pulled the door to behind him and walked slowly down the stairs to the outside door. As he closed it behind him a woman opened the adjoining door. An elderly woman who walked unsteadily with the aid of an aluminium frame.

'Are you the new tenant, may I ask?'

'No ma'am. I'm just a friend of Mr Fisher.'

'It's a nice flat if you're interested. Both of them are.'

'Is it available?'

'I understood it was. I couldn't understand why it hadn't gone months ago.'

'You mean it's been vacant for several months?'

'Oh yes. Mr Fisher left here in . . .' she frowned, '. . . it must have been the end of April beginning of May.'

'Where did he move to?'

'I've no idea. He wasn't a man to gossip.' She hesitated. 'I thought you said you were a friend of theirs?'

'A very casual friend. You said a friend of theirs. But there was only Mr Fisher. Mrs Fisher died some time ago.'

The old lady put her hand to her mouth. Shock in her eyes. 'Oh my God. Bless her soul. What happened?'

'I don't really know.'

'When was this? When did it happen?'

'Several years ago. At least two years.'

The old lady put her hand to her chest, shaking her head. 'No. No. You've made some mistake. You're getting mixed up, young man. She didn't die. They were here until a few months ago. I think they said they were moving because of their work.' She smiled coyly. 'You've got it all mixed up.' She sighed deeply. 'She was such a nice girl. I'm glad we've got that straight. Dear oh dear. Thank heaven for that. It gave me quite a turn. Give them my regards when you see them. I'm Mrs Sewell. They'll remember me.'

'I will. I'd better leave you in peace.'

The old lady nodded and smiled as he turned to walk down the garden path to the street. He was almost at the gate when he heard her call out. When he turned she was beckoning to him to come back. As he approached she looked excited.

'I've just thought of something, young man. I saw her three weeks ago. I saw Mrs Fisher when I was in London.'

'Where did you see her?'

'In Harley Street. I'd just come out of the specialist's. He'd been checking my hip. The receptionist girl was looking out for a taxi for me. One stopped on the other side of the street. A woman got out. It was Mrs Fisher.'

'Are you sure you weren't mistaken?'

'No. My eyes are very good for my age. I saw her quite clearly while she was paying the cabbie. I waved to her but she didn't see me. She went into a block of flats and a wretched man got into the taxi and I had to wait another five minutes. And that's a long time with my poorly hip.'

'You're quite sure it was Mrs Fisher?'

'Oh yes. She was wearing her light coat. A beige colour with black lapels.' She laughed. 'Very smart it was.'

'Thanks very much for your time, Mrs Sewell.'

'You're welcome, young man. It's nice having someone to talk to for a change.'

Back at Century House Thornton went straight to Hallam's office and asked his secretary if Hallam could spare him a few minutes. She spoke to her boss on the internal phone and then told Thornton he could go in.

Hallam pointed at one of the visitor's chairs and as Thornton sat down he said, 'I'd like to ask for that help we talked about, sir. I definitely need it.'

'So soon?'

'Yes, sir. I need a lot of routine ferreting or it's going to take me months.'

'Tell me more.'

'I went to look over Fisher's flat today. It seems that he hasn't lived there for several months. I spoke to the old dear in the twin flat. The records say that Mrs Fisher died a couple of years ago. According to the neighbour she isn't dead. She saw her in town three weeks ago.'

Hallam was silent for several seconds and then he said very quietly, 'Where did they move to?'

'I've no idea. That's why I need routine help. Checking the records for deaths. There are a dozen routine things that can be checked if I had the facilities. There's something very wrong somewhere.'

'What makes you think that?'

'I know it, sir. Instinct, I suppose.'

Hallam sat silently for several minutes before he looked at Thornton again. 'There's a man named Smallwood. Tom Smallwood. He worked for some time for Fisher. He's attached to Alastair Macleod's staff at the moment. He's overdue for retirement but we gave him an extension. He's not what I'd call very creative. Not a thinker. But he's been at it for a long time. I'd let you have him for a few weeks to do your routine work if that would help.'

'It would, sir. Be a great help.'

'OK. I'll speak to Macleod. But don't start empire-building. I don't want this turned into a case. Or anything else official. You understand that, Thornton?'

'Yes, sir.'

Smallwood was waiting for him at the security check next morning. Thornton spent an hour telling him what he had done so far. When he had finished he said, 'You don't seem surprised, Mr Smallwood. Why not?'

'It's Tom, Mr Thornton, if that's OK with you.' He smiled. 'I'm not surprised because I've been around this business most of my life. There's never been a time when there wasn't some internal problem. It's normal. With all the people we've got all round the world doing the kinds of things we do it's not surprising that, when one problem's solved, another one starts up. If we investigated every rumour of suspect officers, breaches of security and a bit of double-dealing there'd be no time for anything else. The public think we're all James Bonds, the politicians think we spend all our time checking on them, and the media are ready to print every fairy story that makes us look inefficient so that it looks like the start of World War III.' He shrugged. 'So I'm not surprised.'

'Mr Hallam told me that you worked for Fisher for some time. What was he like?'

'Just the kind I'd expect to defect to the Soviets.' He grinned as he saw the shock on Thornton's face.

'Why do you think that?'

'Because if you look at his record, his life and his character it's impossible to imagine him as a defector. And I've always remembered something they taught us when I was doing my training way back. They said, "When you've looked at every possibility and got nowhere – start looking at the impossible."' Smallwood laughed softly. 'They call it lateral thinking nowadays.'

'Tell me about Fisher.'

'How long have I got?'

'As long as you need.'

'Well, professionally he was first-class. We were in Hamburg then and he was running a line-crossing network into East Germany. He kept the men's morale up and they got him all he asked for. Everything was well planned down to the last detail and the only cock-ups we had came from London wanting too much too quickly, over-riding his schedule. We had a very mixed bunch of agents but Fisher was good at getting into people's minds. He understood exactly what motivated each one of them. But above all they knew that they'd never be left in the lurch. Total loyalty was what he asked for and total loyalty was what he gave. The few who did get caught were got out no matter what it took. Money, blackmail, a deal – whatever it took, they were released.

'But there's the other side of the coin, of course. If you

understand people as well as he did, there's going to be a snag. Fisher's snag was that, despite the tough appearance, there was a soft spot deep inside him. A soft spot that came out as a loyalty to people who didn't deserve it. Agents who were careless because of worry about some domestic problem. Agents who cut corners to get back quicker to some little chick in Altona. If it was carelessness for any other reason then you'd be for the high jump but give him a human problem and you'd be forgiven.' Smallwood smiled. 'There shouldn't be any room for hearts and flowers on operations.'

'Did it ever damage operations?'

'No.' Smallwood shrugged. 'Not that I know of anyway. But if some bright spark in the KGB had spotted the weakness it could have cost a lot of people their lives.'

'Did you like him?'

'It was good working for him – but I don't believe in liking or disliking people in this business. We've all got a job to do and it's best just to get on with it.'

'I've made a list of things I'd like you to check. You can contact me here or at my flat when you're ready.'

'Have you talked with Macleod about Fisher?'

'No.'

'He's the one. They've known one another for years.'

'Were they close?'

'Hard to tell. My guess would be yes.' Smallwood paused. 'But you can be close and still not like each other. I wouldn't say they were mates.'

Smallwood had done a lot in two days. There was no record of the death of Fisher's wife in the past six years. And what was more surprising was that there was no record of a marriage. Thornton himself had checked that there was nothing about a new address in Fisher's 'P' file. His only address was the flat at Turnham Green and according to the neighbour he had left that some months ago.

Thornton looked at the record of payments to Fisher in the last six months. All the cheques had been sent to Fisher's flat address and they had all been presented at his bank. Thornton made a note to speak to Hallam about getting clearance to look at Fisher's bank account. He had also noted that it was no

43

longer 'Mr Fisher' when he spoke to Hallam and the others. It was just 'Fisher' now, as if they had already decided that he was no longer part of SIS.

The request to look at Fisher's bank account had had to go right to the top. But permission was given provided that some reasonable excuse was concocted that would not bring any discredit on Fisher. Hallam arranged for the SIS pension fund trustee to ask for sight of the account because Fisher was overseas and they needed to check his pension payments.

Thornton had called in one of the Finance men to look over the accounts and they sat together looking at the twelve Photostated pages of statements that covered the previous year of Fisher's account.

There was only one item that had any immediate interest for Thornton and that was a recent monthly standing-order for £420.94 to the Leeds Permanent Building Society which had been cancelled after one payment. It was Smallwood who contacted a friend of his, a surveyor, who worked for the building society on routine surveys. The address of the mortgaged property was 'Little Croft', Makepeace Lane, Wadhurst, East Sussex.

CHAPTER 7

Adam Siwicki had given his report to Schaeffer and Lindgren. Lindgren had criticised some of his conclusions but had congratulated him on his results. The criticisms only concerned his attempts at a mathematical formula relating the research of his experiments with Martinez to the standard formula for Mean Chance Expectation.

Lindgren half-smiled. 'I should stick to your experiments, Siwicki, and leave the math to mathematicians.'

'It was just an attempt to provide data that might convince some of the sceptics.'

Lindgren shook his head. 'Sceptics don't matter in your operation. What you're doing is never going to be published anyway.'

Schaeffer interrupted. 'You say in your report that the target distance isn't significant. He can produce the same standard of result over any distance.' He paused. 'You really think that?'

'I've tried it and it's worked every time.'

'Did you use both methods? Showing him the place on the map and only giving him a map reference?'

'Yes.'

'How much does he know about map-reading?'

'He knew the basics but I gave him several hours of instruction. Mainly on general topography. Contours and so on. He doesn't absorb it. He's not interested.'

'And it makes no difference which way you do it?'

Lindgren interrupted. 'But when you give him grid numbers you're limited. He just describes a large area. That could be anything, or anywhere.'

'It was at first but when it seemed to work I used specific sites. I got grid references from the San Francisco office of the US Geological Survey of specific sites.'

Schaeffer shrugged. 'How about you test him with some grid

points that neither of you know anything about? Do you think that would work?'

'I do.' Siwicki shrugged. 'Do you want me to try?'

'Yes.'

They were eating together later that evening when Schaeffer passed over a sealed envelope to Siwicki.

'Don't open it until you carry out the test. Put it in your safe. There are four cards inside that give eight-digit map references. Give them to him in any order you like and at intervals that suit your conditions. And let us know what he can see. Don't check on where the references are and phone me when you've got his answers.'

'Are the locations in this country?'

'Maybe. Maybe not. It's best you don't know.'

'Do you want me to tape his responses?'

'Why not? They might be useful. Have you got a scrambler down there?'

'Yes.'

'Which model?'

'A Mark Nine.'

'We could use that if we need to. Phone me on the scrambler when you're ready.'

Except for one wall painted white all the walls and the ceiling were painted a matte black so that there were no reflections. And the floor was covered by a fitted black carpet. The only noise was the faint hum of the air-conditioning.

Two armchairs faced the white wall side by side and there was a small low table in front of the chairs.

Siwicki had the four cards in his jacket pocket as he sat alongside Paul Martinez.

'When you slept this afternoon, Paul, did you dream at all?'

'Not that I can remember. I'm pretty sure I didn't.'

Siwicki smiled. 'That's fine, Paul. Are you relaxed and comfortable?'

'Yes.'

'This is just the same as our usual experiments. I'm going to give you a card, four cards, one at a time and I want you to tell me what you can see. They're the map references of various places. I'd like you to describe them.'

'Have I seen these places? Do I know them? How shall I recognise them?'

'I don't know myself where any of these places are but you don't have to identify the places in any way – just describe what you see. OK?'

'OK.'

Siwicki handed Martinez the first card and watched as Martinez looked at it and then Siwicki switched on the cassette recorder.

Martinez leaned forward and put the card on the table. For a moment he stared at the white wall in front of them, then he closed his eyes.

'There's a long line of people. Two or three lines of people. They're waiting to go into a building. A large flat-topped building. It doesn't look like a church. Or a movie theatre. They're moving forward very slowly. Going into the building. It could be a prison. It's some kind of public building from the size of it.

'I can see policemen watching them – or they could be soldiers. It's fading away, getting dark. And now it's gone.'

'OK, Paul. Here's card number two.'

'Was I anywhere near right on that first one, Adam?'

'I told you, I don't know where any of the locations are. The guys at Langley did the cards, not me.'

'Don't they trust you?'

'Of course they do. They just want to see how we make out with us both doing it blind.'

Martinez looked at the second card and kept it in his hand as he closed his eyes. He was silent for several minutes then he smiled and said, 'They're playing games with us, Adam. It's Disneyland or Disneyworld. I don't know which one. There's children and a big Mickey Mouse. And a cowboy. And a lot of kids. It's very crowded. Blue skies and sunshine. Could be California or Florida. There's no way of telling.'

He opened his eyes, still smiling. 'Glad to see they've got a sense of humour. How about the next one?'

Siwicki handed him card number three and they went through the same ritual.

'I can see waves, Adam. Nothing but waves. No beach. No land. There's something way over on the horizon. Could be a ship but I can't really see it. That's all there is. Very grey sky. Could be weather or maybe dusk or dawn. The waves are quite high. Maybe six feet. The light seems to be coming from the right. Some kind of sea, Adam.'

It was the fourth card that was the problem. Martinez just sat with his eyes closed, not speaking for several minutes.

'I don't see a thing, skipper. Not a thing. It's blank. Maybe I've run down my batteries. Give me another couple of minutes.'

But there was no response from the second attempt and Siwicki collected the cards and switched off the recorder. He stood up, amiable despite his disappointment.

'Let's go get ourselves a drink, Paul.'

'Are you disappointed, chief?'

'No way. You were great.'

'I'll be anxious to hear the result. It's like waiting to see if you've won the Irish Sweepstakes.'

It was midnight before Siwicki sat in his office and dialled Schaeffer's number. It took ten minutes to trace him. Siwicki smiled when they told him that Schaeffer was at a stag-party for a friend who was getting married the next day. He couldn't quite imagine the rather pompous Schaeffer at a stag-party. But he sounded sharp enough when he came on the phone.

'Schaeffer. Who is it?'

'Siwicki, Mr Schaeffer. Do you want the result of the test now or shall I phone you later in the day?'

'I'll have it now.'

'It's going to take about an hour to read you the notes.'

'That's OK. Let me get a chair.' There was a pause and then Schaeffer picked up the phone again.

'OK. Fire away.'

In fact it took less than half an hour to read his notes and Schaeffer made no comment between the cards. He was silent for quite a time and Siwicki could hear his heavy breathing.

'That's pretty good going, Siwicki. Not bad at all.'

'Was he on target?'

'Not bad.' He paused. 'In fact he was pretty damn good.'

'Can I ask you what the targets were?'

'I guess so. The first one was Lenin's tomb in Red Square,

Moscow. The second was Disneyland, California. The third one was a reference in the middle of the Pacific.'

'And the fourth one?'

'That was just a check. There's no such co-ordinates. We made 'em up.'

'I don't think he'll like that. He'll feel we don't trust him. That we're checking up on him to see if he's faking or genuine.'

'Well we are, aren't we?'

'I thought we'd got past that stage with my programme.'

'So, if you think he's gonna play the prima donna don't tell him. Tell him it was the Pentagon or something. You know how to handle the fellow.'

'Well I'll sign off now, sir. Have a good party.'

'I will. I'll be down to see you myself in a couple of days. We'll get on to the real stuff.'

'I'll look forward to that, sir.'

'Don't let the little ol' boy get too big-headed or he'll be asking for more money.'

'I don't think he will, sir.'

'Oh. Why not?'

'He's a patriot.'

'A patriot's another name for a fanatic. Never trust 'em, boy. G'night.'

'Goodnight, sir.'

But Schaeffer had already hung up.

CHAPTER 8

Ushi Jaeger had settled easily into her job with Professor Rykov. He was a genial, avuncular man and despite her mother's fears she had proved herself invaluable to the disorganised head of the department. She kept him to his scheduled appointments, reorganised his filing system and tactfully pointed it out when he walked around with his fly-buttons undone. Most days she worked until mid-evening, sometimes sharing a snack and cream cakes with the old man. In fact, he was not all that old, but in his early fifties, although his carelessness about clothes and shaving made him seem much older.

They were sitting together that evening with the professor's favourite snack ·· banana and honey sandwich and Finnish vodka.

'How long since you walked in the forest, little girl?'

'A long time.' She sighed. 'Nearly two months.'

'Don't sigh, my dear, remember what that poet said, "I've no faith in sighing for birch trees – "'

She laughed and continued, ' "Struck dumb, we watch on that shore –"'

And together they said, ' "Where the body seems not to be body, And words are not deeds any longer, They're not even words any more!"'

He had been waving his arms to the rhythm of the words. 'Who wrote that?'

'Aleksander Galich.'

'My God, yes. Wasn't he banned or something?'

'He was banished. He lives in Norway now.'

He frowned. 'I wish our people wouldn't do that sort of thing. What harm can a poet do to the Soviet Union?'

'He shouldn't have disobeyed the rules.'

'What rules did he disobey, little bird?'

'The rules about poking fun at the State.'

'Oh come, come. Surely all that went down into the grave with Stalin.'

'If one person breaks the rules then others will feel free to break other rules. He was well known and well liked, and he set a bad example.'

'That sounds like a line out of some Chekhov play. Anyway you ought to be getting back to your Mama.'

'Don't forget that you are flying to Moscow on Thursday.'

'Am I? I don't remember anything about that. Why am I going?'

'To see Comrade Gavrilov at the Institute. And lunch at the University.'

'Where am I staying?'

'At the Rossiya.'

'I don't like Gavrilov you know.'

'Why not?'

'He is sceptical about our work here. And he's a dull, flat man. Never one to let his mind be clouded by a touch of enthusiasm.' He shrugged his big shoulders. 'Ah well. That's life. That's how it is.'

Ushi laughed. 'And now you're at the Moscow Arts Theatre, playing Uncle Vanya.'

'I'd have liked to be an actor. Maybe . . . ah well. Off you go.'

It was almost eleven o'clock when the door-bell rang and Anna Jaeger put a bow in the belt of her bath-robe before answering the door.

'Why, Professor Rykov, what is it?'

'May I come in? I apologise for the late hour.'

'Of course.'

She led him into the sitting room and poured them both a vodka as he settled himself in a chair.

'Here you are then.' She paused as she sat facing him. 'What can I do for you?'

'Where is she – Ushi?'

'In bed. Asleep by now.'

'A strange thing happened this evening. She reminded me that I was flying to a meeting in Moscow with that wretched man Gavrilov. Told me I'd be staying at the Rossiya for the night. And having lunch at the University.' He looked at her. 'Everything she said is true. It's unbelievable.'

'I don't understand, Professor. Of course it's true if she says so. She's always truthful. Painfully truthful sometimes.'

Rykov shook his head. 'An hour after Ushi had left the office I had a call from Moscow. From Gavrilov. Fulsome apologies for the short notice but the committee had only just broken up. Would I make arrangements to fly to Moscow on Thursday? I would be having lunch with him and the Deputy Minister at the University. They were trying to fix me a room at the Rossiya.' He nodded slowly. 'Twenty minutes later his secretary rang. She had had great difficulty but they had managed to get me a room at the Rossiya for the one night.'

'What are you trying to tell me, Nikolai?'

'Unless she was in touch with Moscow earlier I'm saying that your daughter is blessed with some kind of Extra Sensory Perception.'

'Shall I wake her up so that you can ask how she knew about your trip?'

She saw the eagerness on his face and in his voice despite what he said: 'That would be very unkind, Anna.'

She smiled and stood up. 'Help yourself to another drink. I won't be long.'

It was almost ten minutes before Anna came back with Ushi. When they were sitting Anna said, 'I've told her what happened.'

Rykov reached out for the young girl's hand. 'Tell me, had you spoken to Moscow? Had they contacted you?'

'I haven't spoken to Moscow for two weeks, Professor.'

'So how did you know about my visit?'

'I don't know.'

'You're sure nobody suggested at some time that I might have to go to Moscow?'

'I don't remember it if they did.'

'So what made you – how did you know that I was going there on Thursday?'

'I don't know. It was just in my mind somehow.'

'Was it some sort of voice that you heard in your mind?'

'No.'

'Was it like a dream?'

52

Ushi smiled. 'It wasn't like any of those things.' She shrugged. 'It was just there in my mind.'

'Did something make you think of Gavrilov?'

She closed her eyes for several moments and then said, 'I saw his photograph in one of your science journals.'

'When?'

'This afternoon.'

Rykov smiled. 'Well, you got me into the hotel quicker than Comrade Gavrilov's secretary could.' He paused as he looked at her benevolently. 'You've got a wonderful gift, my dear. We must talk about it. Tomorrow.' He patted her knee. 'Off you go, my dear girl.'

Ushi kissed her mother and left them together. The old man looked at Anna with raised eyebrows. 'You know what we've got there?'

'Tell me.'

'Precognitive or contemporaneous ESP. When she was telling me about my trip to Moscow on Thursday the committee were just finalising the decision. When she placed me in the hotel it was their intention but it wasn't done until over an hour later.'

'Does this mean you'll want to use her?'

'I don't like the word "use", Anna. I'd like her to cooperate with me. She will get all due recognition in anything that's published and I'll see that Moscow recognises her work with me.' He smiled. 'You don't have to worry, Anna. I'll take good care of her.' He smiled again. 'Like she takes care of me.'

Anna sighed. 'How can I object, Professor? I know your work.' She shrugged. 'But she's my only child and I love her very much.'

'You can be there when we do our tests if you wish.'

'I wouldn't dream of it. She's in your good hands, my friend. It's probably because she likes you so much that we have this phenomenon.'

'I'd like very much to think it was that, my dear.' He paused. 'How have you settled down yourself?'

She smiled and shrugged. 'I settled down long ago, Nikolai. A week was enough.'

'Good.'

He stood up, kissed her on both cheeks and she walked with him to the door.

Penny waited until he'd taken off his tie before she told him.

'I've got some good news for you, Sunbeam.'

He turned quickly. 'Is it Jamie?'

'Yes.'

'Tell me.'

'Madam rang. She and Padstow are going for a long weekend to Paris. We can have Jamie from Friday night to Tuesday morning. The weekend after next.'

'That's marvellous, kid. What did she say?'

'I've got a confession to make.'

'You rang her?'

'Not on your bloody life. No, I had a word with friend Springett, the journalist. I thought it would be better if I did it and you weren't involved in any way. Seems he had quite a long chat with Padstow. As a matter of interest he didn't know that she'd been messing you about with Jamie. And, incidentally, he not only never took Jamie to the races but has never been to a race meeting in his life. Springett thought he was telling the truth. Padstow denied any hassle about you seeing Jamie and thought there must be some misunderstanding.'

'She must have hated backing down.'

'I think if you'd answered the phone you could well have got an earful of gutter abuse but as soon as she realised it was me it was all girls together stuff. Weren't men ridiculous? Always misunderstood what was said to them. But – ah, well – men were deceivers ever. And how was I coping with all your funny ways? I asked her what funny ways she had in mind and she backed off.' She smiled. 'Anyway it's worked. We get him for a long weekend.'

'Thanks for saying "we".'

'You're a strange man you know, Robbie.'

'Why am I strange?'

'You're really a very tough cookie. Physically and mentally. I wouldn't want to be one of those naughty boys you spend your time chasing. I'd be very scared. And when you look at people it's as if you know everything that's going on in their minds. All their lies, all their deceits and all their subterfuges. But away from your job all that seems to go. You let people – even nonentities like Elaine – get you down. Why? I've never understood it.'

He sat down facing her. 'What I do in my work means dealing with ruthless people, sometimes thugs, sometimes just very cunning people. I've been well trained to deal with them. We're not sent in like lambs to the slaughter. But it's a different world to all this.' He waved his arm at the room. 'In my job I'm suspicious of everyone. That's part of my training. I was taught that everybody tells lies and it might save me a lot of hassle – or even my life – to find out what they tell lies about. So I do just that. Maybe they only tell social lies to make themselves look richer or nicer or more glamorous than they really are. But at least I know.

'It's not easy to leave all that behind in one's private life. There's a temptation to go on using what you've learned on the people around you.' He shrugged. 'It's fatal to do that. And that often means that you go to the other extreme. You let people get away with things that no normal man would put up with.'

She nodded. 'And because you're tough and capable you go for lame ducks like Elaine and that other one – Paula, wasn't it?'

He smiled. 'I've never analysed why I landed myself with them. But *I've* survived. They won't – in the long run.'

'And what am I? Your latest lame duck?'

He looked at her fondly. 'I may not show it enough but I love you very much.'

'Do you *like* me as well?'

'Of course I do. Do you like me?'

'You're fishing for compliments.'

He smiled. 'Maybe you're right. Forget I asked.'

She shook her head. 'No way. First of all, you're the nicest man I've ever known. You're kind and gentle and I feel safe with you. Safe in every way.' She smiled. 'And apart from all that you're really rather handsome.' She shrugged and laughed. 'You're OK.'

Thornton had checked on the map where Wadhurst was and drove the hire-car down the A21 to the turn-off at Lamberhurst. Wadhurst was virtually a one-street village. Typically Sussex, with small, old-fashioned shops each side of the narrow main street. He asked at the newspaper shop where he could find Makepeace Lane. It was a mile outside the village and 'Little Croft' was the first house past the farm.

As he got back into the car he wondered what it would be best to say if Fisher were there. He parked the car just past the farm and walked on down the lane. The grass verges were thick with dandelion and cow-parsley and the hedges had only been trimmed to the edge of the farm itself.

An oval rustic sign said 'Little Croft' on a post at the side of a five-barred gate with a smaller gate beside it. A gravel path led to the house which was larger than he expected. Either the original owners were unduly modest or given to inverted snobbery, because you would have to be very grand to see it as no more than a cottage. It was built like a small manor house and its windows and doors looked genuine Georgian. He noticed that the lawns were cut and their edges trimmed and a lace curtain fluttered at an open window on the first floor.

The gravel pathway gave way to paving stones and the solid front door of the house. For a moment he stood there undecided whether to use the heavy wrought-iron door-knocker or the brass bell-push at the side of the door. But before he reached a decision the door opened and a man stood there, another young man behind him.

'What can I do for you, sir?'

'I came to see Mr Fisher.'

'There's no Mr Fisher here, sir.'

'May I ask whose house this is?'

'You may.'

When the man stood silently watching him he realised that he was being deliberately bloody-minded.

'So whose house is it?'

'That's no business of yours, sir.'

'How do you know it isn't?'

The man's hard eyes looked back at him. 'Because I say it isn't. Now get off these premises or I'll call the police.'

'That's fine by me. You do that.'

The big man turned and nodded at the man behind him and Thornton heard the sound of his rubber soles on the tiles in the hall. The man was back almost immediately but he didn't say anything to the big man.

There was something odd about the big man. He looked like a typical policeman himself. The short back and sides, the light blue shirt and the navy-blue tie. The air of authority and the 'sirs' that weren't sincere, but a routine. So that a member of the public couldn't accuse you of disrespect or rudeness. And then the police car arrived and a sergeant and a constable crunched their way up the path.

At the porch the sergeant looked at the big man. 'I understand you called the station, Mr Willis.'

'That's correct, sergeant. I asked this gentleman to get off the premises . . .' he shrugged, '. . . and as you can see he's refused to leave.'

The sergeant turned to Thornton. 'Maybe I could help you, sir.'

'I'm looking for a colleague of mine. A Mr Fisher. This is his house.' Thornton paused and said softly, 'Can I have a word with you away from these people?'

'Of course. Let's go down the path.'

A few yards away the sergeant stopped and looked at him. 'What's the problem, sir?'

Thornton reached in his jacket pocket and opened his ID case and held it up for the sergeant to read. He looked at it carefully, checking Thornton's face against the colour photograph. Finally he looked towards the patrol car and then back at Thornton.

'I'd better have words on the radio with my people, Mr Thornton. Just hang on here will you now?'

'OK.'

It was almost ten minutes before the sergeant came back, pursing his lips as he came, as if he was working out what he would say.

When he stopped he said, 'Well, sir. It seems that there's a bit of a mix-up as you might say. I had a word with my bosses in Lewes in view of your identity card. And I think that they spoke to somebody on your side of the fence so to speak. And . . . the outcome is that we'd best leave things as they are for the moment.'

'You mean I've got to get a warrant before I can search the house?'

'I think that could help, Mr Thornton. I think that's the gist

57

of it all.' He smiled and shrugged. 'These things happen, you know. Left hand don't know what the right hand's doing and all that.'

'Do you know who your people spoke to?'

'I don't think I could say anything on that, sir. Not in the circumstances.'

'Who are those people at the house?'

'I suppose by rights you'd have to call them caretakers like.'

'You know them?'

'I think you'd better talk to your people about them.' He looked at Thornton's face. 'Was you given permission to come down here?'

'Not specifically. I don't need any permission. This is a private house. It belongs to a Mr Fisher.'

'What makes you think that, Mr Thornton?'

Thornton opened his mouth to say how he knew that it was Fisher's house and then changed his mind. 'Thanks for your help, sergeant. I'll get a warrant and come down again.'

'Yes. I should do that, sir. Make things easier in the long run.'

He said it as if he were certain that it wouldn't happen. Thornton walked the rest of the way down the garden path and back up the lane to his car. When he drove back slowly past the house the two policemen were talking to the big man, who was laughing at something they had said.

He drove back slowly to London. He knew that he'd been foolish to come down without having the place checked out beforehand. But that was hindsight. There had been no indication that it was necessary. It was Fisher's property so why the heavy brigade? And why hadn't Hallam warned him that the place had been taken over? But taken over by whom? Maybe Five had got in on the act. If they had, then SIS's cat was out of the bag. It would be interesting to see what Hallam's reaction would be.

CHAPTER 9

Schaeffer had come down to the house at LaHonda with mixed feelings. He had been put in charge of the supervision of Operation Aeolus precisely because he didn't believe in ESP or Psi or any other psychic phenomena. For him, those who purported to practise it were no better than the bunco-men who used to con the hayseeds at travelling fairs. What he himself classified as 'reasonable doubt', in fact, bordered on total disbelief. But after seeing the results achieved by Siwicki and Martinez, while he was unconvinced, he was no longer a complete sceptic. His own description of his current attitude was that he was an agnostic now rather than an atheist.

But this visit could be the deciding factor, the litmus paper that settled the issue one way or another. If this experiment failed Operation Aeolus would be allowed to shuffle along for another year or two but if it were successful then its budget could be virtually unlimited. No longer just because the Russians were doing it but because it had a pay-off that was tangible right now.

Schaeffer and Siwicki sat alone in the garden in the shadow of a giant fig that was loaded with purple fruit.

'What's so special about this time, Ed?'

'I'll tell you when we're through. OK?'

Siwicki looked annoyed. 'You know, all this mystery makes it unnecessarily complicated. I've not been working with him like that. It's a joint operation. We're collaborators, not adversaries.'

'Just relax – yes? If this goes OK then you're going to be in charge of a big operation. Recognised as providing a very valuable service to the US of A.' Schaeffer looked at his watch. 'How about you start setting him up and we get going in – say – fifteen minutes. OK?'

'OK.'

*

Siwicki opened the envelope and handed the card to Paul Martinez. As had happened so often in recent weeks all it had on it were the co-ordinates on a Geological Survey map. And as usual Martinez stared at the numbers and then closed his eyes and started to speak. Schaeffer sat in the adjoining office listening on a pair of light-weight headphones.

'Where I am standing there are railroad lines right across the front and a road each side of the railroad lines. Ahead of me is a road that leads to a big building with a flat top. The building is made of stone or concrete. The road splits in front of the building and goes off to each side. There are other buildings away from the main building. And over on my left is a lake. A small lake. There are three sorts of tunnels going down into the ground. Near the main building there is a crane. It must be very high. Maybe a hundred feet or more. It's at the side of the path and on the opposite side is a column. A metal column like a very high electricity supply cable with an arm. A gantry going right across the road like a bridge. There are vehicles – army-type vehicles. Big, long ones and smaller ones. The earth is sandy and there are swirls of dust from a wind. I can't see any people at all. It looks very dry and hot. It's going now.'

Martinez sighed and opened his eyes, turning to look at Siwicki.

'That was a very strange place. I got a feeling of loneliness.'

'Could you do me a rough sketch of what you saw before it goes?'

'I'll try.'

Siwicki handed him a drawing pad and a felt-tipped pen and watched as Martinez started putting tentative lines on the paper.

Siwicki waited until Martinez had put down all he could remember and had taken the drawing into Schaeffer. Schaeffer glanced quickly at the sketch and Siwicki could see that he was pleased with the result but he went back to Martinez and they drove down the road to the coast and lay on the beach and swam until the evening wind started up.

Schaeffer had left by the time they got back to the house but he came back in the early hours of the morning and shook Siwicki awake. He had already switched on the bedside lamp and he sat on the edge of the bed.

'You've done it, Siwicki. I've been in touch with Langley. They're amazed and delighted and rarin' to go. But I tell you this, I doubt if they'd have believed it if I hadn't been here and heard it all myself. I know you think I'm a pain in the ass but it's paid off in the end.'

'Where the hell was the place he saw?'

'What he saw was the site at Semipalatinsk in Kazakhstan where the Soviets do the underground tests for ABM warheads. The other buildings he described are for developing and testing high-energy lasers and charged particle beams.

'The only thing that didn't fit at first was that gantry across the service road. He's really something that guy. They checked the latest satellite photographs and that damned gantry was only erected in the last few days. How's about that for accuracy?'

'How about we talk again in the morning?'

Schaeffer smiled. 'How in hell can you be so calm about it, man? This is a breakthrough. The pay-off. They love you in Langley and they love your little pal too.' He paused. 'Just one last thing, buddy, can he go into those buildings and tell us what he can see?'

'I should think so. I may have to work out some different procedure but I'd guess he could do that OK.'

Schaeffer shook his head in amazement, grinning with undisguised excitement as he said, 'OK. Go back to sleep.' He stood up. 'But I don't know how you can sleep, fella. I thought you'd be running round in your bath-robe shouting "Eureka" or something.'

CHAPTER 10

Thornton wasn't quite sure whether it was just bloody-mindedness or professional curiosity but he made no move to contact Hallam when he got back to Century House.

It was two days before Hallam's secretary rang him and asked him to go over. Hallam was sitting at his desk waiting for him, pointing to a chair without speaking.

'How's it going?'

'Slowly I'm afraid.'

He was determined to make Hallam raise the question of the house at Wadhurst.

'I understand you had a problem a few days ago.'

'I've had quite a number of problems.'

'I meant "Little Croft".'

'I'll just get a warrant and go down there again.'

'What made you go there?'

'I did some checking. Or rather Smallwood did. We traced Fisher as being the owner. I wanted to look it over.'

'There's nothing there that could help your investigation.'

Thornton didn't hide his surprise. 'Am I being warned off?'

Hallam shrugged. 'I suppose if you put it like that then the answer's "yes".'

'But why?'

'Because there's nothing there that could help you.'

'Has it been checked over?'

'Yes.'

'And there was nothing that could give any indication as to why he's disappeared?'

'No. Nothing at all.'

Thornton looked at Hallam's dead-pan face. 'I'd better say for the record that I find it strange that I'm prevented from checking the house and forming my own impressions.'

'When you say "for the record", Thornton, there isn't going

to be any record. If you find him it won't be necessary. If you don't – then there'll still be no record.' He paused. 'I want to make it quite clear to you, here and now, that what you are doing is entirely an internal matter. You may not like having restrictions placed on what you can do, but that's how it is. And how it's going to be.'

'Would you prefer somebody else to take over the operation?'

'Why do you say that?'

'If you don't have any confidence in me, my discretion, or how I operate, I'm not going to get very far.'

Hallam relaxed, visibly. Leaning back in his chair, smiling as he looked across at Thornton.

'Don't take it to heart, my boy. There are good reasons why we have to make these limitations. It's nothing to do with you, either as a person or in your official rôle. Maybe when it's all over, one way or the other, I'll be able to explain. Until then just take it that we trust you implicitly and we'd like you to trust us too. It's unlikely to happen again but if it does, then bear with us.'

Professor Rykov had switched off the tape-recorder as he put the third photograph on his desk in front of Ushi Jaeger.

'Tell me about him.'

She looked at the photograph. 'He's quite handsome, isn't he?'

'I suppose he is. What's he thinking about?'

She smiled. 'He's thinking about a lot of things. Mainly two things. He is wondering if he is going to be promoted. He thinks he will be, but he isn't sure. He thinks – he's a scientist of some kind – at a research laboratory. He thinks that the head of his department doesn't like him and will try to prevent him getting his promotion.

'He is also thinking about a girl. A girl named Natalia. She's a dancer. A ballet dancer. He loves her very much but he's jealous of another man. An actor.' She sighed. 'He's very mixed up and unhappy. He is worried too about his eyes. He uses his eyes a lot in his work. He wonders why he has no close friends.' She sighed and shrugged. 'That's all I can hear.'

'That's very good, Ushi. Very good indeed.'

'How do you know it's very good? Even if you know about the

man how can you know what he is thinking? We don't really know what we are thinking ourselves. Not really.'

'That's a very interesting statement. Tell me more.'

She laughed and shrugged. 'There's nothing you don't know already. It's just that we don't have any control over our thoughts. We can't think good thoughts just because we want to.

'If you ask somebody what they are thinking about they can't really tell you. They can say it was some generality. The weather or some incident. But their real thinking is never that precise and – what's the word – rational. Our thoughts dart about all over the place, influenced by our senses. I'm sure that even with somebody like Einstein, when he was thinking about relativity, concentrating, there would be other thoughts in his mind. Irrelevant thoughts. Thinking is like a music score.'

'Go on.'

'I must be boring you. Or you think I'm crazy.'

'Neither, neither. Carry on.'

'If you look at a music score for an orchestra you see the line of notes for the main melody and then maybe twenty or thirty lines for all the other instruments. They are playing different notes, even in different staves, but we don't hear them separately, we just hear sound, a beautiful sound maybe but unless you are a composer or a musician you never hear the separate strands of the music. And our thinking is like that, drowned by sounds and smells and the world about us. So when I hear somebody thinking it's never quite like I say it is. I only get the theme, not all the diversions. And if I described all the thoughts floating in somebody's mind people would think I was crazy.'

'Nobody will think you're crazy, Ushi. In everyday life there are people who talk interestingly but they need something to be able to do that. They need someone to listen. Some people are good listeners. You're a good listener and you're very special, because you listen with your mind not just your ears.'

'Why do you waste your time listening to what I hear? Most of it's just rubbish.'

The old man smiled. 'There are people in Moscow. In the University and research institutes who know your name. They don't consider anything of what we do, you and I, as rubbish.'

He smiled. 'You got that letter last week from a deputy minister who praised your work.' He paused. 'You're not my little girl assistant any more. You are my collaborator in a new field of research. Scientists in Warsaw, Prague and Sofia know your name and read my reports.'

She shrugged and smiled. 'It's a funny world, isn't it?'

'Do you miss your life in Germany?'

'I don't remember much about it. I miss my father. He seemed a very humble man to most people. Even to my mother. But he wasn't. It was he who showed me the places in the woods where there were badgers and foxes, and told me the names of the wild flowers and the birds. He knew how everything lived and grew. He saw things that other people never noticed.' She smiled. 'He told me that most people looked but didn't see. Like you said about me listening.'

'When you talk to people are you aware of what they are thinking apart from what they are saying?'

'I have to switch off that part of my mind or it gets confusing. Like listening to three or four people all talking to you at once.'

'How do you switch off?'

'I don't know.'

'How do you switch on?'

She laughed. 'I don't know that either. I think I just concentrate on looking at the picture you show me and it's faint at first like a badly tuned radio. And then it becomes clearer.'

Rykov took another photograph from an envelope and placed it in front of her.

'Can you tell me what he is thinking?'

Ushi sat looking at the photograph for several minutes.

'He seems to be a very busy man. He has to make a decision about money. A lot of money. Not his money. He's also thinking about horses. Riding horses. He is in a meeting with a lot of people and he is very bored. He isn't listening to what they are saying. He is nearly asleep.' She looked at Rykov. 'I think maybe I was seeing a film. It was very strange.'

The old man nodded and made a note on the back of the photograph before sliding it back into the envelope. It was a picture of President Reagan.

'Let's talk again this afternoon, shall we?'

She smiled and nodded. 'Who was that last man? Was he a film actor?'

'He was once. It's not important.'

Smallwood went up in the lift with him. He wore expensive clothes that nevertheless didn't suit him. That Monday morning he wore a Harris tweed three-piece suit with a bold check that seemed to emphasise his lack of height and his rotundity.

'You have a good weekend, skipper?'

'Yes. I had my young son for the weekend.'

'Ah. That means the Science Museum, the Natural History Museum and *Match of the Day* on TV.'

'We did a bit better than that. If you've got a nice girl-friend you can spread your wings a bit wider.'

'What did you do?'

'We went down to Marlow and fished, with tea afterwards at The Compleat Angler and Trivial Pursuit and *Match of the Day* in the evening. Sunday we did the Zoo in the morning, lunch at home, a plastic model kit of the *Bismarck* the rest of the day. And today my girl-friend is taking him to the theatre to watch her rehearsing and he goes back to his mother tomorrow morning.'

'If you ever want tickets for the Spurs just let me know.'

'That's very kind of you. He'd be thrilled to see the real thing.'

As the lift doors closed behind them and they got out Smallwood said, 'Tell me what you found at the cottage?'

'Let's wait until we're in my office.'

'OK. I'll get us a couple of coffees from the machine.'

Smallwood stirred the last of his coffee with a Biro before he looked up at Thornton. 'I don't like the sound of any of that.'

'Why not?'

'Either they want you to find Fisher or they don't. If they *do* – then why stop you from looking around his house?' He paused. 'It sounds mighty odd to me.'

'Why do you think they stopped me going in?'

'It's obvious, isn't it? They've got something to hide.'

'Like what?'

'Who knows? Maybe they *don't* want you to catch up with Fisher.'

'Why?'

'Maybe they already know where he is.'

'I'm sure they don't. They're genuinely anxious for me to find him. I'd bet my last dollar on that.'

'They said you could interview the members of the committee. You had a brief talk with Hallam, what about you having a go at the other three? Just a fishing expedition.'

'I'll see what I can arrange. Meantime will you look through his operations files and see if there's anything there?'

'OK. Will you phone Archives so they don't get snotty?'

'I'll give you a note, Tom – "To whom it may concern".'

CHAPTER 11

There were two envelopes addressed to him on his desk. Hallam would like to see him and Mr Seymour would call on him at 1400 hours that day.

Hallam was with his secretary when Thornton went to his office.

'When could I see you, sir, about the assignment?'

Hallam looked at his watch. 'I could give you half an hour right now if that's convenient.'

Hallam's office was spacious but personal. Large pieces of rather grand furniture, and one wall behind the antique partners' desk was covered with photographs of rugby teams and sportsmen. Thornton had been in that office several times in the past and he took the visitor's chair as Hallam sat at his desk.

'So, what can I do to help?'

'Out of all the possible motives for Fisher's disappearance which do *you* think it could be? I don't mean a considered verdict. Just an impression because you knew him so well.'

Hallam leaned back, relaxed, his two huge hands clasped on his desk. Hands that looked as if they were made to clamp round a pint of beer although, in fact, despite the rugby-playing background Hallam didn't drink alcohol of any kind.

'I've thought about it, of course. And I really haven't a clue. I can't believe it was his work. He was particularly successful at everything he dealt with. And much respected by all concerned.'

'What did he cover recently?'

'Well, he'd been a very successful field officer until about ten years ago. In Germany mainly. But he was beaten up – ribs broken, arm broken – the usual stuff. So we pulled him in and put him in charge of most of our operations in Germany. He was in Hamburg, Brunswick and Berlin and the operations were against the Soviets and East Germans. He ran them extremely well – understood his chaps' problems – kept them keen and reasonably happy. Not the kind of man to chuck up his career when he was almost at the tape.' Hallam paused. 'And I told you about the two defectors the other day.'

'What about his politics?'

'I doubt if he had any.' Hallam smiled. 'Like most of us he didn't trust politicians of any stripe. He definitely had no left-wing sympathy that I can recall.'

'What about his private life?'

'He's married. Nice girl. Much younger than he was. Very pretty and highly intelligent. They seemed a pretty solid couple from my assessment.'

'Was he sexually normal?'

Hallam smiled. 'Who the hell is, my friend? As you well know – if you could look into any man's mind you'd be horrified – and so would he. If you mean was he positively abnormal then the answer, so far as I can say, is no. He had to deal with homosexuals, we all do. He was neutral about it. So far as traditional sex is concerned I'd class him as normal and average. Faithful most of the time but on his kind of job – and yours for that matter – a chap can get lonely and may look for something to take his mind off what he's doing for an hour or so.'

'What about money?'

'No private income that I know of. I should say that they got by quite nicely. There were no children.'

'Of all the possible reasons for disappearing which would you say was the least likely?'

Hallam pursed his lips and then said, 'Defection. Of all the reasons a man can have to defect – ideology, greed, ambition – he had none of them.' Hallam paused and looked at his watch. 'I'll have to chuck you out I'm afraid.'

'Thanks for your time, sir.'

'Call my girl any time you want to chat with me.'

'Have MI5 or Special Branch been told anything at all yet?'

Hallam shook his head vigorously. 'Not a word. There's still no call for them to be involved.'

Seymour came in promptly at two o'clock – no knock on the

door. He shifted the chair with his foot before he sat down, then took off his watch and placed it in front of him on the desk.

'Right, Thornton. Twenty minutes.'

'Did you know Mr Fisher well?'

'As well as anybody gets to know a chap like him, I suppose.'

'How long have you known him?'

'Some time before he joined SIS. We were in the Intelligence Corps together.'

'Would you consider him to be a friend of yours?'

Seymour grinned. 'Depends what he's been up to.'

'Was he a likeable man?'

'Depends what kind of men you like.'

'Did *you* like him?'

'He wasn't my type.' Seymour shrugged. 'But he was OK.'

'Why wasn't he your type?'

'He was a loner. He wasn't a team player. Went his own way. Always one eye on pleasing the brass. He was a disappointed man and it showed. Especially when he was passed over for promotion.'

'When was that?'

'Four, maybe five years ago. Bailey got the job. Fisher didn't like that one little bit.'

'Did he say so to you?'

'He didn't need to. Made it obvious in a dozen different ways. He thought they'd marked his card. Couldn't understand why.'

'Who did he think had marked his card?'

'Hallam.'

'Was Fisher working with you? Was that why you shared a secretary?'

'We shared because he seldom needed a secretary. He used the security typing pool for most of his work. On cassette.'

'Was he a good operator in your opinion?'

Seymour folded his arms and looked towards the window before he looked back at Thornton.

'The easy answer is yes. That's the popular opinion. For me I'm not sure. There were flaws.'

'What kind of flaws?'

'Misjudgements of people. Misjudgements of situations.'

'Could you give me an example?'

'Not off the cuff. Give me a couple of days and I could give you something.'

'Have you got even any vague thoughts about why he has disappeared?'

'Oh yes, but not the slightest evidence to support them.' And for the first time Seymour smiled.

'Will you tell me?'

'Why not?' Seymour shrugged. 'I think he's defected.'

'To the Soviets?'

'Who else? I think that Hallam, Macleod and Clayton think the same in the back of their minds. No doubt you'll find out in due course. They won't like it that I've said it out loud and they'll probably disagree vehemently. But they'll know that I'm almost certainly right.'

'But you've no substance for thinking this way?'

'Let's say interpolation rather than extrapolation.'

Thornton smiled. 'OK. I give in. Tell me what that means.'

'At fifty or so it's unlikely to be a beautiful body. He's never struck me as financially greedy. He *is* ambitious, and being passed over really jolted him. There's only one way of getting your own back on an authority that does that to you.' Seymour shrugged his shoulders. 'You join the opposition.'

Professor Clayton had suggested that they had a meal together at his club, the Reform, and he had led Thornton to a table for two in the far corner of the dining room. The soup had passed with Clayton's questions about Thornton's previous experience in SIS, but when the waitress had brought the main course Thornton felt it was time to ask a few questions himself.

'I wonder if you could give me your general impression of Fisher.'

'You mean as a man or as a field officer?'

'As a man.'

Clayton wiped his thin lips carefully with his table napkin before he spoke. 'He was a strange man, Thornton. He had years of experience behind him – successful experience I might add. But I always thought he wasn't suited to the work. I don't think he'd be recruited these days. He'd never get past the initial tests.'

'Can I ask why you think that?'

'Of course. Perhaps I'm being unfair and I'm leaning too heavily on hindsight. He was in the "I" Corps in Germany in the middle fifties. The main denazification operations were over but there were still quite a lot of naughty boys hiding away in West Germany, and Fisher was one of the chaps who had to track them down. And as I said, he was very successful. He was a born hunter. And he was what they call nowadays "a lateral thinker". A mediocre education but a strangely perceptive mind.

'There comes a time when hunters have more in common with the hunted than with their fellows. And that means you get to wonder if the people who decide who has to go in the bag are sticking to the rules. Or you maybe wonder about their competence, those chaps sitting at desks in Broadway House. And that can make a chap think that if anybody's going to play God maybe it ought to be him not some fellow behind a desk.

'I know of two cases where Fisher released a man he had caught because, after interrogating him, he felt his arrest was not justified. You've got to remember that people doing Fisher's job had almost unlimited power. Nobody in Germany could say them nay. Not Milgov, not the Germans, not even the British Army. Your authority over-rode everyone else's. And I'm talking about a chap in his twenties.' He looked at Thornton. 'That's a lot of power for such a young man.' He paused. 'Anyway, I know of two cases where he released people and fiddled the records so that ostensibly they had never been caught.' Clayton shook his head. 'In our business that's not on. Definitely not on.'

'What should he have done?'

'He should have informed London of his views and left the decision to them.'

'Why did he do it his way?'

Clayton smiled wryly. 'If I could tell you that I don't think our friend would be missing for long.'

'Why not?'

'Because there are two likely reasons for how he behaved in those days. It could be a strong sense of justice. An overdone sense of justice. Or it could be no more than a vaunting ego that saw his own judgement as over-riding that of his superiors in

London.' He smiled. 'Not an unusual attitude in field agents even today I understand.'

Thornton smiled his acknowledgement of the dig. 'Who else knew about these cases?'

Clayton shrugged. 'Who knows? I doubt if anyone else knew.'

'How did you know?'

Clayton smiled again. 'Because they were both men I had listed for arrest and interrogation in London.'

'Do you think that he was possibly right in his judgement in either case?'

'First of all he had no authority or right to pass judgement either way. His responsibilities ended when the men were caught. After that it was up to London. But putting that to one side. One of the men was wanted because he was responsible for the deaths of several SOE people during the war. Two girls and two men.

'In the second case the man had been the negotiator between Goering and various Dutch families who had been forced to sell valuable works of art for food coupons. He wasn't vital but he would have helped us establish the legal ownership of paintings and other works of art that Allied forces found down a mineshaft near Hanover. He had little to fear, he had been forced to do what he did.'

'Have you any idea why Fisher released either of them?'

'Not the slightest.'

'How did you find out what he had done?'

'One of his men told me. A long time afterwards.'

'Did you ever confront him about it?'

'As a matter of fact I did.'

'What did he say?'

'He denied it. But I know he was lying. And he said something that I've always felt was very revealing.'

'What did he say?'

'He said – "I departed from legality only to return to justice." It's from the speech by Napoleon the Third explaining the *coup d'état* of 1851.'

'Why is it revealing?'

'Oh, it is. It is. Just to know it. To be able to quote it off pat as he did. And the words themselves. So enigmatic. So typical of

73

the man and his nature.' He paused, looking at his watch. 'I think we ought to get back.'

'What was his wife like?'

'His wife?' He paused for several moments and then, looking at Thornton intently, he said, 'What made you ask about her?'

Thornton shrugged. 'She's recorded in our files as dead but I'm not sure that she is.'

'I don't know about that. I hardly knew her. She was much younger than he was. And very pretty. I don't think she's important, you know.' He picked up his bill. 'Let's take a taxi. After all we're on official business.'

CHAPTER 12

Westphal looked more like Pentagon material than the stuff of Langley. The old-fashioned crew-cut, alert, disbelieving eyes and a slightly prognathous jaw were deceptive. He had been a very successful General but he had been with the CIA for nearly ten years. His official title was DDPSO, Deputy Director Personnel Special Operations, but his actual function was less specific. He was used to ferreting out those odd money-wasting little CIA private circuses that flourished from time to time in semi-official secrecy until they became either fully authorised or were disbanded.

He had direct access to the Director if he needed it but he seldom used the privilege. He was impartial and disinterested and his judgement was respected. And beyond that he had a way of putting these small private empires out of business without causing lasting rancour or immediate resentment. He was in no hurry to abandon some project just because it had virtually no official blessing but he was hard on anyone who tried to bluff him. Open confession of lack of present success was as likely to give some project another year of life as to kill it.

When he had Schaeffer and Lindgren sitting comfortably he smiled amiably.

'Operation Aeolus. Tell me why it isn't being done at Menlo Park under the wing of SRI International.'

They had decided that Schaeffer should be spokesman. He too had been seconded to the CIA from the US Army and they hoped, vainly in fact, that the soldierly background might influence Westphal.

'I was told that originally the thinking had been that there were quite senior people at SRI who would not have approved of our end product.'

'Why?'

'They would have seen it as an abuse of psychic research.'

'Why?'

'Because they would classify it as an offensive weapon with espionage as its main concern.'

'Do they get reports on your work?'

'Not so far as I know. Maybe unofficially by word of mouth. But not from us.'

'Do *you* get reports on *their* work?'

'Yes, sir. We are on their secondary distribution list.'

'Have you seen any evidence of them duplicating your work?'

'They have experiments in our general area but not with our specific targets in mind. Theirs is pure research and not applied research.'

'But they could do what you do if they were so ordered?'

'I imagine they could, sir.'

'You mean you're not sure that they could?'

'No, sir. I think they *could* do our job.'

'So what's the justification for continuing your operation?' He turned to look at Lindgren. 'You, Mr Lindgren. You tell me.'

'I think the real justification is that we are not scientists concerned with research. We have only one objective. To use, or try to use, psychic powers as weapons of intelligence against a potential enemy who is researching the same area with similar objectives.'

'I'd say that that is a first-class definition of what you're doing but it's not an answer to my question.'

Schaeffer took over again. 'I think we're doing this job because Washington doesn't want to go through a mini version of what happened after Hiroshima and Nagasaki when the top scientists who had created the bomb ended up denouncing its use.'

'Enlighten me further, Mr Schaeffer. I'm not sure that I've grasped your point.'

'Like I said, sir, I think that the senior people at SRI might consider that our particular use of psychic power was an abuse of the science.'

'Yes. I thought that was what you meant. Well, that's cleared the decks; let's get down to business. What have you given Langley for its money?'

Schaeffer reached into the open briefcase beside him and

took out a plastic folder, handing it to Westphal, who slid out the several pages and read them carefully. The report was impressive and was headed – 'Installations and Locations where Substantial Information has been Provided of Personnel, Programmes and Classified Documents.' Westphal read every page and then turned back to the first page. That page alone was enough to impress him. The items listed were varied but all of them were of major importance.

1: Kapustin Yar (48.4°N, 45.8°E)
Early test centre for short and medium-range ballistic missiles: Soviet V-2, Shyster/Sandal, Skean. ABM tests with two-stage SL-8 fired towards Sary Shagan. Small Cosmos satellites.

2: Tyuratam (45.8°N, 63.4°E)
Test centre for ICBMs launched to target areas Kamchatka Peninsula and central Pacific; small impact area for short and medium-range missiles angled NE. Cosmos photo-reconnaissance (52°, 65° incl.), SIS, ocean surveillance, FOBS, etc.

3: Plesetesk (62.9°N, 40.1°E)
ICBM base (e.g. 65 x SS-13). Military meteorological satellites. Cosmos photo-reconnaissance (63°, 65°, 73°, 81° incl.), military comsats, early warning, ferret, multiple navsats (74° and 83°) SIS target.

4: Severomorsk
Major submarine base near Murmansk including Delta-class submarines firing SS-N-8 SLBMs.

5: Barents Sea
Firings of SS-N-8 SLBMs from submarine to impact central Pacific (stellar-inertial guidance).

6: Severodvinsk
World's largest submarine yard, near Archangel, building Delta-class nuclear-powered submarines.

7: Chinese facilities
a. Lop Nor nuclear test centre 40°20′N, 90°10′E.
b. Shuang-ch'eng-tze rocket test centre 41°N, 100°E.

Westphal carefully put the papers back in the plastic folder and looked at the two men for several moments before he spoke.

He said quietly, 'This heading, describing what you can provide – have you had requests for information on these locations from anybody in CIA?'

'Yes, sir. On all of them.'

'And you provided that information?'

'Ninety-five per cent, sir. Some cases we couldn't repeat.'

'Why not?'

'We don't know, sir. Not yet.'

'And the information you provided – were the people concerned satisfied with what you gave them?'

'I don't know, sir. We've never had any response from them.'

'What do you think?'

Schaeffer risked a smile. 'I think that if we were wrong they'd have been back at us. And apart from that the number of requests has been increased considerably. We're having to establish a priority matrix.'

'What could we do to help?'

'There's nothing anybody can do to help us. Maybe you'd like to visit the house and meet Siwicki and Martinez. It's so – what's the word – low-key it doesn't seem credible. Unless we found another one like Martinez we couldn't expand in any way. Siwicki has had to take months to develop the right relationship with Martinez. They're like an old married couple.' He saw Westphal's eyebrows go up. 'Not that way. They're just *simpatico*, one for the other. Siwicki protects his chap from us and we keep the engines oiled.'

'How do you divide what you two do?'

'I look after all the administration and Lindgren covers all the technical stuff, weaponry, targets and so on.'

Westphal leaned back in his chair, his hands behind his head, his eyes closed. When he opened them he said, 'You'll have to stay off the official operations list but you'll be funded indefinitely.' He paused. 'I'm sure you know this but I'll risk repeating it – you don't talk about your operation even inside CIA. Is that understood?'

'Absolutely, sir.'

'I don't need to tell you two that a lot of people would not approve of what you're doing. So keep it where it is, under cover.'

'We'll do that, sir. Thanks for your help.'

Westphal shook his head slowly. 'Don't kid yourselves. I haven't helped you. I just haven't hindered you.'

Siwicki was reading through the latest reports to Washington from SRI International. Before he had been given Operation Aeolus he had always envied the people at SRI. When it had been the Stanford Research Institute, they had had a multimillion-dollar programme which covered almost every aspect of Psi, and the reports showed the remarkable range of their current experiments.

When he had first set up the operation, the freedom and scope and the excitement of independence had kept him happy, but now they had settled down to a routine of constructive and creative work he resented the ambiguity of his position. It had a hole-in-the-corner air about it that made him uneasy. He had told Schaeffer of his feelings and he had treated it as no more than a scientist's ego that needed smoothing down.

He turned back to the reports again. He skipped the technicalities of a newly installed binary random-number generator and moved on to a paper describing the results of experiments with telepathy. He noted it as a possible experiment with Paul Martinez. There was a long report from a recent delegation which had visited the Soviet Union where they had compared notes on long-distance telepathy. A note referred to a highly classified report on modifying the breathing and heartbeat of a subject from long distances. A further note had indicated that from hints and gossip it appeared that Soviet scientists had achieved some success in long-distance mind-reading, with a caution that this may be a language misunderstanding and refer to long-distance telepathy.

A general report covered the effects of meditation and cult fanaticism on transpersonal consciousness where the subjects gave up families and possessions as the supposed price of self-awareness. It went on to consider the effect on the public's attitude to the paranormal in general and came to the conclusion that the majority of lay people dismissed the whole subject as belonging to Hollywood and horror-story writers. And those who believed in the paranormal were probably the phenomenon's worst enemies. The cranks, the zealots and the manipulators of the credulous.

He had listed the reference numbers of reports referred to in the general text that he would ask Schaeffer to get for him. He looked at his watch as he walked into the kitchen for a fruit drink from the fridge. It was just after midnight. Time that Martinez was back. He'd gone in the car to see *The Killing Fields* at the cinema in Palo Alto and he should have been back by now.

Siwicki had just reached down to switch on the TV when he heard the car pull in and stop. He knew that he'd have to chat with Martinez for ten minutes or so before he could escape to bed.

And then the door-bell rang and he straightened up, surprised. Martinez must have forgotten his keys. He walked across the tiled hall to the door and swung it open. The young man who stood there had fair hair and freckles that showed up in the light from the porch.

'Mr Siwicki?'

'Yes.'

'Can I come in and have a word with you?'

'What about?'

The young man reached in his pocket and pulled out a leather case, opening it to display the photograph as he said, 'FBI'.

'You'd better come in, mister . . . ?'

'Roberts, sir. Chuck Roberts.'

Siwicki led the way into the living room and switched off the TV before turning to the FBI man.

'It's Mr Paul Martinez, sir. I'm afraid he's dead.'

For a few moments Siwicki didn't speak and then he said slowly, 'Are you sure? He was perfectly OK when he left here a few hours ago.'

'The police in Palo Alto had a call about nine-thirty this evening that a man had died in one of the apartment blocks. The man had been visiting there.'

'But he has no friends in Palo Alto. He doesn't know anybody there. He'd gone alone, to the cinema.'

'The police checked the body and they found an ID card in his wallet that led them to notify my office. I went over and took charge of the card and checked the contents of his pockets. I've got them in the car.' He paused. 'I then phoned Washington and they came back half an hour later and gave me your name and address and told me to see you. They also instructed me to ask for the police to cooperate by not informing the press or the local coroner and to destroy any paper-work. There was no paper-work except the telephone log and that can't be deleted but it doesn't give any details and it's just been logged out as a crank call.'

'And where is the body?'

'It's been taken to Washington, to Langley. They said they'll do the necessary and they'll contact the relatives.'

'He has no relatives that I know of.'

'You'll be getting a phone call, sir. I think they'll want you to identify the body.'

'Who was it called the police?'

'The owner of the apartment where he died.'

'Who was it? What was his name?'

'It was a young woman, sir. She's known to the local police.'

It took several seconds for the facts to register and then Siwicki said quietly, 'You mean a prostitute?'

'A call-girl, sir. She won't be any problem. She doesn't want that kind of publicity.'

'Why didn't she send for a doctor?'

'I understand he died instantly. He was in a state of excitement when it happened. The MO said it looks as if it was a massive cardiac infarction.'

'How did he come to know her?'

'He phoned the girl from a bar. I guess he got her name from the bartender.'

'I can't believe it.'

'These things happen, sir. Especially if they don't do it very often.'

'I didn't mean that. I just can't believe he's not coming back again.'

'Shall I get his things from the car, sir?'

'I suppose you might as well do that.'

Schaeffer phoned Siwicki and told him not to go to Washington; he had already identified the body as Martinez' and they wanted Siwicki to stay where he was until things had been sorted out and the dust had settled.

Professor Rykov disliked having to share a bedroom, especially with Abromov. The meetings would last a week and he had hinted that unless he was found better accommodation he would be flying back to Novosibirsk the next day. There had been profuse apologies but he had to suffer one night with Abromov, a man he disliked intensely. Not only disliked but despised. He was a man without scruples who was prepared to carry out experiments that others wouldn't accept. Experiments which ignored any pretence of ethical acceptability. Experiments whose sole purpose was to destroy minds, not to extend human awareness and perception.

The participants in the Moscow conference were the heads of the most important institutions concerned with parapsychology and the paranormal in the Soviet Union. They and their senior staff were to meet daily in small discussion groups to exchange information and ideas on present and future laboratory work. There was Vagner from the Bauman, Sokolov from Moscow Energetics Institute, Gulyaev from Leningrad, Inyushin from Alma-Ata – all men whom Rykov respected. But at lower levels he found third-rate thinking, a willingness to let ends justify means.

It was the programmes for the third day that began to disturb him. He looked through the options for the day and the brief subject précis that went with them. A short discussion on autogenic training, another on factors affecting electro-bioluminescence. A report on successful experiments to produce a psychokinetic burn on the body of a female subject unaware of the experiment. The experimental results of stopping the hearts of different animals over long distances using only a woman psychic's psychokinetic powers. And then the final item that disturbed him deeply: proposed experiments to influence the health and thought-processes of specific subjects over long distances. The subjects to be unaware of their participation. Experiments which would be carried out at Akademgorodok. The scientist-in-charge not yet appointed.

Rykov attended only the discussion on autogenics and took no part in it, leaving before it was over. He walked out of the university grounds and crossed the road to the bank of the Moskva. He sat down, knees drawn up, and stared unseeing at the river. There was something wrong. Was it he who was wrong? Old-fashioned, hiding away from the realities of life in the laboratory at Akademgorodok, not facing the facts of life in Moscow. Or was it others who were wrong, non-scientists, administrators who decided what should be done or not done? Men who were ambitious for promotion and indifferent to the morality that they trampled so clumsily. But it was a harsh world that the men in the Kremlin had to face every day. A world that had no scruples in its determination to destroy the Soviets and their way of life. If this was work that would arm them against their various enemies who was he to indulge in the niceties of morality and scientific ethics? His mind went to Mikhail Lomonsov who had helped to found the University. He had a picture of him on his wall at home. Not just a scientist, but a poet as well. An eighteenth-century man who said that science and the arts were one, an amalgam of vision and practicality.

Rykov looked at his watch and then stood up unsteadily. It was time to get back to the arena.

He had had a snack in the cafeteria and then it was time for the discussion of the work to be carried out at Akademgorodok. If he was lucky he could avoid being involved and Simonov would be assigned to the new work.

Simonov had given the opening talk, mainly about his own work on long-distance telepathy, but then he had turned to Rykov's work with Ursula Jaeger. He described the early work with randomly chosen subjects and had then described the experiments using photographs of foreign politicians. The academics had been amused at her analysis of President Reagan's thoughts. The man who was bored by a meeting he was at and whose mind had gone to horses rather than the Federal budget discussions. Several people had turned to look at Rykov as he sat there with his eyes closed. He knew it was irrational to resent hearing Simonov describe his experiments with the girl. But it seemed like an intrusion. She was listed as his collaborator but she was just a young woman with a special talent trying to please an old man whom she liked. Simonov seemed to Rykov to be like those men who talked obscenely about their relationship with a woman to their friends.

And then another man had taken the chair. He gave his name as Litovkin, an officer in the KGB. He talked about the importance of this new development to the men in the Politburo. The security services were the guardians of the Soviet Union. The KGB and the GRU had all the resources they needed for obtaining information on the capitalist world's weapons and technology. What they needed now was 'the intelligence of intention'. What was in the minds of their enemies? What would be their reaction to the Soviet Union's policies? Thanks to the work of Professor Rykov a new weapon of defence had been forged. He was pleased to inform his audience that no such work had been undertaken in the USA. At the last estimate the total US budget for parapsychology was about three million dollars. The budget for the Soviet Union in this area already exceeded $338 million. He was also pleased to inform the meeting that, from now on, the work on long-distance mind-reading at Akademgorodok was to be funded by the KGB as well as the Ministry. Rykov suddenly felt cold as he heard the words and the murmurs of approval from the audience.

He barely heard the summing-up by Simonov, and when the latter had called for questions Rykov had been relieved when the KGB man had intervened and said that questions on any work involving the KGB were not in order.

Later that evening the KGB man had come to his room at the hotel. Major Litovkin was in his early fifties.

'I thought we should talk, Professor. Get to know one another so that we can work together constructively.'

'Do you have any experience in this kind of work?'

Litovkin smiled amiably. 'Why do you ask that? Are you worried that my big heavy boots will be trampling all over your laboratory?'

'I asked out of curiosity.'

'I had a two-year psychology course at the Quantum unit in Krasnodar and for the last four years I've been responsible for

monitoring what is being done in the US in parapsychology.'
He smiled. 'Does that do anything to calm your concern?'

'I must be frank with you, Major. I'm not happy about my work being used as a weapon.'

'I understand that when you lived in Moscow you were a frequent visitor to the Bolshoi Ballet?'

'Yes, I was.'

'Do you disapprove of the Ballet's tours overseas?'

'Of course not.'

'Well, they are a weapon, Professor, a weapon of diplomacy.'

'I don't understand.'

'When our ballet dancers or our orchestras are sent overseas they are ambassadors for the Soviet Union. They let people in other countries see that we are not the savages that we are painted. All our women are not digging up the streets of Moscow. They see that we have pretty girls and good-looking men. People with talent and charm. It's not a pretence. Both the charm and the talent are genuine.' He smiled. 'The other side of the coin from the news-reel shots they see of our leaders who are not appointed for their looks or their charm. Our creative people are a weapon. Not a weapon of war but, like I said, a weapon of diplomacy.' He paused. 'When a music-lover in another country enjoys the music of Tchaikovsky, Rachmaninov, Glazunov or even Shostakovich, he might wonder just for a moment how our nation can produce such talent if our people are all the modern equivalents of Genghis Khan.'

Rykov smiled despite himself. 'You are a very good advocate, Major Litovkin.'

'Now about your work.' Litovkin smiled. 'And your fears. Let me say first that your only KGB contact will be me. I shall not interfere in any way with your work. That will go on exactly as you intended. But if you need help or resources you only have to contact me and they will be provided immediately.'

'And what do I do that would interest the KGB?'

'Can I ask you a question first?'

'Certainly.'

'When your collaborator hears a target's thoughts, what language does she hear them in?'

'She doesn't hear them in any language. She's not hearing the person speaking, she is just hearing their thoughts. We

85

don't think in a language. We just think. When she relates the person's thoughts, she speaks to me in German or Russian. She's beginning to pick up English but that's nothing to do with the experiments.'

'So the language of the target is no problem. He could be Chinese, Japanese, anything, and she would be able to comprehend his thoughts and pass them to you?'

'Yes.'

'So. Back to your question. The only cooperation I shall ask of you will relate to your collaborator "contacting" specific targets at specific times. They will tend to be heads of foreign governments or senior politicians who can influence events.' He paused. 'Is that agreeable to you, Professor?'

'I don't see any difficulties, Major.'

Litovkin stood up and held out his hand. When Rykov took it, the KGB man said quietly, 'I'm just a man, Professor. We both love our country, we both work to protect it. Each in his own way. Thank you for being so patient with me. And remember – I'm on your side.'

CHAPTER 13

Schaeffer didn't have access to the Moscow embassy reports but he was on a restricted list of recipients of a weekly digest of embassy material. In the limbo after Martinez' death he took the opportunity of reading and clearing his desk of the backlog of reports. Somebody in Evaluation at Langley had side-lined in red any references to Soviet or Warsaw bloc experiments in parapsychology.

It was one of those items that caught his attention.

Two recent reports have suggested that the KGB has taken over control of a small unit experimenting with long-distance mind-reading. The unit is reported as being based just outside Novosibirsk. (Probably Akademgorodok. See several previous reports.) It is rumoured that the psychic involved is a young female of non-Soviet nationality.

Source reliability: One source of proved reliability. One new and untested. The circumstances under which information was passed on indicate that it is unlikely that this is an attempt at disinformation. Further RL074.

Schaeffer phoned the Research Liaison Officer and was shown the original embassy report. It named a Professor Rykov as the scientist in charge and gave a brief résumé of his academic career. A special note had been added that, for security reasons, Rykov's name should not be identified with the reported operation.

He phoned Westphal who saw him for ten minutes. The General was cool, almost as if he blamed him for Martinez' death. Implying that somebody had been unobservant in not recognising Martinez' needs. Completely ignoring the fact that Martinez was a civilian and free to go wherever he liked. But

Westphal had agreed to let Schaeffer go to Moscow and talk with the attaché who had put in the report. He also gave permission for Siwicki to accompany him, provided he was given false documents that would not give any indication of his area of expertise.

Schaeffer had been surprised that the attaché concerned was not only a woman, but not CIA, despite speaking fluent Russian. Melanie Tuchman had taught art history at Boston University and had been with the State Department for five years. Attractive and intelligent but not drawn to Schaeffer and his rather macho approach. But Siwicki was another matter; he knew what he was talking about. The questions he asked were relevant and informed. After ten minutes Schaeffer got the message and diplomatically excused himself and went to talk with an old friend, one of the CIA men at the embassy.

Melanie Tuchman smiled at Siwicki. 'Let's start again from square one.'

Siwicki grinned. 'Forgive him, it was just an alumnus of Fort Bragg trying to be civilised.'

'And failing miserably. What is it you want to know?'

'About the girl in the parapsychology experiments. What can you tell me about her?'

'Not much I'm afraid, or I could be compromising my informants. One of them anyway.'

'How did the subject come your way?'

'I heard about it first as a piece of gossip at a French Embassy party. A group of people were talking about pseudo-religious cults, particularly the Moonies. Somebody asked me if it was true that people sold all their possessions and gave the money to the cult. I said that it was true and somebody from the Bulgarian Embassy said that the Moonies' recruits were mainly impressionable girls. I asked him if that was a fact or a guess. He quoted figures and was obviously extraordinarily well informed. An American asked him if he knew how the Moonies did it. Got a hold on the girls' minds. Was it sex? He said that sex might come after but they used parapsychology to control the girls.'

Siwicki interrupted. 'Have you got the Bulgarian's name?'

'Yes.'

'Was he your source?'

'No. If you'll just listen I'll explain.'

'Sorry.'

'Then somebody, a Russian, made some crack about the Bulgarians only using pretty teenagers in their experiments and said that maybe they got them when the Moonies were finished with them. The Bulgarian took it badly and said something about Professor Rykov screwing the brains out of his little blonde at Akademgorodok. It was beginning to turn nasty and one of the French diplomats cooled them all down with a joke about Nancy Reagan.

'I found out later that the guy who made the original crack was a Soviet scientist. But nobody could remember his name.'

'Can you check the French Embassy's invitation list?'

'I've already done that and drawn a blank. Too many people go to those things with just word-of-mouth invitations. The Bulgarian's name was Talev, Nikola Talev.'

'The report said you had another source, could you tell us about that?'

'Yes. I gave a talk to a group of students at the University on the "American way of life" theme and afterwards there's always a lot of questions. It goes on for hours. Mainly about Bob Dylan, Pete Seeger and the pop scene. But that night the question of equal opportunities for girls came up. How did the two countries compare? I quoted the girl tennis players and athletes and got back the girl cosmonauts. And it became quite serious, not jokey any longer. Percentages of women doctors in the two countries, lawyers, factory bosses and I was taking quite a beating. I shifted into creative things, quoting women writers, Mary McCarthy, Joan Didion, et cetera and they quoted names of Soviet females in creative areas. The ballet, film and science. Somebody said science wasn't creative and there were loud protests with people shouting names I'd never heard of. And amongst the names was a German name, Ursula Jaeger. I asked who she was and there was a long silence and somebody said that she was Professor Rykov's assistant at Akademgorodok. After that – silence. We carried on for another half-hour and that's about all I can tell you.'

'What can you tell me about Professor Rykov?'

'I put a career resumé with my report. That's all I know. I've dropped his name around with Soviets but either they've never heard of him or he's under wraps.'

'And the girl?'

'Nothing. Just the name.'

'Could you find out more? Ask around a bit?'

'I could but I'm not going to. I'm Assistant Cultural Attaché, not CIA.'

'You'd only be gossiping.'

She shook her head and smiled. 'No way, honeychile. I like my job and I'm not going to mess around. Not for anyone.'

Schaeffer had persuaded Westphal to let Siwicki tell him what he had learned in Moscow from Melanie Tuchman. It was hard to tell whether Westphal was interested or not. He listened impassively and then turned to look at Schaeffer.

'So what is it you want, Schaeffer?'

'I'd like the Soviet section to find out more about Rykov and the girl. And what they're doing.'

'And then what?'

Schaeffer shrugged. 'It depends on what they turn up, sir.'

'I'll think about it, and let you know.' Westphal paused. 'There's a Brit coming over next week. A specialist on Soviet affairs. I've given him permission to visit with you. He's OK. SIS. But he's got nothing to trade. They've got no programme on parapsychology. Just desk research on what other people are doing. We want to look cooperative but don't go over the top.' He smiled. 'We may want a few favours from them in the next month or so. His name's Clayton. He's a professor of something or other.'

Schaeffer had picked up Clayton at Dulles and transferred them both to San Francisco flights where they had spent the night before driving down to Siwicki's place. Schaeffer had not taken to the tall dour Brit who wore a light-weight safari suit that looked as though it had seen a lot of wear and tear in darkest Africa. And owing to Schaeffer mishearing and misunderstanding a passing remark of Clayton's they had spent an uneasy evening on a tour of some of San Francisco's gay bars.

Having handed over his guest to Siwicki the next day Schaeffer had left an hour later.

As they sat together with a jug of orange-juice Clayton said tentatively, 'A strange fellow that Schaeffer.'

'Is he? In what way?'

'He asked me if I'd like him to fix me up with a girl for the evening. Right out like that. I'd only been with him for a couple of hours. I told him I wasn't interested, and then what happens? I have to hang around with him all evening at those all-male dumps down by the harbour. Why didn't he just say outright that he was a queer?'

Siwicki grinned. 'You mean you think Schaeffer's a queer?'

'We spent the whole damned evening with queers.'

Siwicki was laughing. 'He must have thought that that's what you wanted when you said you weren't interested in a girl. Old Schaeffer is so square he would have had to get somebody else to find out for him where the gay bars were so that he could keep you happy.'

'I hope you're right, Mr Siwicki.' Then he paused. 'You mean he still thinks I'm a queer?'

'Probably. I'll make sure he knows that it was a misunderstanding. Let's talk about your visit. What is it you want to know?'

'Anything you care to tell me. Maybe you could just put me in the picture about your work.'

'D'you want to start now?'

'If that's convenient to you.'

Clayton had spent four days with Siwicki, listening to tapes, reading his notes and talking. Siwicki got to like the reserved Englishman with his stiff, formal ways and his precise clipped accent. Clayton was no fool and there was a hint that if the British set up a parapsychology operation they would be interested in hiring Siwicki as a consultant. And in his present ambiguous situation that was good news.

When Clayton had asked him if there was anything he could do in return for his help, Siwicki had told him about Rykov and the girl. He asked if SIS could find out anything about the operation. And Clayton had said that he'd see what could be done.

CHAPTER 14

Schaeffer was surprised when he got the first report from Clayton and astonished at the information that SIS had gathered in a few weeks. He caught a plane and hired a car to drive down to see Siwicki.

There were eight pages of single-spaced typewriting and two photographs. One was of an elderly man with glasses, at a podium, addressing a meeting. On the back was a gummed label that said: 'Professor Rykov addressing delegates of seminar on Parapsychology at Irkutsk University. Photo from *Stroitelnaya Gazeta*. Recent.' The second photograph was of a young girl, blonde hair waving in the wind, looking from a bridge over a river. From the coarse grain it looked as if the original photograph had been much enlarged. The label on the back said: 'Jaeger, Ursula, on bridge over River Ob. In original the subject is with her mother and a German Shepherd Dog. Recent.'

Apart from a description of the kinds of experiments that were being carried out, there was a list of known subjects who had been targets for long-distance thought-reading by the girl. Those asterisked had been used frequently. There were thirty names on the list. All of them except three were public figures. They included President Reagan, the US Secretary of State, Olaf Palme the Prime Minister of Sweden, the Israeli Prime Minister, the Heads of State of the People's Republic of China, the Federal Republic of Germany, France and Finland, several American scientists, the captain of a Polaris submarine, two Democratic Senators, several senior members of the Polish Politburo and several people whose names and locations were given but whose significance was not explained. The three men who were not internationally known were all Soviet officials. One a senior member of the KGB, one a minister and one who was only identified as a librarian working for the GRU.

When Siwicki had finished reading the report, he said quietly, 'How the hell do these people get this kind of information in weeks when we don't have a clue?'

Schaeffer shrugged. 'First of all they've been at this game for centuries and secondly they're Europeans, on the spot. They've been filtering people into the Soviet Union from the day the war ended. They can't compete with us in our own backyard – South America. Or even the Far East.' He smiled. 'You notice that there isn't a single Brit name on that list. They aren't giving those to us.'

'They've given us enough here for God's sake. It's handsome payment for Clayton's visit.' Siwicki paused. 'What are we going to do with it?'

'What would you do with it?'

'I'd show it to Westphal.'

'And what would you get from that?'

'At least he'd take us off the hook and let me go looking for a replacement for Martinez. And start the operation again.'

'Did you notice the other significant thing about that list apart from no Brit names?'

'No.'

'I'd guess that that operation is being run by the KGB and somebody very high up.'

'Why that?'

'No tame scientist in Siberia is going to have the girl mind-reading KGB top brass unless somebody with a lot of clout tells him to. Playing games with us is one thing, probing KGB brass is a very different ball-game. And that means that they're getting useful results. They take notice of what the girl says. They'll have tested her. Checked on her. Like it says in that report from Clayton. When they showed her the photograph of a man who was already dead she cried and was ill for days. They're putting their silver dollar on that little gal, that's for sure.'

'So what would you do with this?' Siwicki gestured at the report lying on the coffee table between them.

'I'd talk to some friends before I went to Westphal.'

'What friends?'

'Oh, let's say friends on the operational side of CIA.'

'What could they tell you?'

'Not tell – do.'

'Do what, for Christ's sake? Why the guessing game?'

Schaeffer half-smiled. 'What would you most like right now, for your work?'

'To raise that poor bastard Martinez from his grave.'

'And failing that?'

'Find someone just as good.'

'Would the girl be just as good?' Schaeffer said, softly.

Siwicki looked at him, frowning. 'I don't get it?'

'Say we lifted her for you?'

'You're crazy, Schaeffer. She'd never agree. Why should she?'

'She doesn't have to agree.'

'You mean kidnap her?'

'Yep.'

'Kidnap a girl in Siberia under the noses of the KGB. You're dreaming dreams, Schaeffer. Dangerous dreams.'

'But you could use her?'

'Of course. Provided she hadn't been scared out of her mind.'

'It's been done before.'

'Westphal would never agree. Not in a million years.'

'I wasn't thinking of Westphal. I was aiming much higher than that.'

'How much higher? Who?'

'The Director himself.'

'You think he'd listen to something like that?'

'Provided my friends say it could be done, yes, I think he'd listen. We'd be offering quite a handsome prize. Just imagine tuning that little gal onto the top brass of the KGB and the Politburo.'

'Are these friends of yours what they call the "Dirty Tricks" people?'

Schaeffer grinned. 'They call themselves the Clandestine Operations Committee.'

'Count me out, old pal. That sort of thing's not for me.'

'But you'd use her if we got her?'

'I'd have to think about it.'

'You do that, my friend. We'll talk about it tomorrow. Now tell me what you've been doing down here on your own.'

CHAPTER 15

Macleod had put off several meetings with Thornton but he had eventually agreed a time and they had met in Macleod's office.

'Right, Thornton. What is it you want?'

'Just a chat with you about Mr Fisher.'

'A chat? I don't go in for gossiping about fellow officers. Can you not be more specific?'

'I'd like your impressions of him as a field agent.'

'I'd better say right at the start that I was not an admirer. We worked together on several occasions but only for short periods.'

'Mr Hallam suggested that you were quite close to him at one time.'

'Me? Close to Fisher? I don't know where Hallam got that impression. I saw a lot of him on one operation but that doesn't make us close. He must have got that impression from Fisher. He certainly didn't get it from me.'

'Did you actually dislike him?'

Macleod hesitated, then said, 'Yes. I suppose I did.'

'What was it you disliked?'

'I think his success in the field had gone to his head. I thought he was arrogant. A law unto himself.'

'Did he dislike you?'

'That was part of his arrogance. Despite our differences he seemed to take it for granted that I was one of the fan club. To him I was just another chap from behind a desk at Century House – issuing orders – or "interfering" as he would put it.' Macleod shrugged. 'Let's just say we didn't get on.'

'How long ago was this?'

'About three years ago.'

'He must have been in Germany at that time.'

'He was. In Hamburg.'

'Why had you gone out there?'

'He was being very obstreperous. Refusing to carry out London's orders. Arguing the toss, putting up difficulties. I was sent over to sort him out.'

'Didn't he eventually do what was wanted?'

'We thought he did. But we found out afterwards that he'd had his own way in the end. Like I said – he was arrogant.'

'Did you have much to do with him when he came back to the UK?'

'None at all. I did my best to steer clear of him.' He gave a rueful smile. 'And he was promoted over my head as so often happens in SIS. We seem to like the chaps who don't stick to the rules. As long as they bring home the bacon all is forgiven. That, of course, is why you're having to waste your time on this little venture now.'

'Why do you think he's disappeared?'

'Whatever the reason it'll be because it suits him.'

'Mr Seymour thinks that he's defected. He thinks that all four of you think that he's defected but don't want to admit it.'

'Seymour should speak for himself.'

'*Do* you think he's defected?'

'No. That's the last thing I would expect. He knows too much about the Soviet Union and the KGB to want to spend the rest of his days there.'

'What about his private life?'

'What about it?'

'Money, sex, family.'

'Well, he certainly wasn't a big spender. Like most agents I imagine he lived off his allowances and banked his salary. It wouldn't be sex. He wasn't immune to pretty faces but I'd guess he took sex in his stride. Let's just say he didn't inhale.' Macleod paused. 'And he was married after all.'

'And family?'

'There was no family. Just a wife.'

'Did you meet her at all?'

Macleod looked towards the window and then back at Thornton.

'I met her a couple of times,' he said quietly.

'What was she like?'

'Very pretty, much younger than he was.'

'Likely to be an influence on him?'

'The other way round I would say. Entirely dependent on him. He was very obviously the White Knight so far as she was concerned.'

'Can I ask you about the cottage at Wadhurst?'

'I knew nothing about it until a few days ago.'

'Why was I prevented from checking it out?'

Macleod looked genuinely surprised. 'Were you? I didn't know that.'

'Mr Hallam told me that the sub-committee had decided that it wasn't necessary for me to check it.'

'Well, I certainly wasn't asked. But I would have gone along with it if that was what Hallam wanted.'

'Why would you go along with it?'

'Because that was Hallam's problem not mine. If he didn't want you nosing around that's his prerogative.'

'It doesn't help my research much.'

Macleod stood up, half-smiling. 'You'll find a lot of things don't help your research much, my boy. When the skeletons start rattling in the cupboards SIS are old hands at closing the cupboard doors. I'm afraid I'll have to throw you out. I've got another meeting.' And Thornton had the feeling that Macleod himself was closing a cupboard door.

Thornton had taken to meeting Smallwood away from Century House, usually at the cafeteria at Victoria Station. But they had met that day at the coffee room at the Hilton. A plate of Danish pastries on the table between them.

Smallwood put down his cup. 'I made a little trip down to Wadhurst at the weekend. And very interesting it was.'

'Did you go to the cottage?'

'No. I went to a couple of estate agents. Told 'em I was looking for somewhere nice. They showed me the details of a few places and I mentioned that I'd noticed a nice place called "Little Croft" when I was coming into the village. Had they got something like that? Even "Little Croft" itself.'

'Cut out the drama, Tom. What did you find?'

'The first guy looked through his records. He discovered that it was owned by a Mr Fisher and he remembered then that he'd sold it to Mr Fisher about three months ago. He didn't think

97

Mr Fisher would be interested in selling. I took the details of a couple of other cottages.

'The second guy was younger and much more on the ball. He knew all the property in the area and he knew "Little Croft". He'd heard in the local pub that it had either been sold or was coming on the market a few months back. He'd phoned the owners and been told it wasn't for sale. But while I was there he rang the chap he'd met in the pub who'd told him it might have been sold and asked him what he knew. The chap worked for the Land Registry in Tunbridge Wells and he'd registered the sale of "Little Croft" about three months ago. He couldn't remember the name of the purchaser. But he gave the name of the local solicitors who handled the conveyancing. My chap has a girl-friend who was a clerk at the solicitors and he said he'd ask her what the current position is. It cost me an expensive dinner but it was sold to Fisher and then sold three days later to Sir Arthur Beagley, KCB.'

'Who the hell is Sir Arthur Beagley?'

'Sir Arthur is one of the top brass of Her Majesty's Property Services Agency, and . . .' he paused for effect, '. . . and, he bought it from the previous owner, to wit a Mr David Fisher, for ten thousand quid more than the said Mr Fisher had paid for it only a few days before.' Smallwood helped himself to another pastry as he said, 'What d'you make of that, Mr Thornton?'

'What do you make of it?'

'I've thought about it a lot over the weekend. There's two things come out of it for me.'

'Go on.'

'First of all it looks like SIS wanted to do Fisher a good turn. Ten thousand quid's worth of good-will. Tax free.'

'And the second?'

'The second is that somebody's playing silly beggars with you and me.'

'Why should they do that?'

'I reckon they don't want us to find friend Fisher. They may even know where he is.'

'So why put me on his trail?'

Smallwood shrugged. 'Something for the record to show that they tried to find him – could even be one bit of SIS is trying to keep him away from some other bit.' He smiled. 'You never know with our chaps. They look like innocent overgrown schoolboys but they ain't innocent. None of 'em.' He sighed. 'That's my experience anyway.'

'Did you have any luck tracing relatives?'

Smallwood shook his head. 'I've seen death certificates for both his parents. There are no relatives alive. I'm sure of that.'

'You worked for Macleod for some time, didn't you?'

'Yes, I've done his leg-work from time to time.'

'How did he get on with Fisher?'

'They had some flaming rows. At least Mac would be flaming and Fisher would be surprised and amused. But they respected one another. In their own ways I think they liked one another.'

'When I spoke to Macleod he gave a totally different picture from that. He actually said he disliked Fisher and that didn't fit in with something that Hallam mentioned.

'I asked Hallam who first noticed that Fisher wasn't around and he mentioned that Macleod was probably the first because Fisher hadn't turned up for a game of chess.'

'Like I said, you can't trust those bastards an inch when they're up to their tricks. I've seen Mac and Fisher together. They got on all right and Mac definitely didn't dislike Fisher. They had their differences but it never lasted. There was a bit of frostiness on Mac's part when Fisher was promoted above him but he settled down. Fisher deserved the promotion.'

'Nobody has really seemed to like Fisher except you.'

Smallwood laughed. 'Maybe they didn't know him as well as I did. I've seen him in action, under pressure, and he is like a rock. I respect him and I like him too.' He smiled. 'And of course, they could be lying for their own good reasons. Whatever those might be.'

'There was nothing unusual in his case files that I read.'

'I know. I looked through the files.' He grinned. 'The ones that matter aren't there of course. Just the routine stuff.' He paused. 'You knew he lit out once before?'

'You mean this isn't the first time Fisher's disappeared?'

'Yes. He went missing for about three weeks.'

'They didn't mention that to me.'

'They probably thought you knew.'

'What happened?'

'Just that. I was working for him at the time. We were in Hamburg. He'd been pulled out of the operation by London for some emergency job. I think it was in Berlin. He was away for a few weeks, came back for a few weeks, and then disappeared. We thought he was back on the special and London thought he was in Hamburg so it was some time before everybody realised that he'd done a bunk. By the time we knew he was off he'd been away for a couple of weeks or more. The panic had been on for a week or ten days when he just walked back in at Hamburg as if nothing had happened?'

'Did he give any explanation?'

'Not in Hamburg anyway. Not that he needed to. He was boss. I think he told London he'd just gone on leave and forgotten to inform them. He wasn't the sort of chap who forgets things but he hadn't had any leave for five years so there wasn't much they could do about it. So it all died down.'

'Where did he live at that time?'

'He had a house just outside Hamburg. In Blankanese.'

'What was it like?'

'I never went inside. I drove him there a couple of times and picked him up once, but I wasn't invited in.'

'Could you find it again?'

'Yes. No problem.'

'Let's go there and have a look at it.'

Smallwood looked surprised but he said, 'D'you want me to lay on tickets with Facilities?'

'OK. You do that.'

As Smallwood got to the door Thornton said, 'Hold on, Tom. I'd like to think about all this for a couple of days. I don't want to rush in and get a bloody nose again. OK?'

'Whatever you say, squire. I'll get on snooping around in the records.'

'OK. But keep in touch.'

Smallwood smiled, clicked his heels and did a mock-salute as he opened the door.

Long after Smallwood had left Thornton still sat there thinking. Trying to arrange and re-arrange all the conflicting information that he had gathered about Fisher. Arrogant, tough, soft-hearted, a loner, a successful field officer, a flouter of orders, a ruthless operator, liked and disliked for almost the same reasons.

Smallwood had seen more of Fisher than the others and he'd seen him in action, not from a desk in London. Then there was the cottage at Wadhurst, the field reports that apparently were not available, the death or non-death of Fisher's wife. That disappearance in Hamburg. And the attitude of the self-appointed committee of four and their conflicting views of the man they were all supposed to know so well.

But even Smallwood wasn't totally reliable. Tough and cynical as he was he was the kind of man who would tend to hero-worship a leader he admired and who was successful at what Smallwood set store by. And Smallwood's views on Hallam and the others were typically biased. Suspicion and cynicism were bred in the bones of SIS field operators because it might save their lives, but Hallam and the other three were not as black as Smallwood painted them. They had to make tough decisions: that was part of their jobs. But they were honest men at heart and were as moral and concerned as any man could be doing their kind of work.

But there was definitely something wrong with the whole set-up and he had no idea what it was. It would be fatal to leap to conclusions, and he knew that at that moment he didn't even have any conclusions to leap to. There were times with all operations when you had to just free-wheel and wait for a sign from the good Lord. Just charging around could do more harm than good. For some reason he wished that he could talk about it with Penny. Unlike other men he had no office gossip to relate, the chat was all hers. What made it worse was that she obviously hoped that he might relax from time to time and tell her about the goings-on of some public figure. Sometimes she'd show him some item in a newspaper about a West German defector, a minister's elderly secretary, and ask him how such ordinary-looking old bags could be modern-day Mata Haris. And all he could do was fend it off with a smile and a shrug. He wondered if Hallam told his Gabriella things that he shouldn't.

He phoned the theatre and spoke to Penny to suggest they met in town for dinner but she was in the last week of rehearsals and would be finishing late. He had heard the clamour of voices in the background and a piano playing one of Penny's songs to the shuffle of the chorus's feet. It sounded warm and friendly. Maybe he'd pick her up from the theatre and some of the enthusiasm and excitement would rub off on him.

CHAPTER 16

After the first flush of information from SIS about the work of Professor Rykov and the girl, there had been high-level criticism inside the CIA that they had not been able to uncover such important material themselves. The counter-argument was that it was of only marginal importance and not of major concern to the CIA. Westphal's response to that had been that if you want something at all then it's important enough to find it.

When the dust had settled some lessons had been learned on both sides. Westphal realised that he would have been wise to use his privilege and go right to the top to the Director himself. And the opposition recognised that Operation Aeolus, whatever that might be, had enough potential clout to warrant more effort than they had expended.

In not much more than a couple of weeks the CIA had made a contact. In terms of hard intelligence, the contact was useless and the information that came back on the experiments was no more than servants' gossip. But it provided a detailed picture of the girl's everyday life and her movements.

As the information accumulated Schaeffer and Westphal argued the case for kidnapping the girl. And finally Westphal agreed to put the proposal to the Director CIA.

The then Director had been specifically appointed by the White House to breathe life back into an organisation that had been battered by the Puritan ethos of the Carter administration. In the Marines he wouldn't have been rated as 'gung-ho' but by the standards of politicians that was how he was seen. He listened to Westphal's case attentively and pursed his lips when it ended.

'What's the likelihood of success?'

'We shouldn't carry it out unless we were absolutely certain it would be successful.'

'You realise that if it went wrong the Soviets would have us for breakfast?'

'Yes, sir.'

'Have you discussed this with the people who might have to do it?'

'Yes, sir.'

'And they said they could carry it out?'

'Provided they controlled the timing, yes.'

'I'll put it up to the man and see what he thinks.'

'Do you need any more information, sir?'

'No. I've got all I need.'

There had been four other items on the agenda before the two men came to point five – Operation Aeolus. The President pointed at the file on his desk.

'I read it very carefully.' He paused and gave a wry smile. 'And I don't like it.'

'You saw the kind of intelligence we could get. No more trying to guess what those guys in the Kremlin are thinking.'

'Yep. I saw all that.'

'Are you worried about the repercussions if we didn't bring it off?'

'Yes. But I'm equally worried about the repercussions if we *did* pull it off.'

'The girl's still an East German national. She's not a Soviet.'

'I appreciate that. Frankly I find this whole parapsychology business abhorrent. It may be sheer old-fashioned prejudice on my part, but for me it's like one of those wretched horror films. *The Exorcist.* That sort of crap. I'd hate having to defend this sort of stuff to Congress.'

'OK, Mr President. I'll close the file on it.'

'I'd like you to go further than that, Joe. I'd like you to close down the whole operation. See that the guys involved are not disadvantaged but no more of this guff. It's unAmerican. And it's obscene.' He sighed. 'If it's any consolation to you I'm going to have somebody look at what Stanford are doing too.'

The Director stood up. 'Thank you for your time, sir.'

'That's OK. You're entitled. How's that family of yours?'

'They're fine, Mr President. Sailing around somewhere in Massachusetts Bay.'

The President grinned. 'Just make sure they don't come back with Boston-Irish accents. I couldn't stand that.'

The Director's meeting with Schaeffer was uncomplicated. The President had given his orders and there was no room for argument or discussion. Schaeffer was obviously surprised and shocked that his venture had led to the abandoning of the whole operation. But he had been around long enough to know that these sorts of things happened. And when they did, you retreated gracefully and waited for a change in the weather.

'How long have I got to close down, sir?'

'Operation Aeolus is written off as of now, Schaeffer. Today. So far as the practical arrangements are concerned just be as quick as you can. I'll instruct Accounts to release six months' budget cash as the cost of closing. How you apportion that is at your discretion. But you'll render a proper account when you've wrapped it all up.'

'Thank you, sir.'

'And regarding your own position – you'll be posted to another appointment. Upgraded.'

'Thank you, sir.'

He spent half a day in his office working out the practicalities of what he had to do, and then took the afternoon plane to San Francisco. As he drove down the freeway he knew that Siwicki would be a problem. The Director had been careful to quote very little of what the President had said, but he had mentioned that he had found it 'unAmerican' and 'obscene' just to make sure that Schaeffer realised that there was no room for argument. But when Schaeffer came to dealing with Siwicki he toned down the dislike, for Siwicki was already depressed, and to hear the President's comment would demoralise him completely. But Schaeffer knew from experience that bringing bad news without revealing the facts always led to a lot of recrimination. He'd just have to play it by ear.

Siwicki was out when he arrived and one of the servants told him that he'd gone to see a friend at Stanford, and Schaeffer guessed that Siwicki was testing the water to see if there was any chance of an opening there for him. And if that's what he wanted Schaeffer would pull all the levers to make sure he got it.

It was nearly 1 a.m. when Siwicki got back, hurrying into the house when he saw the hire car, eager to see if there was some new development.

'Hi,' he said, smiling. 'I've got a feeling you're bringing good news, Schaeff.'

So much for parapsychology, thought Schaeffer, but he managed a relaxed smile.

'How were things at Stanford?'

'Overloaded according to what my friend tells me.'

'Have you got designs on working for them?'

'I'd be glad to if our thing doesn't work out.'

'I've had orders from the top to put the whole thing on ice.'

'What does that mean?'

'There's a big economy drive on at the moment. Our operation is one of the victims. Indefinite suspension.'

'Despite all we've been able to give them?'

'I'm afraid so. And with Martinez dead we can't give them any more.'

'What about the Soviet girl? The plan to lift her?'

'That's not on for political reasons. With a new guy in the Kremlin they want to wait and see if he's going to be interested in negotiations. And nothing's going to be done that could upset them unnecessarily.'

'And for me? What do I do?'

'If you want to go to Stanford I can see that you go. If you'd prefer to act as a consultant neurologist to Clandestine Operations I can fix that too. You'll get three months' pay clear of tax, and any kind of reference you might want.'

'How long do I have to make up my mind?'

'I guess you could think about it overnight. We can talk again in the morning.'

Siwicki opted for Stanford and duly went down in Schaeffer's estimation for so doing. But he reckoned that any man who could choose the academic life rather than the CIA was no great loss to Langley.

Despite his feelings Schaeffer pressed the appropriate buttons and pulled the right strings to make sure that Stanford not only took Siwicki on board but was made aware that he had the approval of influential people in the CIA. An accolade that didn't endear Siwicki to his peers at SRI, but which its administrators bore in mind.

Siwicki settled in quickly, moved into a pleasant apartment in Palo Alto and was assigned to a team evaluating the application of intuitive data.

Schaeffer was, on principle, moved to a different office, and his old one was cleared out and redecorated, as if someone feared contamination by osmosis. He was put in charge of routeing agents' reports from Warsaw bloc countries to their appropriate recipients. He was given Head of Department status. The rest of his department consisted of a secretary and two clerks. After a few days he knew that he was relieved to be away from the mysteries of the human mind. He could see the uses but it had made him uncomfortable. It wasn't work for a real man.

CHAPTER 17

Anna Jaeger looked at the handwritten letter on her desk and then reached for the phone and dialled Rykov's number. Rykov himself answered.

'Professor, it's Anna, Anna Jaeger.'

'How nice to hear from you.'

'I've had a letter from my husband, Ushi's father. He's in East Berlin. He'd like to see her and he doesn't like travelling. He asks if it would be possible for her to visit him for a few days.' She paused. 'Would that be convenient to you?'

'Of course. Of course.'

'I was thinking of in about a month's time. Over the May Day holiday.'

'Whenever you decide, my dear. No problem. Have you told her yet?'

'No. I'll tell her tonight.'

'She'll be very pleased, I know. She talks about him often.'

'Thanks for your cooperation.'

'Not at all. A break will do her good.'

In the end Ushi's plans had to be changed so that the visit would take place six weeks ahead, but in the meantime there was much excitement and many preparations to be made for the journey. Passport, permits, foreign exchange and even a concession of 'hard' roubles for gifts, and new clothes to be chosen and bought. The servants had joked that the journey to East Berlin needed as much preparation as the launch of Sputnik I.

The only person who seemed immune to the excitement was the old man who swept the yard, brought logs for the stoves and looked after the garden. He also did the odd repairs around the house: plumbing, gardening and unblocking drains. He never gossiped with the other servants and seldom spoke. There were people who said he was mentally defective but he did his work thoroughly and did what he was told. Nobody knew what nationality he had originally held – he spoke rough ungrammatical Russian and some German – but nobody really cared. He was quite harmless.

In fact he was originally Polish but that was a long time ago. He had been taken prisoner when the Russians eventually swept into Warsaw and with others he had been herded onto the train that finally dumped them at a prisoner-of-war camp near Novosibirsk. And, like the others, he had worked on building roads and clearing forests for almost ten years. When the slave labourers were given the option of being transported back to Poland he had no reason to go. By then he knew enough Russian and enough of bureaucracy to walk out of the virtually empty camp one day and head for the city. There were too many foreigners of one kind or another in Novosibirsk for him not to be absorbed easily into the population. There was what amounted to a Polish ghetto in the city. Three or four back streets where Polish was spoken more than Russian. Inevitably there was a black market and he had been involved on the fringe of it. Running messages and negotiating small deals for food and alcohol.

There were two men, both Poles, who ran the black market, and it was one of those men who had told him about the new town that they'd built on the other side of the river. There were opportunities for work in the new town. The old man could earn more money there than in the city. When he had hesitated the Pole told him that he would not only get his pay for the light work that he did, but the Pole would pay him too. He had winked and grinned. He wanted information about certain things. He'd be told what things as they became necessary.

The old man had made the Pole wait for a day or two before he agreed. The Pole had been sure that the old man would do what he wanted. What he was offering was irresistible. The old man would make more in a day than he normally made in a week. But he'd raise the stakes gradually. He didn't want to arouse the old man's suspicions. The Pole was not a good judge of character. He assumed that every man in the ghetto was as avaricious as he was. The only difference was that they were happy with food and roubles. His money went into a Swiss bank account.

As with many people who are misjudged by their fellows it didn't really matter to the old man. He went as ordered to Akademgorodok. Did his work and kept his ears open. Everything from the writing on a blackboard in a lecture room to hints of adultery were grist to the Pole's mill. He never knew that the old man had a good idea of what his 'gossip' was used for. And the old man's motivation had never been the money. It was the memory of his young wife being raped by the three Mongols from the infantry that Zhukov had sent in to relieve Warsaw. He still had the faint marks on his chest where their boots had caved in his ribs. And that was why he never went back to Poland. And why, after years of indifference to his own fate, he relished the chance of revenge on the Russians.

It was the old man's information on the life-styles of the community of Akademgorodok and the home-life of Ushi Jaeger that eventually ended up in Langley, Virginia.

The Pole's brief was wide and non-specific. If anything he passed back to the man in Moscow was worth pursuing there were other means to do it. The intermediaries were comparatively innocent, assuming that what they carried was to do with the black market. Satisfied with supplies of fruit and vegetables for providing a link in the chain. The thought that they were part of an intelligence network would have horrified them.

The man in Moscow was the foreman in charge of the stage-hands at the Bolshoi Theatre. He was a 'fixer', an expert in the game of *blat*, the Soviet equivalent of the 'old boy' network. Seats at the Bolshoi were his basic currency, exchanged for scarce goods, petrol, permits, 'hard' roubles, Levis, pop records and anything that could return him two or three hundred per cent on every transaction. The last link in the chain was a technician in the maintenance section of Radio Moscow. He picked up the coded messages at three-weekly intervals. Sometimes taped under the slats of a bench down by the Moskva River where it flowed past Gorky Park. Sometimes from a rubbish bin at the Pavlersky railway station in Leninskaya Square. And in emergencies the American would stand alongside him in the interval, in the toilets of the old Moscow Circus on Tsventoi Boulevard. Except for the old man, nobody in the chain did what he did for ideological reasons. Greed was their only motive.

The information about Ushi Jaeger was already five days old when it landed on Schaeffer's desk with a batch of other reports. It was five hours later when he read it, and knew that it would have been the perfect opportunity for the girl to be lifted.

If distance makes the heart grow fonder it was also distance, distance in time, that had made Schaeffer realise the value of the information that Siwicki and Martinez had provided. They had mentally looked at some of the Soviet Union's most secret installations. Described in detail what had only been a rumoured complex at some site in the Urals. Operational headquarters, missile-testing bases, had all been open for inspection. The Operations people had been amazed and delighted the first few times but in the end they had treated it as if it were some normal service provided by Central Archives and their computers. It had all been taken for granted. It had suited them all at Langley to let it stay a secret. A dilettante experiment in the house on the West coast. If the success had been properly acknowledged and the top-brass had known about it then maybe the Director himself would have been anxious to have the girl brought over.

Despite his ex-soldier's attitude to life Schaeffer was not given to self-deception and as he watched another re-run of *The French Connection* on TV he came to the conclusion that if anyone was to blame it was him. He had done nothing to promote the importance of the work that Siwicki and Martinez had been doing. He had just accepted others' advice to keep it all low-key. It had been bad advice and he had been gullible in taking it. It had suited them to have it that way. They got the kudos and Operation Aeolus never received the recognition it was due.

If he had done the right things Washington could be tuned into the mind of the new Soviet President right now, not playing guessing games and trying to make sense out of a hundred different and conflicting views on what Soviet intentions were at the nuclear disarmament talks. He had been at least a fool and perhaps even a coward. He'd stood on the side-lines and let Siwicki and Martinez be seen as cranks when he should have had them lauded as heroes. It was time to put things right.

He had had to look back in his diary to recall the name of the Brit but once he had found it he lost no time in taking action. He checked by phone that Professor Clayton was in London. Actually spoke to him and arranged a meeting without telling the Brit what it was about.

He used his Head of Department rating and booked a seat on the morning Concorde flight from Dulles. He'd taken a taxi to the London Hilton and booked himself a suite for a week. He had a shower and a hair-cut and then he'd waited for Clayton and his friend.

They had arrived promptly at eight o'clock as arranged. Schaeffer thought the Professor looked a shade smarter in a suit and on his own home ground. After shaking hands Clayton turned to introduce the other man who was with him.

'Let me introduce my colleague. Bill Hallam.'

'Glad to meet you, Bill. Won't you both sit down?' He waved towards the armchairs. 'Can I fix you a drink?'

Clayton had a neat malt, not even ice, and Hallam had opted for an orange juice. As Schaeffer handed round the drinks he sat down facing the two men.

'Does Hallam know about the work we showed you in the States, Professor?'

'Yes. I put him in the picture after I got back.'

'Am I right in thinking you still don't have a similar operation here in England?'

It was Hallam who replied and Schaeffer guessed that he was the senior of the two. 'We've got a couple of psychologists reading the books and checking the international scientific papers but that's all we've got.'

'Have you got any information on what the Soviets are doing in this area?'

'Nothing except that they're spending large sums of money on parapsychology experiments.'

'Have you heard of a Professor Rykov?'

Hallam looked at Clayton who in turn looked at Schaeffer.

'We sent the CIA information on him some time ago and on a young German girl name of Jaeger, Ursula Jaeger.'

'And you've heard of Akademgorodok?'

112

Hallam again looked at Clayton who said, 'Yes. Two of our universities have sent people to seminars in Kiev on criminal psychology and they met people from – "Science City" I think they called it.'

'That's the place, my friends. And it's Rykov and the girl that I wanted to talk with you about. How long can you give me?'

Hallam smiled and shrugged. 'We're at your disposal, Mr Schaeffer.'

For an hour Schaeffer had told them all that he knew of the long-distance telepathy experiments and the set-up in Rykov's laboratory and the girl's background. He reminded them of the information that they had originally passed to Langley. And then told them of his own shortcomings in emphasising the importance of Siwicki's work in the States.

He made the demise of Operation Aeolus just a touch less permanent than it actually was, but made clear that for the time being the CIA had no authorisation to experiment with parapsychology as an arm of intelligence although he hoped that that would not last for long.

Schaeffer then plunged into the deep end and suggested that if the British would pick up the girl on her visit to East Berlin the CIA would send over Siwicki to operate the girl and the information would be shared between SIS and the CIA. The CIA would fund most of the cost of the ongoing operation.

When Schaeffer had finished his pitch he was longing for another drink but he was shrewd enough not to let the atmosphere relax. It was Hallam who broke the silence.

'Tell me, Mr Schaeffer, what happens if when you've got her the girl refuses to cooperate?'

'Siwicki thinks he could overcome any problems in that area.'

'How exactly?'

'He's a likeable young fellow and he took his time building up a good relationship with Martinez who wasn't all that keen in the early days. He is sure that he could do it again with the girl.'

'Would this have the approval of Langley? At the top level I mean?'

'No, sir. It would come under Clandestine Operations and the top-brass wouldn't want to know.'

'Have you got the authority to do this yourself?'

'Yes, sir.'

'You say we've got about four weeks and a few days before the girl is in East Berlin?'

'As of now it's four weeks and three days.'

'That doesn't give us much time for planning.' As Schaeffer opened his mouth to speak Hallam interrupted. 'Anyway that's jumping fences. I'll have to discuss this with one or two of my colleagues before giving you an answer.'

'You'll appreciate the time factor, Mr Hallam?'

'Certainly. Could we meet you here about five tomorrow afternoon? Would that be convenient?'

'I'm at your disposal, Mr Hallam.'

Hallam stood up and then Clayton, and as they headed for the door Hallam said, 'You'll find us a dull, cautious lot compared with you lively chaps in the States. You'll have to be patient with us if we seem to be taking our time.'

'If I could point out, sir, that if we succeed we've got a prize almost on a level with Enigma. And if we don't. Well, we've lost a little time and a little money but that's all.'

Schaeffer walked with them to the lifts and when the doors closed behind them Hallam looked at Clayton. 'Just a little time and a little money and we could be putting a spanner in the works for the FO and the Moscow Embassy that they'd never forgive us for.'

'But he wasn't far wrong in comparing it with Enigma.'

Hallam looked down at his big shoes and then at Clayton as he said quietly, 'It's almost incredible, isn't it? Sitting in a room at the Hilton talking about reading Gorbachev's mind. What a world, Clayton. What a crazy, bloody world that makes it not only possible but almost certainly feasible that we can do such things.' He smiled. 'Can you imagine Seymour's face when we explain it to him?'

Hallam had phoned Macleod and Seymour to meet him and Clayton at the Travellers' Club, and while they were waiting Hallam booked a private room and Clayton booked rooms for himself and Seymour at the Piccadilly Hotel.

It was Hallam who explained the situation and Clayton who filled in the experimental background and the possible rewards.

When they had finished Seymour said quietly, 'You two aren't serious about this are you?'

Hallam shrugged. 'Why not?'

'If the kidnapping went wrong can you imagine the repercussions? They'd crucify us. And rightly so.'

'Who would do the crucifying?'

'Parliament, the media, the public, the Government, the United Nations, the German governments – both of them – and the Soviets. Think of a name and they'd crucify us. Nobody would dare to say a word in our favour.'

'Clayton read you the list of our people who Rykov and the girl are supposed to have been mind-reading. The Prime Minister, the Foreign Secretary, the CIGS, scientists, several MPs, the Minister of Defence. Why is it OK for them to do this to us and yet you're so sure that it would be wrong for us to do it?'

'I'm not talking about that – I'm talking about kidnapping the girl to do it.'

'You mean that it's OK for our people to kill the opposition but not kidnap them?'

Macleod interjected, looking at Seymour as he spoke. 'Are you worried about the kidnapping or that it might go wrong?'

'That it might go wrong of course.'

Macleod raised his eyebrows. 'So let's cut out the holier than thou stuff and talk about the kidnapping.'

Hallam sighed. 'Before we do that are we all agreed that if it all worked then it would be worth having the information? Seymour?'

'Yes, of course it would.'

Hallam looked at the other two who nodded. 'So let's talk about the kidnapping and some precautions if it went wrong.'

'Are you going to tell the DG or the Minister if we go ahead?'

Hallam shook his head. 'Of course not. It's between the four of us and whoever does the job.'

Seymour said, 'Who's going to pick up the girl?'

Hallam looked at him. 'I've got somebody in mind but we've got to decide the main issue first. Do we do it?'

Macleod looked at Clayton. 'You haven't said a thing, Professor. And you know more than we do about whether it will work if we do it.'

Clayton was silent for a few moments. 'I can't guarantee it but from what I saw in the States I'd think that Siwicki was quite capable of doing it. We know that the girl is already performing successfully. It could take time before she settles down but I'm sure that, given time, Siwicki could gain her confidence.'

Macleod said aloud what was in all their minds. 'We'd be ahead of the Yanks and ahead of the Soviets and we'd have taken away the KGB's advantage at the same time. It would be crazy to miss this chance.'

Seymour nodded. 'I guess you're right.' He looked at Hallam. 'Who's going to lift the girl?'

'Fisher's the only one I'd trust to do it.'

'Where is he now?'

'In Hamburg.'

'What's he doing?'

'Running a line-crossing operation. But his deputy can take over.'

Hallam looked from one to another. 'And we agree that we and Schaeffer and Siwicki will be the only ones who are in the picture.'

'And Fisher,' added Seymour.

Hallam shook his head. 'No. He doesn't need to know why we want the girl.'

'Will you leave the planning to him?'

'Of course.' Hallam smiled. 'You know Fisher as well as I do. Whatever we suggested he'd still do it his own way. And he'd probably be right too.'

They talked for another half-hour, beginning to be confident and enthusiastic.

Fisher had landed at Heathrow two days later and Hallam had met him. He used one of the security offices at the airport to brief him. The photograph, the description of the girl and the date of the planned trip to see her father. He could even give her father's address in East Berlin and a rough description of him.

Fisher had listened without questions until Hallam had finished. He asked only two questions.

'How soon shall I know her actual travel arrangements?'

'I'm not sure. Probably some time in the next week.'

'And what sort of outcry will there be when she disappears?'

'In public, nothing. But the KGB and the East Germans will

116

be mounting a full-scale search for her as soon as she doesn't turn up at her father's place.'

'There's a flight back to Hamburg in an hour's time. Do you need me any more?'

'No. Get your seat booked and we'll go and have a meal and a drink in the restaurant.'

'I don't need it.' Fisher stood up. 'I'll wait for you to contact me. See you.'

In the taxi back to London Hallam wondered what it was like to be a man like Fisher. So admirable but so aloof. Ruthless but strangely vulnerable. He was the living proof that John Donne was wrong when he said that no man was an island. He wondered how Fisher got on with women. He was a handsome man and Hallam knew that he had had several girl-friends, but none of them had lasted long. But the odd thing was that from what he had heard, Fisher's ex-girl-friends went on liking him even after it was over. He must be very attractive to women. Not just the good looks but the independence of the man. Fisher always seemed entirely self-confident. Needing neither help nor advice from anyone. A whole man. A man you could trust and rely on.

CHAPTER 18

Thornton was surprised when he got the telephone call from Arthur Padstow at the office. And even more surprised when Padstow had asked if he could see him urgently. Padstow had suggested that they meet early that evening at the Connaught. He had asked what it was about but Padstow had just said that it was a personal matter. Thornton agreed to see him at six.

Thornton was ten minutes early but Padstow was already there, sitting in the far corner of the lounge. He walked over to Thornton and led him back to the two armchairs and ordered their drinks. A Glen Livet for himself and a Perrier for Thornton. When the waiter had brought the drinks Padstow leaned forward.

'It was good of you to come. I'm very grateful.'

'That's all right.'

'You must wonder what I wanted to talk about with you?'

'You said it was a personal matter.'

'It is. It is.' He paused and looked at Thornton. 'Can I ask you at what point you decided to divorce Elaine?'

'I don't understand. It was she who divorced me. Because she wanted to marry you.'

'Is that so?' He paused. 'She told me that you were going to divorce her and name me as co-respondent and she only divorced you to get in first and prevent that happening.'

'We never discussed anything about a divorce. I was just served with the notice out of the blue.'

'Did you try to persuade her to stay with you?'

'No.'

'Why not?'

'It suited me not to. I'd had enough.'

'It's very embarrassing to ask you this, but what sort of things did she get up to when she was with you?'

118

'I think you'd better tell me why you're asking these questions.'

'Because I've had enough too. I'm going to divorce her.'

'On what grounds?'

'Normally I'd only need to give irrevocable breakdown as the grounds. But we've not been married long enough so I need to convince the court of unreasonable behaviour.'

'Unless she's changed that shouldn't be difficult.'

'She hasn't changed, believe me. She was no problem for the first few months. I'd heard things about her when she was still married to you but I assumed that either you didn't care what she did or maybe were the cause of it. She told me that she was lonely because you neglected her.'

'I didn't neglect her but it's possible that she was lonely. My job takes me away a lot. Generally without notice.'

'*Did* you mind what she did?'

'Of course I did. I tried to stop it until I realised that it was impossible.'

'That's my experience too, Thornton. Believe me, I really tried. But nothing's going to change her.'

'You've got actual evidence of this?'

'My God, yes. I spilt some coffee over my suit at lunch a few weeks back. I went back to the house to change. She was on our bed with a bloody Frenchman from their embassy. He's five years older than I am.' He shrugged. 'And there were others. She'd stay out all night with the bastards, with me not knowing whether she had been hurt in an accident, or what. I tell you, it's been a bloody nightmare. I wish I'd never met the bitch.'

'I'm afraid that there's no helpful advice that I can give you.'

Padstow shifted in his chair and Thornton's mind registered the guilt reflex.

'As a matter of fact I wondered if we might cooperate with one another.'

'In what way?'

'My chap – my lawyer – tells me that it would strengthen my case a lot if I could show that she was given to this kind of behaviour. Not just with me, but previously as well as now.'

'And?'

'And you could either appear for me or do an affidavit.' He

laughed nervously. 'Not asking you to say anything that isn't true of course. Just giving your experience.'

'I don't think a court would much like the idea of a man giving evidence against his ex-wife.'

'It could help you with your son Jamie.'

'How?'

'With my evidence of Elaine's behaviour and your own evidence you would have a good case for applying for custody.'

'Jamie's her son as well as mine. And I didn't contest custody when we were divorced.'

'Do you think that she is a suitable mother for your boy?'

'She's not ideal but I think she cares about him in her own peculiar way.'

'How will she provide a good home for him? Tell me that.'

Thornton took a deep breath. 'Mr Padstow, what happens to Jamie will depend on a number of factors. But one of them will not be me giving evidence against his mother. I'm genuinely sorry about your domestic problems. You must be very worried and very sad that it's turned out the way it has. But you must let your lawyer deal with it without my help. I'm sure you'll do the right thing.' He paused. 'And now I'll have to leave.' He stood up. 'Best of luck. And I mean that.'

She had listened carefully as they finished the meal to his retelling of his meeting with Padstow and he sensed as he finished that she didn't agree with what he had said.

'What do you think?'

She looked at him, shaking her head slowly. 'I don't know, Robbie. I just don't know.'

'You don't think I did the right thing?'

'Oh, you did the *right* thing all right.'

'So what did I do wrong?'

'You left Jamie to Elaine's erratic whims and fancies. To the vagaries of an obviously neurotic and unstable woman. You know what she's like better than I do. You got out from under. But you didn't do what you could for Jamie.'

'She's his mother, sweetie.'

'There's more to being a mother than giving birth, my love.'

'You think I should have gone along with Padstow?'

'Yes. I do.'

'And what if Jamie finds out when he grows up that I went to court to give evidence against his mother so that another man could divorce her?'

'What of it? Either he'll be grateful that you did it or at least he'll know you cared enough about him to put up a fight on his behalf.'

'What if he likes her? Or likes being with her? Children don't see parents' behaviour the same way adults do.'

'It's not a question of liking her. He can be with you and still see her. But he doesn't have to grow up thinking that getting pissed every night, lying for the hell of it and sleeping with every creep who makes a pass at you is the best way to live your life.'

'I doubt if the court would give me custody anyway. She's married and a mother. I'm single.'

For long minutes she looked at his face, waiting for him to continue. And in the end she gave up.

'It's last rehearsal tomorrow night. I've brought you a press pass. It's on the mantelpiece.' She smiled. 'Cheer up. Don't take any notice of me airing my views. I'm partisan. And probably wrong.'

It seemed like a week for strange telephone calls. When he got back to the flat the next evening there was a note in Penny's handwriting on the table. Elaine had phoned. Was desperate to talk to him. Would he call her at her girl-friend's place. And the girl-friend's telephone number.

He dialled the number and the girl-friend put Elaine on the line. She wanted to see him urgently. She was desperate. She was crying. He arranged to see her in the lounge at the Charing Cross Hotel. This wasn't exactly grim but it was old-fashioned and solemn and both guests and waiters tended to talk in not much more than a whisper. She wouldn't put on one of her exhibitions there. It lacked the atmosphere for theatricals.

Her tears would no longer move him. She was a talented crier and could run the whole gamut from large individual tears rolling slowly down her cheeks to tear-filled eyes to sobbing inconsolably.

He sat at a table for two near a window and ten minutes later she swept in in a swirl of lime-green and Rive Gauche. But her make-up couldn't hide the red-rimmed eyes and he realised that she must have been crying quite genuinely at some time in the past hour or so.

He stood up and pulled out her chair. 'What would you like to drink?'

'I'd love a Bloody Mary.'

'I doubt if they've ever heard of them here but I'll see what I can do.'

He pressed the bell-push on the wall and then turned to look at her.

'I can't stop long, Elaine, I'm on my way to the theatre.'

'That bastard's been in touch with you hasn't he?'

He smiled. 'Which particular bastard have you got in mind?'

'Padstow. The shit. I got a note from his solicitor asking me to see him. He told me that you might be giving evidence for Padstow, telling the court that I was a nympho and a drunk, to back up what Padstow says about me.'

'Go on.'

'He said I might lose Jamie if I didn't play ball. That you'd have him.'

'What's their idea of playing ball?'

'Me divorcing Arthur with only a nominal claim for maintenance.'

'How nominal?'

'Two thousand a year unless I marry again. Then it would stop.'

'What did you say to the lawyer?'

'I told him to get stuffed.'

'Now tell me what you really said?'

She smiled. 'I told him I'd consult my solicitor.'

'Who is he?'

She shrugged and giggled. 'I haven't got one. I just wanted to talk to you about it. Are you going to do what they say?'

'No.'

She frowned. 'Why not?'

'Why should I help Padstow? Why should I get involved at all? It's nothing to do with me.'

'But Jamie. He said that you could go to the court again and with me . . .' she shrugged, '. . . messing about you'd certainly get Jamie.'

'So?'

'So you could get him off me.'

'If I wanted to do that, that isn't how I'd go about doing it.'

'What's that mean?'

'I mean that Padstow's lawyer was lying. Padstow did meet me and did talk on those lines.' He paused. 'And I turned him down.'

'I knew that old fart was lying.'

'Who was he?'

'Sir Nicholas something or other. Logan. Sir Nicholas Logan. All the time he was talking to me he was trying to get his hand up my skirt.'

To Elaine every man wanted to get her into bed. Dozens of times she'd told him about some man who'd tried to get his hand up her skirt. In the old days it had made him angry despite the fact that he knew it wasn't true. It had angered him then because it was so revealing of her mind. But now it seemed merely pathetic.

'Where is Jamie now?'

'He's with me at my girl-friend's house.'

'Have you moved out of Padstow's place?'

'Yes. I moved two days ago.'

'I'll have to be going.'

She looked at his face. 'How are things with you, Robbie?'

'I'm fine.'

She sighed. 'I'm sorry about the mess I made with you.'

'Forget it. It's done and gone.'

'Thanks for not doing what Arthur wanted. You must have been tempted, because of Jamie.'

He stood up. 'Can I get you a taxi? And I'm sorry about the Bloody Mary. It's quiet here but the service is terrible.'

She stood up facing him. 'Give me a kiss, Robbie. Just for old times' sake. Just a peck on the cheek.'

He looked at her lovely face and smiled. 'You're still very beautiful.'

And then he left.

They had taken Jamie to the Zoo on the Sunday and Penny Lambert sat on the bench watching the man and his son. Robbie had his hand on the boy's shoulder, his eyes on the boy's face as he watched the keeper throwing the fish to the sea-lions. He so obviously cared about the boy. Whenever they were together Robbie was relaxed and young, smiling, ever ready to laugh. And yet he was prepared to leave the boy to the mercy of his mother. That neurotic, totally selfish bitch who had so nearly ruined him by her feckless, uncaring behaviour. She was sure that most men would have grabbed the opportunity of saving the boy from a life with that psychopathic woman who told lies, not for gain, but just for the hell of it.

He had told her of an incident when they were at a party and she had left surreptitiously with some man and flown to Paris that night, slept with him and come back the next day, phonily contrite but, in fact, amused and delighted by the scandal she had caused. She had once read *The Pursuit of Love* by the Mitford girl and she saw herself as a similar *femme fatale* to The Bolter. Admittedly she was very pretty but she had the mind and the instincts of a whore.

She wondered for a few moments if he still cared about Elaine but dismissed the thought. He saw her as a victim. A victim of her feckless parents and her genes. Most men would have hated the woman, but not Robbie Thornton. He said that hate was a sign of weakness and a reluctance to face facts. Facts that must sometimes mean that whatever had happened was the result of your own bad judgement or weakness of character.

In a way she envied him his self-assurance and his steadfast holding to his own values. When he saw weakness in others he had an instinct to protect. A knight in armour. Although she wished sometimes that she was the beneficiary, but at least it meant that he didn't see her as a lame duck.

She was standing in the small bathroom wiping steam from the mirror so that she could see how the ear-rings looked. The one on her left ear was a large, bright-red plastic heart on a gold-plated swivel. On her right ear a modest cultured pearl in a setting of small yellow petals seemed to her a little too modest. Born to waste its sweetness on the Dorchester's desert air. She changed them both for a pair of gilt stars. She turned her head to look at him. He was sitting in their only armchair looking at a model locomotive in its plastic pack. She walked over to him, smiling.

'What's that?'

He smiled up at her. 'It's a Hornby Dublo "Duchess of Athol" for Jamie.' He laughed softly. 'I longed for one of these when I was a kid.'

She pulled one of the Habitat chairs away from the table and sat down, looking at him.

'Why that?'

'It seemed beautiful to me. All those valves and its neatness. The paint.' He smiled. 'And I suppose part of its attraction was that it was unattainable. I used to dream about having one.' He smiled. 'I still do, sometimes.'

'Tell me about when you were a kid.'

He shrugged. 'There's nothing really to tell.'

'What was your father like?'

'I only saw him once that I can remember. He was a merchant sailor. Rather jolly and beery.'

'And your mother?'

'She was very pretty but she wasn't very keen on children. Not on me anyway.'

'What makes you think that?'

'There was always some new man in the place. A series of "uncles". I guess I got in the way. She was always threatening to have me adopted or put in a children's home. She wasn't any good with kids. She was out most of the time.'

'Who looked after you when she was out?'

'I looked after myself.' He stood up. 'It's time we went, I booked the table for eight o'clock.'

CHAPTER 19

Fisher had taken a double room at the Schweizerhof that looked out onto Brandenburgerstrasse and across to the Zoo and the gardens. There were a table and two comfortable chairs set by the window. Fisher sat there, and on the table were several passports, a bundle of documents and a tray with a coffee pot, sugar, cream and a cup and saucer. After he had stirred the coffee slowly in the cup, his eyes on the traffic in the street below, he lit a Stuyvesant from the red and gold pack on the table by the sheet of handwritten notes.

He reached for these as he inhaled and then for the small thin calculator. He had been over the schedule a dozen times and in the previous week he had gone over the route and timing half a dozen times. It could be completed in just over two hours from when she came through security provided nobody was there to meet her. If there was, it would mean another half-hour. He had checked the punctuality of the Moscow-Warsaw-Berlin flight and it had been on time for the past two weeks.

A taxi would get them away quicker but the S-Bahn was safer. They wouldn't be able to talk much with the noise of the train and he didn't want to do much explaining until they got to Alexander Platz and the café. Judy Miller and Miles Putnam would be there before him and could cover for him. The phone rang and he walked over to answer it. It was reception. His two guests had arrived. He asked the porter to send them up to his room.

He cleared the papers and all but two of the passports from the table and put them in the worn briefcase in the wardrobe.

When Miller and Putnam arrived Fisher drew up another chair.

'Do you want to go over the schedule again?'

Putnam shook his head. 'We checked it out again today. You realise that if anybody's there to meet her and we have to cut

126

them out we won't be able to cover for you after that. Not in the café or at the check-point.'

'That's OK. I've made allowances for that.'

'Who is this girl? She doesn't look like our kind of material.' Putnam leaned forward as he spoke, reaching for Fisher's cigarettes.

Fisher ignored the question. 'Don't forget to leave your currency slips inside the passports and don't go through together.'

Judy Miller smiled. 'It was a lousy photograph but she looked like Garbo when she was young. Another Ninotchka maybe?'

Despite his annoyance at their probing Fisher smiled back at the young woman. 'You're fishing for compliments. It's you who looks like Garbo.'

She laughed and Fisher said quietly, 'I'll see you both tomorrow.'

They knew they were being dismissed and as they headed for the door the woman turned, smiled, and said, 'Best of luck.'

Fisher nodded and half-smiled and then turned to look out of the window.

Fisher used the US passport to go through the check-point and walked on up to Friedrichstrasse and turned right into Leipzigerstrasse. At the bridge at Mühlendamm he stopped and looked at the river. There was no sign that he was being followed and he took the back streets up to Alexander Platz.

At the station he bought a ticket for Jannowitzbrucke, one stop down the line. And there he walked out of the station and stood in the spring sunshine before walking down to the river bank. Half an hour later he returned to the station and bought a ticket for Flughaven Schönefeld.

The arrival board showed that the Moscow-Warsaw flight was on time. Due in twenty minutes. There were groups of East German workers waiting for the return flight to Moscow, and family groups waiting for planes due in from Prague and Budapest and domestic flights from Dresden and Rostock.

He stood watching the passengers from earlier flights coming through customs and immigration. It seemed that all luggage, including hand-luggage, was being checked. There were several plain-clothes security men watching the queue of people at the check-points. Speaking into their hand radios from time to time. The glass windows gave a good view of the arriving passengers and once they were cleared by the officials, they came through to a general area that was railed off from people waiting for passengers. It shouldn't be difficult to spot her well before she came through to the public area.

He walked back to the cafeteria and sat with a coffee. There was a temptation to go over the routine one last time but he resisted it. Everything that could happen he had allowed for. He glanced towards the exit and saw Judy Miller and Miles Putnam talking together by the row of taxis, a bunch of red carnations in Judy's hand. They looked so unconcerned, the young woman laughing at something that Putnam was saying, like any couple waiting for relatives or friends.

Then the loudspeakers were announcing the arrival of the Moscow flight in German, Polish and Russian. He waited ten minutes before he walked slowly to the barrier. There was only a trickle of people passing through the four check-points but a few minutes later he saw the first group coming through from the Moscow flight. And then he saw her. She was far prettier than in the photograph, smiling and talking to an Aeroflot stewardess as she headed towards the security check. She seemed to be answering several questions as the security man leafed through her passport. But then he handed it back and she picked up her case and walked to the customs bench. The case and her hand-luggage were examined by a woman with a sullen face who nodded and then turned to the next passenger, leaving the girl to repack her belongings.

He took a deep breath as she walked out through the door to the reception area. She showed no sign of expecting anyone to meet her but he had to wait until she headed for either the taxis or the U-Bahn. She was taller than he had expected and quite smartly dressed as she walked across the foyer. She was heading for the taxis and he caught up with her a few yards before the exit doors.

'Ushi.'

She was so intent on what she was doing that it was several seconds before she turned and looked at him.

'Ushi Jaeger?'

'Yes,' she said doubtfully. 'Who are you?'

'I came on behalf of your father.' He paused. 'There's a small problem, so I came to give you a hand.'

She frowned. 'What's the problem?'

Fisher pointed to the door and picked up her case. 'Let's take the train into the city. I've got tickets.' He smiled. 'Did you have a good flight?'

She smiled, 'Yes. I had a drink of champagne. French champagne.'

He took her arm and led her towards the station. 'Did you like it?'

She laughed. 'Not really and Mama told me not to drink fizzy drinks on a plane as it can give you terrible stomach pains.'

'Do you feel OK?'

'Yes. I'm fine. Tell me about the problem.'

'When did you last hear from your father?'

'We had the last letter about ten days ago. Maybe two weeks.'

'He had a slight accident. Nothing serious but he had to stay in hospital for treatment.'

She looked shocked. 'What happened?'

'He fell down some stairs. He's broken an ankle so he's in a kind of sling.'

'Can we go straight to the hospital?'

'We'll have a cup of coffee in town and work things out.'

They passed through the barrier and a train arrived as they reached the platform. As the train pulled out she sat by the window, watching the houses with their neat gardens alongside small workshops and industrial estates. They were almost at Karlshorst before she turned and said, 'Is he in pain?' He could only just hear what she said because of the noise of the train. He shook his head. 'Not really.'

She sat with her chin resting on the palm of her hand, still looking out of the window. And then they were in among the tall city blocks through Warschaustrasse and the Ostbahnhof and finally Alexander Platz.

As they came out into the square he said, 'Have you eaten?'

'Yes. Too much.' She laughed.

'Let's just have a coffee and do a bit of planning.'

129

She looked surprised but said nothing as he led her down one of the side-streets, through an alleyway and into a narrow passage. He saw Judy Miller and Putnam sitting in the far corner as he opened the door of the café for the girl and took her to a table by the kitchen door.

When he had ordered their coffee he excused himself and walked to the far side of the room to the men's toilets. Putnam came in a few moments later and they exchanged the two sets of passports without speaking.

Back at the table he helped himself to cream and then looked up at her face. 'I'm afraid the broken ankle wasn't the only problem.'

'Tell me,' she said.

'You know that he's a Party official?'

'Yes, of course.'

'He was sent into West Berlin to deliver an important confidential message. That was where he fell down the stairs. He was unconscious and when a passer-by phoned the hospital the ambulance took him to the emergency ward at the Wilmersdorf Hospital. That's where he is now.'

'But that means he's in West Berlin and I won't be able to see him.'

Fisher shook his head. 'I've pulled some strings, Ushi. I'm going to take you, but we'll have to be back through the check-point before they close tomorrow. I've booked you a room in a quiet hotel and I'm hoping to fix things so that your father can come back into East Berlin tomorrow.' Fisher paused and sighed. 'It's not easy because he had to use false papers to go over. But I've talked to some friends of mine and I think they can fix it for me.'

'Was it illegal what he did?'

'I'm afraid so.'

'What a silly thing to do.'

Fisher smiled. 'He couldn't know he was going to fall down some stone stairs, my dear. He was doing what the Party required him to do.'

'So why don't they do something about it?'

'They have, my dear. That's why I'm here.'

She sighed. 'I was so looking forward to this week. And now it's all spoilt.'

'Drink up. It isn't spoilt. Let's get on with it.'

'What happens now?'

'In my pocket I've got two passports. One for you. One for me. British passports. We'll go through what they call Check-point Charlie. So listen carefully to what we have to do. It's quite easy really.'

For five minutes he explained the procedure. She asked questions and he then rehearsed her about the times and the money.

'Any more questions, Ushi?'

She shook her head. 'I wish I'd never come here. I don't think I'll stay for the whole week.'

'See what you feel like tomorrow.' He paused. 'Are you ready?'

She nodded. 'Yes, I suppose so.'

They walked to Alexander Platz and took a taxi direct to Check-point Charlie. There was no longer any point in any kind of evasion. Miller and Putnam would have checked that he was not being followed.

They joined a group of tourists at the Check-point. Fisher went first and the guard had noticed the Penguin translation of Marx's *Surveys from Exile* as he rested it on the counter to count out his Ostmarks. When he was through he stood waiting for the girl, smiling as she fumbled with her money. Then she was through.

He took her arm. 'We'll get a taxi.'

In the taxi she turned to look out of the window as they passed the airfield at Tempelhof and then turned back to him to speak, her mouth opening until she saw his finger go to his mouth as he shook his head and pointed to the driver.

The evening traffic was building up and it took just over twenty minutes to get to the patchwork of squares that had names like Alpental, Sorgenfrei and Roseneck. More or less the German equivalents of Dunroamin. He stopped the taxi about a hundred yards from the house.

She stood looking around as he talked to the driver and then walked with him to the tall wrought-iron gates and watched as he turned the big old-fashioned key in the heavy lock.

For a moment she seemed to hesitate as he swung the door

open and nodded to her to go inside. And then she shrugged, went in and stood watching as he locked the door again.

She followed him up the gravel pathway to the house and seemed relieved when the door was opened by a middle-aged woman.

Fisher said quietly, 'That's Miss Makinen. She's Finnish. She speaks good German. And she'll be looking after you while we're here.'

'Is this her house?'

'No. She's the housekeeper. Go on in.'

The girl walked into the hall and Fisher brought in her case. 'Let me show you your room, Ushi.'

She followed him upstairs to the open door of her room. It was large with well-preserved old-fashioned furniture. A comfortable room. Flowers in a vase on the bedside table, the windows open, lace curtains lifting fitfully in the breeze.

The girl walked over to a window and looked out at the gardens. They were almost twice the size of those of the adjoining houses.

She turned slowly towards Fisher. 'You said I would be staying in a hotel tonight.'

'I thought that you'd like it better here. It's more comfortable than a hotel.'

She shook her head slowly. 'There's something wrong about all this.'

'In what way?'

'This was all planned. It's waiting for me.' She paused. 'I'd like to phone my mother.'

'The phone here isn't connected, Ushi.'

'There'll be a phone in one of the streets. I'll find it.'

'Ushi, if we were stopped by the police we should be arrested. Our passports are forged. We'd both end up in prison.'

'What about when we go to see my father? They could stop us then.'

'I'm thinking about that. It's a problem I've got to work on.'

For long moments she looked at his face and then she said quietly, 'I don't believe you. There's something wrong about all this. You'd better tell me what it's all about. I shouldn't be here in West Berlin. It's crazy. Like you said – I could be arrested and I've already broken the law by using false documents.' She shook her head. 'I don't do things like that. I want a proper explanation.'

Fisher looked back at her, his eyes hard. 'You'll do as I tell you, Ushi. Then you'll come to no harm. But I warn you – if you set foot outside this place you'll be arrested in a matter of minutes. You've committed a number of serious offences and you'll certainly end up with a severe prison sentence. In a few days' time I'll be able to let you know what happens next. Until then, relax and do as you're told.'

And suddenly she was no longer a young woman but a child, standing there with her blue eyes filled with tears, her lips quivering as she said, 'Why are you doing this to me?' and she turned away as if she didn't expect an answer.

He gave some brief instructions to the housekeeper. She was used to the things he was involved in and he had brought her from the house in Hamburg because he could trust her. She was like an old family retainer. Not part of SIS but trusted because of long years of satisfactory service. Only vaguely aware that from time to time strange things happened she got on with her daily routines uninvolved and unconcerned.

He had had to walk to Ullsteinstrasse before he got a taxi and he went directly back to the hotel. He had kept the room on for another ten days. He dialled Hallam's direct number and was transferred to his home number. It was his wife who answered.

'Gabriella Hallam. Who is that?'

'It's Fisher, Mrs Hallam, can I speak to your husband?'

'Of course. Just a moment.'

Hallam must have been right beside her because he came on almost at once.

'Hallam. How did it go?'

'OK. I've got the parcel.'

'Good show. Any problems?'

'There will be.'

'Why?'

'She's not one of us. She's very naive. Very unsophisticated.'

'Why's that a problem?'

'She's upset about the situation. Not seeing the father and all the rest of it. She hasn't a clue about what's happening so she's very worried. Scared even.'

'Can't you soothe her down?'

'I need to know something about the situation. I'm just free-wheeling, stoogeing along. The scenario I painted is now obviously untrue. I'm running out of road. I need to start talking turkey or she's going to disintegrate.'

'Are you sure you're not exaggerating, David?'

'Quite, quite sure.'

There was a long silence and then Hallam said, 'I'll send the Prof over tomorrow. He'll put you in the picture. You can put it over to her yourself. Use the Prof as well if you think it will help.'

'Tell me something.'

'What?'

'Is she with us permanently now?'

'Yes.'

'She ain't gonna like that. Not one little bit.'

'Too bad.'

'She's only a kid, H.'

'She's twenty-two.'

'She's still a kid.'

'That's how it is, my friend.'

'Tell the Prof to come direct to the house. The rented one.'

'OK. Leave it to me. Anything else?'

Fisher sighed, hesitated and then said, 'No thanks,' and hung up.

'Did you sleep well?'

She shook her head. 'No, I couldn't sleep.' She sipped at her coffee and then looked across at him. 'At five o'clock this morning I heard a nightingale singing. In the morning, mind you.'

And Fisher realised that she was talking to shut out the fear of what was happening to her.

'I thought they only sang at night.'

'Usually they do. It was very beautiful. Do you know Galich's poetry?'

'I'm afraid I don't.'

'He has a verse about a nightingale in a poem called *White Night*.'

'Tell me.'

134

'I only know it in Russian. Do you understand Russian?'

'A little bit. I'd like to hear it.'

She leaned forward and closed her eyes, smiling to herself as she said softly –

> 'There, far off in the misty distance
> Of this night of Spring-like whiteness
> The nightingale with glorious thunder
> Announced the frontiers of Summer.'

Then she opened her eyes and looked at his face expectantly. 'Did you like it?'

'Yes. It's very gentle.' He paused. 'You've got a beautiful voice for reciting poetry.'

She smiled. 'My Russian's very poor. Very primitive. Do you like poetry?'

'I don't know very much poetry.'

'Music? What music do you like?'

'Just the obvious things. Elgar, Tchaikovsky and Rachmaninov.' He paused and shrugged. 'And jazz.'

She smiled. 'I've not heard of the first name but it sounds like you must be a romantic. Except for the jazz.'

'You don't approve of jazz?'

'I like old jazz not new jazz.'

'Tell me some jazz you like.'

She laughed. 'Maybe it's not real jazz but I like a song called "Manhattan".'

'Why that?'

'It has a lovely melody and the words make me feel that I know New York very well. Have you ever been to New York?'

'Yes, I lived there for a short time.'

'The song says – "And tell me what street compares with Mott Street in July."' She paused. 'You understand English?'

'Yes.'

'Tell me about Mott Street. What is it like?'

'The words are a piece of New York humour. Mott Street is not very nice. It's the street where they make cheap clothes.'

She smiled and shook her head. 'Not for me. Mott Street is very gay. With silver-birch trees and street cafés with coloured blinds.'

135

Fisher laughed softly. 'I'll get it changed.'

'Tell me about me.'

The blue eyes looked intently at his face and he said, 'What about you?'

'I'm a prisoner, aren't I? But why?'

'There's somebody coming to talk with you today.'

'What about?'

'About the situation. Your situation.'

'Tell me about my situation.'

'We'll talk about it later today or tomorrow.'

'Is the man coming from Moscow or Novosibirsk?'

For a second he hesitated. 'He's coming from London.'

He saw the surprise on her face turn to disbelief and then, slowly, to outright fear. The coffee cup clattered as she put it down and she folded her arms across her body as if she were trying to hold herself together.

'Can I ask you your name?'

'I'm afraid I can't tell you – as yet.'

'Please tell me. I'm very frightened. I feel cold and faint.' She was trembling now, quite visibly. He said, 'Don't be afraid. You won't be hurt or come to any harm, I promise you.'

She bowed her head, the long blonde hair trailing across the plates and dishes. Then she looked up at him. 'I thought the nightingale was a sign that today would be a good day for me. I almost trusted you. I was a fool, wasn't I?'

'Wait until you've talked to the man.' He looked at his watch and stood up. 'If there's anything you want, the housekeeper will get it for you.'

'I want my Mama,' she said, 'I want to go home.'

Fisher called to the housekeeper and when she came in he pointed silently to the girl, sobbing, with her head cradled in her arms, seemingly oblivious of the spilt cream and sugar beneath her arms. As the woman put her arm round the girl's shoulders Fisher walked away. Angry, but not sure why.

Clayton arrived just after noon and Fisher took him into the study, obviously impatient to hear what he had to say.

'They haven't given you any background at all?'

'None. Just the bare essentials for me to pick the girl up.'

'How is she responding?'

' "Responding" isn't the word I'd choose. She's upset and scared, and my not being able to talk sense hasn't helped.'

'OK.' Clayton smiled. 'Calm down, old chap. Let me fill you in.'

Clayton had talked for twenty minutes, only partly explaining the situation and avoiding answering many of Fisher's questions. Giving only a bare outline of what the girl had been doing and how they intended to use her. When it was over Fisher sat silent for several minutes, then he looked back at Clayton.

'She really can do this mind-reading business? It's not some fancy trickery made to look like science?'

'It isn't mind-reading, David. At least not what people know as mind-reading. It may not be valid but it certainly isn't trickery. We don't know exactly what they've got from Rykov's work with the girl but they're still doing it – or they were. The KGB and the Politburo wouldn't be letting them carry on all this time if they didn't feel that what the girl is producing was worth the time and money.' Clayton smiled. 'You can bet they were as sceptical as you when it started.'

'And you reckon this Yank – Siwicki – can produce similar results?'

'We think so. He thinks so too. He's been very successful in a similar set of experiments.' Clayton shrugged. 'A lot depends on his ability to create an atmosphere that the girl will accept and respond to. It's going to take time.'

'What if she refuses to cooperate?'

Clayton shrugged. 'Let's jump that fence when we meet it. Do you want to put the girl in the picture yourself or shall I do it?'

'You do it. I'll just sit and listen.'

Clayton had talked quietly and courteously to the girl for over an hour; tears ran slowly down her cheeks, a sopping wet handkerchief held in her hands. And when there was nothing more he could say he sat waiting for a response. But it was Fisher she turned to, her voice quavering as she said, 'It was all lies that you told me about my father, wasn't it?'

Fisher nodded. 'Yes. I'm sorry I had to do it. He's not had an accident either.'

'How can you sit there, both of you, knowing that I shan't see my mother and my home ever again?'

Clayton, obviously moved, opened his mouth to speak but it was Fisher who spoke. 'Ushi. I've told you that you won't come to any harm. You'll be well cared for. But you have to remember that you were part of an espionage organisation – the KGB. You were actively involved in intelligence work. You were as much a spy as any little KGB stooge hanging around the embassy in London or Washington.'

'I have never even spoken to a KGB man in all my life.'

'Ushi. Professor Rykov's whole operation with you was funded by the KGB and controlled by the KGB. You were being used to attempt to read the minds of Presidents, Prime Ministers and dozens of other significant people. Why do you think Rykov chose them as the targets?'

'I was never told who they were. I recognised some of the people in the photographs but not many.'

'Believe me, Rykov knew who they were.'

Clayton leaned forward towards the girl. 'Ushi, if they had wanted just to carry out a proper scientific set of experiments they would have chosen subjects they could check on. People in the Soviet Union, not foreigners. They seem to have been very satisfied with what you and Professor Rykov provided but they couldn't ever know if it was reliable.'

The girl shook her head. 'But what about my mother – and my father? They will be terribly worried. They won't know what's happened to me. They won't even know whether I'm alive or dead. Doesn't that matter to you people? Don't you care about people's feelings?'

Clayton looked uncomfortable. 'Maybe there's some way we can set their minds at rest when things have settled down.'

Fisher was angered at Clayton's glib response. He must know that it wasn't on. It was typical of a desk-man's evasion of the unpleasant facts of espionage. Tough on paper but weak as water when they were face to face with their quarry. They were like people who liked a good steak but were shocked when faced with an abattoir. Rigid in theory but weak in practice. But that was why they sat behind desks and called themselves 'case officers', and left it to people like him to do the dirty work. To mop up the tears and clean up the blood.

He stood up. Clayton, who was obviously glad to have the excuse to leave, followed Fisher to the door. At the door Fisher turned to look at the girl, sitting there with her head bowed.

'I'll be back in a few minutes, Ushi.'

She didn't respond and he closed the door and led Clayton into the small study.

'Don't ever offer people things that you know you can't deliver. It might make you seem a good guy for a couple of minutes but it makes it worse afterwards when somebody else has to pick up the pieces.'

'I'm sorry, old chap. I was very sorry for her, that's all. It must be a terrible situation for her and she's only a kid.'

'When will this guy Siwicki be coming over? She needs to have something to occupy her mind and her time. Stop her brooding.'

'What if she won't cooperate?'

Fisher smiled grimly. 'Even non-cooperation will occupy her mind and if this chap's any good they'll have things in common to discuss.' He paused. 'So when can he get here?'

'A matter of days I should think. Hallam's looking after that end.'

'Are you catching the evening flight?'

'Yes.'

'I'll walk up the street with you and get you a taxi.'

By the time Fisher got back the girl had gone to her bedroom and he didn't see her again until the next morning. She had refused to speak to him all day and he'd not pressed her. But she seemed calmer now after yesterday's traumas. She joined him for the evening meal. When she was drinking her coffee Fisher looked across the table at her.

'Do you want to talk about anything?'

'Can you tell me your name now?'

'I guess so. It's David Fisher.'

'And you are British KGB, yes?'

'I'm an intelligence officer if that's what you mean.'

'You are trained to deceive people? To tell lies? To kidnap them?'

Fisher put down his coffee cup slowly and looked at the girl's face.

'Ushi, I might just as well say to you: Are you employed by the KGB? Do you supply information to the KGB about what you know of President Reagan's mind? Or Mitterrand's mind or Chancellor Kohl's mind? If you were truthful you'd have to answer "yes" to both questions. You use a talent, a sensibility, your mind, for the most ruthless invasion of a person's privacy that one can think of. You abuse another·human being without knowing or caring if it damages them. Yes?'

She shook her head. 'You argue too well for me.' She shrugged. 'You are trained to do that.'

'Ushi, I'm talking to you as one person to another. I'm just trying to help you to understand that you yourself can be viewed in more than one way. A gentle, perceptive and very pretty young girl. Or a willing employee of an espionage organisation. A very ruthless one. Both statements are true but neither of them are the whole truth. You don't feel that you are part of an espionage exercise. You don't believe that what I describe is you.' He paused. 'Just as I don't believe that your description of me is true.'

'How do you see yourself then?'

Fisher shrugged. 'I'm just an ordinary man and I'm employed to defend my country against people who would like to destroy our way of life.'

'The Russians would say the same. That they're defending the Soviet Union against the capitalists.'

'Let's talk about your situation. I want to make it as tolerable as I can for you.'

'Tell me about the American.'

'You mean Siwicki?'

'Yes.'

'He's much the same as your Professor Rykov. But he's much younger.'

'Has he done parapsychology research before?'

'Yes. It's been his speciality.'

'When does he get here?'

'I've asked for him to be sent over soon. In the next few days.'

'Are you married, Fisher?'

'No.'

'Have you been married?'

'No. Never.'

'Why not?'

'I wouldn't want to take on the responsibility of another person's life with my sort of job. It wouldn't be fair to them.' He looked at the girl. 'What about you?'

'No, I'm not married.'

'Why not? You're very pretty. You must have had plenty of men running after you.'

'The kind of men that I've met don't interest me.'

'Why not?'

She shrugged and smiled. And Fisher noted the smile. It was a good sign. 'Either they've been scientists who I find rather boring or they're just louts who want to go to bed with me.' She smiled. 'The only man I really like is Professor Rykov, and he's happily married already.'

He wanted to keep her occupied and talking. 'Which did you prefer, living in Germany or living in the Soviet Union?'

She shrugged. 'It was a very closed community in Akademgorodok. It wasn't typical. But I think of it as "home" rather than Dresden. There were fields and woods where I walked. And time to read and to think.' She sighed. 'I don't think I appreciated how happy I was.' She shrugged. 'Until now.'

He reached out and put his hand lightly on hers where it lay on the table. 'We'll make it as easy as we can.'

She looked surprised. 'You're a strange man, Fisher. A very strange man.'

'You'd better get a good night's rest.'

She smiled. 'And that's typical of you. Any man I've met if he was told he was a strange man would have wanted to know why I thought he was strange. But not you. You know exactly what you are. No little doubts. No uncertainties. Fisher is Fisher and that is that.'

Fisher stood up. 'Sleep well, Ushi. See you tomorrow.'

He walked out into the garden. He stood on the lawn looking up at the sky. There were no clouds and the moon was almost full and he saw the winking lights of a plane on the flight path to Tempelhof. It looked like a heavy-bodied troop carrier. Probably American. And as he stood there he heard the nightingale. The rich tones seeming especially strong in the quiet of the garden. Short musical phrases and then single notes increasing in volume. It made him think of the girl and he looked up at her room. She was standing at the window. He could see the pale wan oval of her face and the white of her dress. And as he looked up at her she waved to him before she drew back into the room. There was nothing that he could think of to make it easier for her. Her unhappiness was like a wound. Only time would turn it into just a scar. He hadn't been told whether she would be based in Germany or the UK or whether he would have to stay in charge of her once the scientific stuff started.

CHAPTER 20

Thornton had several meetings with Smallwood. None of them establishing much that was new. Smallwood, having checked public records for Fisher's marriage certificate, had eventually come to the conclusion that Fisher must have been married overseas and the certificate had not been registered in the UK.

The photograph from Fisher's office had been shown to the neighbour at the flat who had claimed to have seen Mrs Fisher recently in Harley Street and she had confirmed that the photograph was of Mrs Fisher.

When they met that day it was Smallwood who raised the question of the missing operations files covering Fisher's work.

'I asked a girl in Central Registry what happened to withdrawn operational files and she said it was very rare. She didn't actually know what happened to them but seemed to think that they'd be destroyed.

'But I did a bit of sniffing around and I gather that there's a place somewhere in Wales — a bunker of some sort where high-security files are kept. It's listed as . . .' Smallwood paused to open his diary and find the entry, '. . . yes, it's listed as the "Discretionary Archive Unit".' Smallwood smiled. 'Could mean anything or nothing.' He shrugged. 'Who knows?'

'I'll ask Hallam if he knows anything more. He obviously didn't want to discuss the missing files when I first raised them with him.'

'I shouldn't, skipper, if I was you. Hallam isn't going to come clean.'

'Why do you say that?'

'I'm bloody sure he won't.' Smallwood looked at Thornton. 'They're giving you the run around, skipper.'

'Go on.'

'I've seen it all before. I know the signs.'

'What signs?'

'Oh, the missing records. Vague and maybe misleading answers to questions. Limited resources.' Smallwood shrugged. 'You don't think that if Fisher really was missing they'd leave it to just you and me? They'd have forty or fifty people on it, working like beavers.'

'Anything else?'

'Yes. For the last ten days or so I've been under surveillance. Two men and a girl.'

'Are you sure?'

'Yes, of course I'm sure.' He smiled. 'Fortunately they're not much cop. They obviously don't know London like I do. They're probably new boys from Five trying their 'prentice hands on me instead of doing training exercises in Southampton.' He paused. 'And then there's that so-called cottage at Wadhurst. They've been in there for weeks. Anything we could have found they will have found long ago. So why do they still keep us out?'

'Maybe it's time I had a serious talk with Hallam.'

'Can I make a suggestion?'

'Do.'

'Don't mention that I've rumbled the surveillance team. Let's just keep it to ourselves.'

Hallam had listened carefully as Thornton talked and when he had finished Hallam said, 'Is that the lot?'

Thornton nodded. 'Yes, sir.'

'Right. Let's go over the various points. First of all what you describe as the missing files. They aren't missing. They're withdrawn. And I thought that I'd already explained why. They cover operations concerning defections and I'm not prepared to jeopardise people's lives by revealing names and intentions when they are in no way relevant to what you've been given to do.

'Then what you call lack of cooperation or reticence by the four of us on the committee. For most of his recent career Fisher was overseas. Mainly in Germany. None of us had all that much contact with him. And to pass comment that could influence attitudes to a chap who, to some extent, is under

144

suspicion would be irresponsible. You also have to bear in mind that, like you, Fisher was a field officer and the four of us have been administrators for a long time. The two parts don't always see eye to eye. Either side can get a jaundiced view of the other. And our side is desk-bound in London while the other can be hundreds or even thousands of miles away for most of the time. Distance doesn't always lend enchantment. You can work with a man for years and still not know much about him.

'And finally, this cottage at Wadhurst. Is it all that important in your opinion?'

Thornton shrugged. 'I don't know, sir. It was a place that belonged to Fisher. There might be some evidence, some clue, that could indicate where he might be.'

Hallam reached into the top drawer of his desk and threw a couple of keys down. They were tied together with string.

'There are the keys to the cottage. There's nobody there. You're welcome to go down and look it over if that will ease your mind. Was there anything else?'

Thornton hesitated, took a deep breath. 'Have MI5 been brought in on this?'

'Good God, no. What made you ask that?'

'Smallwood tells me that he's under surveillance. Has been for the last ten days or so.'

Hallam looked relieved, shrugging as he said, 'Those old China hands like Smallwood can see spooks behind every door. The training in the old days put great emphasis on surveillance methods. And give them their due – there was a lot more of it in those days.' Hallam smiled. 'Plus, of course, the traditional and permanent suspicion by SIS that big brother might be watching them too. Anyway, I can assure you that Five have not been informed and I'm pretty sure that between us we've kept this wretched business inside this building. OK?'

'Yes, sir.'

As Thornton stood up Hallam pointed at his desk. 'Don't forget the keys. Let me have them back in due course.'

It was mid-morning when Thornton and Smallwood got to the house at Wadhurst. As they walked up the path Thornton

145

noticed that the lawns had been recently cut, and trimmed, and the flower beds were well-tended.

The big key turned easily in the main lock and the Yale had obviously been recently oiled. Diamond-paned windows gave plenty of light to the hall. There were heavy beams across the ceiling, supported by massive king-posts. There was a distinct smell of floor polish and some kind of disinfectant.

Thornton turned to Smallwood. 'I'll do downstairs, you do the rooms upstairs.'

'Are you looking for anything special, chief?'

'No. Nothing, anything.'

Thornton smiled as he watched Smallwood walk carefully up the wide stairs, treading as near to the wall as possible. Just like the training course way back had recommended, to avoid the stairs creaking.

Despite the oak beams and the polished wooden floors the kitchen and breakfast room were modern with fitted cupboards in white Formica and a line-up of brand-new kitchen appliances. Unlike the flat at Turnham Green the cupboards were well stocked with china and cutlery, packets and tins and all the necessities for a normal family existence. A greater variety and quantity than the two men guarding the place would have needed.

In the other rooms there were all the signs that the house had been lived in on a permanent basis. Books on shelves. Pictures on walls. Ornaments, vases and the bits and pieces that are the signs of the owners' personalities.

The books were mainly paperbacks. A dozen or so Penguin classics. A wide range of modern novels. A few hardbacks in German, again mainly classics – Thomas Mann was well represented. And half a dozen current Ullstein paperbacks. Several books on natural history and two or three AA publications on touring in Britain and the British countryside.

On a long white shelf was a mini hi-fi unit, its small twin speakers at each end of the shelf. It included a record-player but there were no discs, just a couple of dozen prerecorded cassettes. They included the standard concertos and symphonies as well as a selection of Fats Waller and Duke Ellington. Thornton tried a couple of tapes and they were what they were supposed to be – the Rachmaninov First Piano Concerto and the Dvořák Violin Concerto.

The decor and furnishings gave an impression of unadventurous middle-class taste. Rather old-fashioned, as if much of it had been bought second-hand at sales. The kitchen was the only place where money had been spent lavishly. Maybe Fisher's wife had been a keen cook.

Smallwood reported that there was nothing of any interest in the bedrooms, one of which was empty. Two double rooms and a single room were furnished and there was a good-sized bathroom and a separate shower room.

Thornton went upstairs and looked around casually. It was just as Smallwood had described. It was when they were both standing on the landing at the top of the stairs and Thornton had looked up at the ceiling that he saw the wooden insert.

'Looks like a trap-door to the attic.'

'You want me to nip up and have a look, skipper?'

'See if you can find a ladder in the garage.'

When the light aluminium ladder was in place Smallwood tussled with the catch on the trap-door. 'You usually get a pole with a hook on the end to pull these things down. Hold on, it's coming.'

As Smallwood moved to avoid the trap-door he saw that there was a light metal extending ladder attached to the door itself. He pulled it down after him as Thornton moved the other ladder out of the way.

Smallwood went up first and found a switch fixed to the floor at the top of the ladder. The fluorescent lights flickered and hesitated before they came on fully. Thornton came up slowly after Smallwood.

The room was quite small, about eighteen feet square. The ceiling and walls were covered with white acoustic tiles and the floor with deep rubber-backed carpet from wall to wall.

There were two comfortable armchairs, side by side in front of a low table. On the side wall was a deep shelf running the whole length of the room. The shelf was covered with a layer of cork. Just above it was a line of white plastic ducting that held cables leading to four double mains sockets spaced along the wall. On the bench itself was a Revox tape-recorder with empty oversized reels, an ICOM IC-R70 short-wave receiver, two telephone receivers, one white, one red, with a standard black scrambler between them. On a small shelf above was a BIB demagnetiser, a Leitz 35 mm projector and six grey plastic slide boxes, a cordless telephone, four standard A4 W.H. Smith Jumbo pads and a clip-board.

Thornton switched on the radio. Some music faded and then a voice said, '*Hier ist der Sender, "Frieden und Fortschritt"*.' It was Radio Moscow's overseas propaganda service in German on 11860 kHz. The aerial cable at the back of the set led under the acoustic panels. There were no reels of tape and no slides in the grey boxes and both telephones had been disconnected.

There were two framed prints on the facing wall. Both modern in style and both showed scenes of the countryside. One was of mist rising in the tall trees at the edge of a wood and one was a realistic painting of a hedge with brambles and wild flowers alongside a field of corn. Obviously by the same artist but the signature was illegible.

'What do you make of this lot, Mr Thornton?'

'I've no idea. The radio's just a receiver, there's no transmitter.' He shrugged. 'Could be a hobbies room. Photography and music. It's too comfortable to be a work-place. I expect you noticed that there's no TV in the house but there's a double aerial on the roof so that they could get both TV channels of the BBC plus Thames from London and TVS from Maidstone. And there's no aerial to the hi-fi. Just the set's internal aerial.'

'There's a fold-up bed and mattress under the shelf at the far end.'

Thornton bent down and looked.

'So there is. I hadn't noticed it. What was the garage like?'

'Untidy, typical garage stuff. Petrol mower, odds and ends of oil, a few tools, a worn tyre. Nothing of interest.'

'What's your impression of the place?'

'I'd put it down as just a domestic. Except for this room.'

'Me too. But there's something odd. This room is nothing like the rest of the house. It's like somebody else lived up here who was different, trendier than the Fishers. A lodger. But there's no facilities for living up here. No toilet, no cooking stuff.

But it all looks cleaner and less dusty than the rest of the place. And why did somebody remove the pole with the hook and make it more difficult to get up here? Whoever removed it must have known that it was still easy enough to get in here if you really wanted to.'

CHAPTER 21

When Schaeffer got the phone call from the Director's assistant to go over at once he assumed that it concerned the suggestion he had made about using a dedicated section of the main-frame computer for routeing field reports. The computer people were against giving up any main-frame capacity for a single function but they had had to agree that the idea was feasible and would cut down distribution times by at least half.

O'Hara was on the phone when Schaeffer was shown into his office, nodding as he listened, responding in monosyllables. He sighed as he eventually hung up and pointed to one of the chairs facing his desk.

'Sit down, Schaeffer.'

Schaeffer turned the chair slightly to face the Director, aware of the brown eyes studying his face. He knew that those soft brown eyes were deceptive. Thomas Fitzgerald O'Hara was a politician who had played a major part in the President's election campaign. His talent had been for sorting the sheep from the goats. And despatching the sheep without hesitation.

'Tell me what your department is doing at the moment, Schaeffer.'

'It's a small department as you know, sir. We've been examining and improving the routeing of field intelligence to those who can make best use of it.'

'Are you running over budget?'

'No, sir. We're dead on target.'

'Have you any other responsibilities?' He waved a casual hand. 'Any peripheral responsibilities?'

'No, sir.'

O'Hara folded his arms and leaned forward on his desk. And then he said very quietly, 'What happened to one hundred thousand dollars of the winding-up money for Operation Aeolus?'

'I don't understand, sir. It's all in the accounts rendered.'

'So how come one hundred thousand dollars end up in a special account with a merchant bank in London?'

'It was a reserve in case my old operation was ever revived.'

'Why is it in London?'

'SIS had considered offering to fund the operation on a joint basis if Langley agreed. That was our contribution.'

O'Hara nodded slowly and for a fleeting moment Schaeffer thought that he'd escaped. Then he heard the words and saw the anger.

'Mr Schaeffer, one of my personal assistants is in your office right now. As of now you are dismissed from this agency. There will be a recommendation to the Pentagon that you are dishonourably discharged from the US Army with a reduced pension. Consider yourself fortunate that it doesn't suit either the Pentagon or the CIA to indict you at the moment. You have lied, deceived and conspired in a manner that I found almost incredible when I was informed of what had gone on between you and the people in London. You lied even to them that you had some kind of *sub-rosa* approval from this agency.' O'Hara leaned back until his heavy chair creaked. 'Now get out of my sight.'

'I assure you, sir, that my intentions were . . .'

'Get out, man. Get out. You will be escorted to your car after you've been searched; and if you ever communicate in future with anyone here I swear I'll have you arrested.'

Schaeffer stood up slowly, opened his mouth to speak, saw the pent-up anger on O'Hara's face and walked unsteadily to the door.

The man who searched him in the small office and took his ID card before handing over his personal possessions from his office was a man he had known for years. When he was escorted to his car he turned and said, 'I never imagined it ending this way, Brett.' The other man shrugged. 'You must have been out of your fucking mind, man, with the summit due in a couple of months. They've raised hell at State and there's God knows how many senior people trying to put out the fire you started.'

He saw the tears on Schaeffer's leathery cheeks and said no more. He continued to watch as the car tail-lights faded into the dusk.

It had been 2 a.m. when Hallam was wakened by the call from Langley. He sat on the edge of his bed trying not to think of the implications of what the CIA man was telling him. When it was over he put the receiver back on the phone, walked slowly and quietly to the bathroom, washed, shaved and dressed. He left a note for Gabriella before driving to Century House.

In his office he sat thinking, wondering what to do. Several times he had reached out for the telephone and drew back. There was no need to get them from their beds. There was, in fact, no urgency. But the indecision was almost unbearable. He was tempted to phone Fisher and put the process in train. But the others might have some better suggestion. Not that he could think of any sensible alternative himself. But there were other alternatives that were unthinkable, lurking at the edges of his mind.

He left a message at the security check-in that he wanted to be told when they arrived and the duty-officer reminded him that Seymour was in Canberra and wouldn't be back for at least ten days.

Hallam waited until 10 a.m. before he phoned Macleod and Clayton to come to his office. As the two of them settled into the leather armchairs facing him Hallam said, 'I had a call from Langley in the early hours of the morning.' He paused. 'Not good news, I'm afraid. They've called the deal off. In fact, according to the fellow who spoke to me there never was a deal. Schaeffer was playing it by ear. Hoping that it would all turn out a success. But nobody, not at any level, had authorised him to do any of it. Nobody even knew of it until yesterday.'

Clayton said quite calmly, 'What's happened to Schaeffer?'

'Apparently they've given him the works. Dishonourable discharge. Reduced pension. Never darken the CIA's door again. Friend Schaeffer's backside is out in the snow.' Hallam looked at them both. 'But Schaeffer's their worry, not ours. Ours is the girl. What the hell do we do with her?'

Macleod shrugged. 'We send her back. Shove her over the border.'

Hallam looked at Clayton and said, 'She'd end up in some Gulag camp brothel. Nobody would believe her story that she'd been kidnapped. And even if they did she'd be suspect. They'd assume that we'd turned her. You might just as well finish her off where she is. You can imagine what the KGB would do to her.'

Clayton shook his head. 'We can't afford to speculate, Bill. Let's just put her through the Wall and then it's up to the KGB what happens. It's on their head not ours.'

Hallam said, 'Suppose we just let her loose in West Berlin. Pay her a lump sum. Fix her a new identity.'

Clayton shook his head. 'They'd still get her. Sooner or later. And before she was shipped off to a labour camp they'd have one of those show press conferences where she tells the world's press what's happened to her.'

Macleod said, 'They'd probably do that anyway if we send her back over the border.'

Clayton shook his head. 'I doubt it. If they picked her up in West Berlin they'd have watched her before they took her. They'd see that she wasn't working for us. If she goes back cold they'll never really be sure if we used her, or maybe turned her.'

Hallam said quietly, 'So what do we do with her?'

Macleod said, 'We send her back.'

Clayton shrugged. 'I think that's the only way.'

Hallam sighed. 'OK. I'll tell Fisher to arrange it.'

When the others had left Hallam moved back to his desk and then stood, looking across the river. They hadn't discussed it thoroughly. They'd dodged the issues. All of them were too long in the game not to be used to violence and the callousness that went with it. But that was against professionals like themselves. Field agents of any espionage organisation knew the risks they were running and what would happen if they were hunted and caught. They were trained to protect themselves and they neither gave nor expected quarter from the other side. But the girl wasn't in the business. She was just an innocent bystander. Despite that, the convenient rationalisation was there. She wasn't just an innocent bystander. She was controlled by the KGB. She spent her days providing the KGB and the Politburo with what purported to be the private and innermost thoughts of world statesmen. The men who decided their nations' attitudes to the Soviet Union. She was as much part of the KGB as the cypher clerks who coded and decoded without knowing, or caring about, the significance of what they were dealing with.

Hallam looked at his watch. It was nearly eleven and Fisher checked the hotel for messages at noon. He'd leave a message for him to take a call at 4 p.m.

There was no way of communicating with Fisher apart from the telephone. The house in Berlin did not have a scrambler, and Hallam couldn't use the Security Signals Unit because nobody could even be told that Fisher was in Berlin, let alone where he was. It was four ten when Fisher answered the phone call in his hotel room, giving the room number in German.

'It's Hallam. Something's come up. I can't go into details on the phone. Our overseas friends have pulled out of the deal. You'll have to put the parcel back again.'

There was a long silence and Hallam eventually said, 'Can you hear me OK?'

'Yes. I can hear you.' He paused. 'You know what this will mean. The parcel will be destroyed in transit.'

'I hope not. But that's the way it is, I'm afraid. There's no alternative.'

'There must be a dozen alternatives, Hallam. They just need working on.'

'We've decided, F. That's what we want to do.'

'How much time do I have? I don't want to rush into it and make it worse.'

'There's no need to rush into it.'

'So how long?'

'The sooner the better. A week to ten days at the longest.'

'I'll maybe come back to you.'

'It's an order, F.'

Hallam toyed with hanging up to end the conversation to demonstrate that there was to be no discussion. But that could get Fisher's hackles up even more. And as he hesitated he heard the phone go down at the other end. Fisher had beaten him to it. But he was relieved that he'd done it. And in a week's time they could forget it. Fisher would know how to handle it.

*

154

Hallam had contacted Fisher every day to ask if he had carried out his orders and Fisher's laconic and evasive replies had finally provoked him.

'Have you told her what the plan is?'

'No.'

'Why not?'

'Because I haven't decided yet what I'm going to do.'

'Look. I don't want to make something more out of this than it calls for, but I have no intention of changing my decision.'

'Maybe you people should come over and deal with it yourselves.'

'Is that a serious suggestion?'

'Why not?'

'OK. I'll send Macleod over tomorrow. He'll tell the person concerned what we're going to do. We'll get her agreement and then you can put her through and your conscience can be clear.'

'What about Macleod's conscience?'

Hallam hung up.

That night Fisher had talked to the girl. Well aware that he was warning her against his own people.

'There's a colleague of mine coming from London tomorrow to talk to you. His name's Macleod. He's going to tell you some news that I think you'll quite like.'

'So why do you look so angry?'

'Just listen to what I tell you, Ushi. I'm not going to tell you now what he's going to suggest or he'll know from your face that you already know.' He paused. 'When he tells you what's going to happen I want you to go along with it. Whether you like it or not – just agree. Understood?'

'Yes.' She paused. 'It sounds as if you don't agree with it yourself.'

'You'll have to trust me, Ushi. Just do as I say and appear to go along with what he suggests. OK?'

'Of course.'

Macleod had telephoned from Tegel but Fisher hadn't offered to pick him up.

He had introduced Macleod to the girl and had sat impassively, listening to Macleod.

'We do quite genuinely apologise, Fräulein Jaeger. It was a foolish mistake. We should like to return you as quickly as possible. In the next few days. Is that convenient for you?'

Fisher watched her nod. 'Yes, thank you.'

Macleod smiled broadly as he gave her an envelope. 'There's a thousand D-marks in there, Fräulein. You might like to buy something to take back for your parents.'

'Thank you very much.' She put the unopened envelope beside her on the couch.

Macleod stood up, holding out his hand to the girl and when she took it he said, 'Have a good journey, my dear, and again our apologies.'

He turned to look at Fisher and they walked together into the hall. 'What was the problem, David? She swallowed the bait easily enough.'

Fisher pointed. 'The phone's over there, Macleod. I've activated it. The taxi number's on a card by the phone. Have a good flight back.'

Macleod looked at Fisher. 'Are you OK, pal? You seemed kind of subdued in there.'

Fisher took a deep breath, opened his mouth to speak, then closed it so hard that his jaws snapped together like a trap.

'I'll see you some time, Macleod.'

Macleod shrugged. 'OK. Where's the phone again?'

Fisher pointed, turned away and walked back into the room where the girl was still sitting.

CHAPTER 22

Fisher waited until they had finished breakfast and then he said quietly, 'If I took you back to the Check-point what would you do?'

She shrugged. 'I'd just walk through and tell them what had happened.'

'And what do you think would happen then?'

'I'd go back to Moscow and then I'd go back home.'

'You really think that they would let you do that?'

'Of course. Why not? I've done nothing wrong.'

'You think they would believe your story?'

'It's not my *story*,' she said indignantly. 'It's the truth.'

'And you think they would believe you?'

'Why shouldn't they believe me?'

'They might think that you had defected and were sent back to spy on them.'

She smiled. 'I don't even look vaguely like a spy, I'm just an ordinary girl.'

'What do spies look like?'

'They're aggressive and they're usually men. Tough men.' She smiled. 'Men like you.'

'You don't think that they might assume that people over here might have questioned you about the work you do with Professor Rykov?'

'If they thought that, I'd be able to tell them that no such thing had happened.'

'And they would just accept your word on that?'

'Of course. Why should they think I'm not speaking the truth?'

Fisher looked at her for a long time. She was incredibly naive. But with her sheltered life with her mother in Siberia, politics and real life must never have touched her. It was more innocence than naivety. She was intelligent but she had never had cause to be suspicious or shrewd or defensive. She was like some character from a Louisa M. Alcott novel. How the hell could he convince her of what would really happen? If it was left to London they would be delighted with her innocence. Just take her back to Check-point Charlie, shove her through and let the Vopos take over. What's the problem?

Fisher stood up. 'Let's go in the garden before it gets too hot.'

There was a bench under a weeping willow tree and he led her there. It was too good a morning to be doing what he had to do. A pair of blackbirds listened, heads cocked, for worms on the lawn, and a thrush sang in the hawthorn hedge.

He turned his head to look at her face. 'I want you to pay close attention to what I'm going to say, Ushi. And before I start I want to tell you that I shall say nothing but the truth. I swear it. I ask you to believe me. Not for my sake but for yours. OK?'

She shrugged. 'OK,' she said, but without conviction.

'First of all – my people in London have told me to take you to the Check-point and put you through our side of the barrier. Like the man Macleod told you, they want me to do this as soon as possible. In the next two or three days.'

'So what's the problem? That's what I want too.'

'OK. And now I'll tell you what will really happen on the other side of the Wall.' He paused. 'When you give them your name and tell them that you've no identification papers and no permit to enter West Berlin they'll take you to the headquarters of the East German secret police – the MfS – in Normannen-allee. When they've interrogated you briefly they'll hand you over to the KGB in the same building. They'll interrogate you for several days and pass the details to Moscow. Then the next thing they will do is arrest your mother and maybe your father too. If they've not been arrested already.'

'Why should they do that?'

'Because they will assume that your parents were accessories to you defecting.'

'But I didn't defect.'

'They won't believe you, Ushi.'

'Why not?'

'Because when they catch a defector he always swears that he was kidnapped. My people are just the same. If I went into East

158

Germany without being ordered to do that, and I was caught and I got back, they wouldn't believe me either.'

'That's crazy.'

'Maybe, but it's what always happens. There are no exceptions. But let's get back to you in Moscow. You'd be put in the KGB's own prison – the Lubyanka. They would interrogate you for weeks. Maybe months or even longer. They would apply physical pressure and psychological pressure to make you confess that you defected. They would tell you that you were causing your parents to undergo the same treatment. You would be offered a pardon if you signed a confession that you defected and that your parents knew about it.'

'What do you mean by physical pressure and psychological pressure?'

'Physical pressure – they'd beat you up. Psychological pressure – they'd confront you with your mother, her body and face covered with bruises. They'd tell you it was your fault for not signing the confession.

'This could go on for months. No matter what you said they wouldn't believe you. Let's say that in the end you are so ill and so confused that you surrender and sign the confession. Then you'd be sent to one of the slave labour camps run by the Gulag organisation. Your parents would be sent to other camps.'

For several minutes she was silent, her head bowed. Then she slowly lifted her head and looked at him.

'How can I believe what you say?'

'I don't know. You'll have to decide for yourself.'

'Why have you told me all this when you could have just taken me to the Wall like your people have told you to?'

'I suppose that the difference between the London people and me is that for them you're just a name and for me you're a person.' He paused. 'And I don't think you deserve to be sent back to face all that.'

'Why not?'

'Because you were kidnapped by us. You were totally innocent. And talking to you in the last few days I've realised that you have very little knowledge of the real world. You lived a kind of fairy-tale life in Siberia. And even people who have to face life as it really is in the Soviet Union don't really know how the KGB acts. They know that they are to be feared but they are sure that, provided they do nothing wrong, they are safe from the secret police. They can't, or don't want to, believe that they treat innocent people as criminals if they choose to.'

'What will your people in London do to you if you don't push me back through the Check-point?'

'I shan't tell them that I haven't carried out their orders. They'll never know.'

'Would they beat you up if they found out?'

He smiled. 'Let's say they wouldn't be very pleased. But they won't find out.' He shrugged. 'I've been in this game a long, long time.'

'Why was I kidnapped?'

'Because of your work with Professor Rykov.'

'But I'm so unimportant in his work. Why didn't you kidnap *him*?'

'There was no way we could do that. He's in Siberia but you were coming to East Berlin to see your father.' He paused. 'And in any case your contribution is far more important than Rykov's.'

'How did you know about me coming to East Berlin?'

'Somebody who works for the Americans in Akademgorodok told us.'

'Why should they do that?'

'Because he happens to hate the Russians.'

'How is it my father didn't meet me at the airport?'

'I had somebody tell him that you were coming in on a later flight.'

'So some men in London who have never met me or my mother and father can just decide to do something that will ruin my whole family. Our lives – everything.'

'I'm afraid so. To them you are not just Ursula Jaeger.'

'What am I to them?'

'You are a young woman with a special talent, an extra sense, who works for the KGB.'

'How can I be working for the KGB? I've never spoken to a KGB man in my life.'

'Rykov's experiments with you are paid for by the KGB.'

'You mean they see Professor Rykov as KGB?'

'Yes. He is – indirectly maybe, but he's a KGB employee, doing what the KGB tell him to do.'

'He's a quiet, gentle old man who wouldn't hurt a fly.'

'Nevertheless – that's how the people in London see him. A KGB man, and you're his assistant. And the work you both do was intelligence work. There's no doubt about that.'

'And all your people wanted was to stop our work?'

'No. It was more than that. The Americans have been doing experimental work of a similar kind. They wanted to persuade you to collaborate with them.'

'It's fantastic, isn't it?'

'What is?'

'There's me sitting in a room with a professor in Siberia. Talking and working. Going home at night. Talking with my mother. Reading books. Walking in the forest. And there are some men in America and Britain who can just decide that it's all going to end.' She snapped her fingers. 'Just like that. You don't need to ask or persuade, you just do it.' Her lips quivered and tears trembled in her eyes. 'It's just not fair.' She paused. 'Is it?'

'I guess not, Ushi. But that's what wars are all about. Hot wars or cold wars. People get trampled on.'

'Innocent people?'

'Sometimes. But you don't count as innocent. They consider you fair game. You are part of Soviet intelligence and this is part of the price you have to pay. If your people caught me they'd put me through the KGB's mincing machine without a second thought.'

'Do people in your country know that these things go on?'

'Not the general public. It's about the same as in the Soviet Union. People suspect that it goes on. When the other side does it it justifies your own secret police. When your own side are caught out doing it you're sure that they only did it for the best of reasons.' He shrugged. 'It's been going on for a long, long time, Ushi.'

She looked away from him towards the house. It looked calm and peaceful, the curtains lifting gently in the mid-day breeze. When she turned to look at him he saw the tears on her face and her voice trembled as she spoke.

'What shall I do? Tell me what to do.'

'Don't go through the Check-point.'

'But then what? Where do I go? How do I live? I've no

money, no skills to earn a living and I'd be an illegal immigrant.'

'I can provide genuine documents for you to live here without any problems.'

'And then what?'

'Do I take it that you won't go into East Berlin?'

She nodded, and sighed. 'I'm too much of a coward. I'm afraid.'

'That means that you believe what I told you?'

'Yes.'

'Why?'

'Why do I believe you?'

'Yes.'

'First of all because it sounds true. And secondly because I somehow do trust you.' She shrugged. 'And I've nobody else but you.'

'In that case I'll think about what you should do and we'll talk about it again. Maybe tomorrow. I'm going into the city now and I'll be back about nine this evening. Is there anything I can get for you?'

She shook her head slowly. 'Maybe a book. A poetry book.'

Fisher nodded, turned away, walking to the house, leaving her sitting under the weeping willow tree.

He took a taxi to the cemetery in Spandau and walked to the grey apartment block on Kronprinzenstrasse, knocked on the door of No. 139 and waited until the man opened the door after looking through the spy-hole.

An hour later he left with the West German passport. The photograph was of a pale young blonde. Nothing like the girl, but passport photographs were seldom like their holders. And the passport was genuine. It would be good enough for a couple of days. He'd get it 'improved' in Hamburg. He stopped the taxi just before the Kurfürstendamm and bought a bunch of red roses.

She was asleep when he got back but he got the housekeeper to put the flowers in a vase and put them on the table by her bed. When she came down she smiled at him. 'She needs all the red roses she can get, that girl.'

'Did she talk to you?'

'A little.'

'What about?'

'No need to worry, my friend. She only talked about you.'

'She must hate my guts.'

'She's not the kind that hates. And whatever *you* tell her she believes.' She smiled. 'She says she could hear your thoughts when you talked to her. She says that you tell her the truth. She believes you.'

'We'll be moving to Hamburg tomorrow. See that she's up early.'

The plane to Hamburg was half empty. Fisher sat with the girl, and the housekeeper sat behind them. When they landed he took them by taxi to the Inter-Continental and gave the housekeeper a wad of D-marks and told her to take the girl round the shops and buy her clothes and whatever else she needed. They were to meet him in two hours' time at the Fontenay Grill.

While he was waiting he phoned Hallam and told him guardedly that the parcel had been returned early that morning and he was now back in charge in Hamburg. As he hung up he realised that Hallam had sounded relieved, and that angered him. Angered him that Hallam should think that he would carry out such an order. If it had been a man, a man in the business who knew the rules of the game, who expected no quarter, it would have been different. But it was none of those things. It was a girl whose mind had been abused by her own people and who his people would happily have abused the same way. And because of some back-off by the Yanks she was unhooked like a fish and thrown back in the water. Hallam would now have a good lunch at his club, his mind on other things. While if he had carried out Hallam's orders the girl would be screaming her head off by now in some KGB interrogation room. He shook his head in anger as he walked down the hotel corridor to the bar.

When he had ordered a drink he went to the phone at the door of the bar and dialled a local unlisted number.

'*Ja, bitte.*'

'It's Fisher. Who's that?'

'Smallwood, sir.'

'Tell them I'm back. I'll be in tomorrow morning. Get

somebody to drive my car to the parking lot at the Inter-Continental, and give the keys to the doorman.'

'Yes, sir. Do you want Mr Mitchell to come over to your place?'

'No. Everything will keep until tomorrow.'

He opened the big wrought-iron gates of the house himself and drove up to the twin garages at the side of the house, opening the boot of the car and telling the housekeeper to take the bags and parcels to the spare room and make the girl comfortable.

He sat on his bed with his accumulated mail and read through it briefly. Offers of loans from finance companies who were sure that he was eager to buy a new car or have an extension to his house. Bank statements from four different banks. Two in the UK, one in Jersey and one in West Germany. Two personal letters from girl-friends. One a Dutch girl, and one a girl from what used to be Saigon. There were three pay-slip notifications from the merchant bank that SIS always used. Just a code-number without a name. A Road Fund Licence renewal reminder. A suggestion from BUPA that in the light of increased costs he should upgrade his medical insurance. And a letter asking him for a reference for a man who had once worked for him who was being considered as an investigator for an insurance company.

He pushed the mail to one side and turned to look out of the window to where the spacious garden lay half in shadow from the late afternoon sun. On the plane from Berlin he had mentally listed just over twenty-five offences that he had committed by what he had done in the last two days. At least half of them would justify his dismissal from SIS. He was used to defying London when he was sure it was necessary, but the criteria that he applied had, up to now, always concerned some aspect of the success of his operations. The field-wisdom that came from long experience, against the security logic of a desk-bound controller. But this was nothing to do with his work. It was a personal judgement that flowed, not from experience, but from his character. Against the grain of all his professional attitudes. Never emotion, always facts. Something that he had constantly instilled in his own men, time and time again.

For the first time in many years he thought about himself. And came to the conclusion that such virtues as he had were allied to his job. Talents and virtues that made him a successful intelligence officer. There was nothing that he could think of that made him a successful man. Or even a good man. He was aware as he looked out at the garden that it made him think of the girl. She was at home in a garden. She knew the names of flowers and shrubs and birds. She reminded him of the word 'tranquil'. Despite all the terrible pressures on her, when she had time to recover from some new blow she came back to being herself again. Innocent and naive, but a whole person. Absorbing her unhappiness with a special kind of fortitude. In her fragile way she seemed to have more strength than he had. His was toughness, hers was strength. An inner strength that seemed impervious to outside influences.

After their meal that night he walked with her in the garden and asked her to tell him the names of the things that were growing there. She showed no surprise that she should know so much about natural things when a much older man knew nothing about them.

When they stood by the pool in the light from the house he said, 'Why didn't you become a botanist?'

She smiled. 'Nobody ever suggested that I should.'

'You could have suggested it yourself.'

She looked at him calmly. 'I don't believe in making things happen. I think that whatever is meant to happen will happen. If you force things it can lead to disaster or unhappiness.'

'Are you a fatalist?'

She laughed softly, 'I don't even know what that means.'

'A person who believes that what will be, will be.'

'In that case – yes. I'm a fatalist.'

He walked her inside the house and took her to his study. As he poured two Cokes she looked around the room and when he handed her the glass she said, 'Is this your home?'

'It is for the moment. I don't have a permanent home.'

When they were sitting, facing one another, she said, 'Are you happy?'

He turned quickly to look at her face. 'What on earth made you ask me that?'

'I'm sorry. It was thoughtless.'

'Why thoughtless?'

She waved her arm slowly, encompassing the room. 'Because it's all so obvious.'

'What is?'

'That you're not happy.'

'How do you make that out?'

She shrugged. 'No books. No music. No pictures on the wall. No photographs. No pleasures. Just a room. A space. A cell.' She paused. 'And then one has to think about what kind of cell. A monk's cell or a prisoner's cell.'

For long moments Fisher was still and then he said quietly, 'And what kind of cell do *you* think it is?'

'Perhaps a bit of both. A monk and a prisoner are very like one another. They are cut off from the world. They live by man-made rules that are unnatural and, in some ways, cruel. In your case I would think that physically you're a monk. And mentally a prisoner.'

'Whose prisoner? Who are my jailers?'

'Prisoner of your life, your experience. And your jailers? The men in London who tell you what to do.'

'So why aren't you being interrogated by the Volks Polizei right now, in East Berlin?'

She smiled. 'The same mixture. The monk's purity and the prisoner's feeling for a fellow-victim.'

'Nothing more than that?'

'Yes. Of course. A thousand other things. But they all come under one of those two conditions.'

'Are you scared?'

'Scared of what?'

'Anything. Me. Your situation. The future?'

'I *was* scared of you at first. But not now.'

'Why were you scared?'

'I'd never met a man like you before. So determined. So – so implacable. It was like meeting face to face with a dinosaur or something like that. Something that you've heard of, or read about, but never really believed existed in real life. I just couldn't connect with you.'

'And your situation?'

'I don't think you saved me from what was going to happen to me to do me harm. I think you will help me if you can.'

'How can I help you?'

She shrugged. 'I don't know. I'll leave it to you. I'll do whatever you want me to do.'

'Is your room comfortable?' he said lamely, aware of its banality.

'Yes. I like it very much.'

CHAPTER 23

Fisher's operational HQ was the top floor of an apartment block. Two adjoining flats with four average-sized rooms each. One given over as a radio room, another for administration and the other two, with bunk beds, for sleeping and living quarters. They had an extensive array of aerials on the roof partially concealed by an attempt at a roof garden. Confidential conversations often took place in the corridor.

As he went into the radio room he could smell the ozone from a recent transmission and switched on the extractor fan. They got so used to the sharp smell of ozone that they didn't notice it. But he'd seen too many cases of ozone nausea and headaches to ignore it. There was a pile of papers in the wire basket with his name on it and he sat at the table looking through them. Taking out a sheet from time to time, making a separate pile of papers that he needed to read carefully. When Roberts, the clerk, came in he pointed to the wire basket.

'I'm finished with those . . .' then he pointed at the separate pile, '. . . register those to me.'

'Right, sir.'

'Who's here?'

'Mitchell and Smallwood – Pritchard's on leave for another two days.'

'OK. Tell 'em I want to see them all in ten minutes.'

'Yes, sir.'

'What about "Rheingold"?' Fisher looked at Smallwood.

'I sent the cash across. They seem OK.'

'How much cash did you send?'

'They asked for ten thousand D-marks and I sent them five.'

Fisher made a note on his pad. 'And you, Mitchell? What are you up to?'

'I've been servicing the network working out of Lübeck.'

'Any problems?'

'Yes. One of them didn't report in for three days. I'm not too happy about him.'

'What was he doing for you?'

'He was at Wismar checking on the port facilities. There was talk that it was going to be developed as a base for Soviet fast patrol boats.'

'Who was he?'

'Biedemeyer.'

'Was that the red-haired chap?'

'Yes.'

'What's worrying you about him?'

'He wouldn't give any explanation of what he'd been doing in those three days.'

'And what have you done about it?'

'I've left him there but I've pulled the rest of the network back over the border.'

'And?'

'I'll go over and sort him out myself.'

Fisher nodded. 'OK. I'll talk again when I've had a chance to read through my backlog.' He paused. 'One other thing. Have there been any signs of this place or yourselves coming under surveillance?'

There were negatives from both of them and Fisher picked up his papers which were now in a plastic folder and went into his office. As he opened the file of backlogged reports he wondered for a moment what the girl was doing. He was thankful that she was too calm and too sensible to do anything stupid. He knew that he'd have to start thinking about what she should do to make a new life for herself. She was young and pretty and intelligent but she had no idea of what the world was really like. She needed some sort of inoculation to counter the world's virus of greed and selfishness.

He watched her face as she looked at the chessboard on the table between them. She was playing White and he had got her in a corner, one move from mate. There was nothing she could do. Her hands supported her face, her elbows on the table. And he was struck once again by her aura of calmness. The blue eyes intent on the board, the long sweeping eyelashes and the neat turned-up nose. It was the first time that he realised how extraordinarily pretty she was. It was a typically German girl's face. Young and innocent, gentle and endearing.

Then she made her move. The wrong move. He moved his Queen to N3, pinning her Knight and threatening to take it with his advanced pawn. But she unpinned the Knight by sacrificing her Queen in an exchange for his. Her next move checkmated him with her Knight.

He looked up at her from the board. 'That was fantastic, Ushi. I was sure I'd got you pinned down ready for me to pounce.'

'It's very old, that combination. We call it "Philidor's Legacy". It's quite neat, isn't it?'

He smiled. 'Next time we play I'll expect you to give me a Bishop or a Rook advantage.'

She smiled. 'Perhaps a Knight to start with.' As she re-set the pieces on the board she said, 'What can I call you?'

'You mean my name?'

'Yes.'

'It's David.'

'Can I call you David?'

'Of course.'

'It's a nice name. David and Goliath. It suits you.'

'Are you tired?'

'No. Not yet.'

'Have you thought about what you'd like to do? Remember that you're free now. You can do whatever you like.'

She shrugged. 'I don't know what to do, David.' She smiled. 'In Siberia I was valuable – here I have nothing anybody would want.'

'You speak some English already. It would be very useful if you could speak fluently. I thought that you might like to go to language classes.'

She smiled. 'But I need to earn money, to pay for the lessons.'

'I'll pay for your lessons. We owe you that.'

'When can I start?'

'I'll phone the people I have in mind tomorrow. You could start the next day. If you're sure you want to.'

'I told you. I'll do whatever you say.'

Fisher sighed as he stood up and looked at the girl.

'You don't *have* to do what I say, Ushi. Do what *you* want. Make your own decisions. I'll just help you do whatever you decide to do.'

He was standing in the kitchen drinking a glass of milk as the housekeeper laid out the breakfast things for the next morning.

'What does she do when I'm at the office?'

'Reads the books you bought for her, listens to the music broadcasts on your hi-fi and walks around the garden.'

'Have you made it clear that she can leave the house?'

'Of course. Says she's not interested. That this is where she belongs.'

'Does she talk to you about what she wants to do?'

'All she talks about is the garden – and you, of course.'

'I think she's beginning to trust me, don't you?'

She turned and looked at him, hands on her ample hips. 'You know, for an obviously intelligent man you still don't have much common sense in that head of yours.'

'How come?'

'I saw a film once about some Viennese scientist who studies animals. He had half a dozen ducks waddling around with him everywhere he went. He said it was "imprinting" or some such word. The ducks thought he was the mother duck because he fed them when they were first hatched out.' She looked at his face. 'You're stuck with her, Mr Fisher. And she's stuck with you.'

Fisher smiled and shrugged. 'D'you want a lift into town tomorrow?'

'No. I've done the shopping locally.'

Elaine was still camped out with her girl-friend Joanna in her flat in Fulham and she had put no difficulties in Thornton's way when he wanted to see Jamie. It was much easier when he didn't have to limit their outings to weekends. They were walking back with the crowds after watching Chelsea play an evening match against Everton.

He took the boy into a small restaurant in the Fulham Road

for a snack. As usual Jamie had Diet Coke with baked beans on toast. When they got to the ice-cream Thornton said, 'How are things at the new place?'

Jamie shrugged. 'They're OK.'

'Are you doing your homework?'

'Yeah.'

'Does anybody help you with it?'

Jamie grinned. 'Momma helped me with my arithmetic one night. I got two out of twenty. Did she ever go to school?'

'Why do you ask?'

Jamie laughed. 'She doesn't know anything about anything. Joanna's just the same. We had Henry the Eighth as our term project and Momma kept ringing up people about where we could see this film about him and Anne Boleyn.' He grinned. 'They're real daft those two. But they're good fun.'

'Tell me.'

'Oh, just funny ways. Aunt Joanna always brings back sweets for me and they play Monopoly with me. They're gonna teach me how to play poker.'

'Do you like it there?'

'Yeah. It's OK.'

As Thornton walked towards Fulham Broadway after he had taken Jamie back he thought about the boy's mother. Daughter of a drunken father and a jealous mother, she had never had much of a chance. The family moving from one lodging house to another. The father pimping for his fifteen-year-old daughter until he was arrested and sent to Wandsworth jail with a three-year sentence. The young girl, with her good looks and young body as her only assets, picking her way through the men to try and achieve some sort of stability. Often succeeding in building some sort of relationship but throwing it all away with compulsive infidelity. She was at home at all levels of society and was familiar with the best hotels and the sleaziest night-clubs. And always she had that little-girl-lost look. The look of helplessness that attracted many different types of men who were tempted to play God and cure all her problems. Another Marilyn Monroe in the making.

He was sure that there were times when Jamie was neglected but the boy seemed happy enough and she was always there waiting for him when he took him home. And he noticed that once the door opened the boy automatically moved to stand by his mother as they exchanged a few words before he went on his way.

For the next five months Fisher was deeply involved in the defection of a senior East German agent.

He spent a lot of time in West Berlin but was back in Hamburg most weekends. As the plane took off for Berlin for what he hoped was the final stage of the defection he leaned back in his seat and thought of the girl. She had made tremendous progress with her English lessons. They spoke to each other in English now. There was a faint, attractive accent but her English was almost as good as his German. He had taken her to the Zoo and once to the cinema to see a re-run of *Gone With the Wind*. She didn't like Hamburg. The noise and the neon lights and the crowds scared her. Just once she had asked if he knew what had happened to her mother and father and in a weak moment he'd said he would try and find out. Maybe Lemke could check before he came over. Or maybe it was better left alone. He didn't have any doubt about what would have happened to them.

CHAPTER 24

Fisher had always avoided being seen in Hamburg with the girl but he had taken her that night for a meal at Oelmann's Strandhotel and afterwards he'd driven along the river road and parked where they could see the big freighters with their pilot boats thumping their way slowly up the Elbe to the main docks.

After watching for several minutes she turned to him and said, 'Tell me about when you were a boy. Your parents and what you did.'

'Well, my father was a schoolteacher and my mother was just a housewife.'

'Were they good parents?'

'Yes. I liked them both a lot. Maybe I liked my mother more because she was around all the time.'

'Were you good at school?'

'Not particularly. About average I would say.'

'Did you go to university?'

'Yes. I went to Oxford.'

'What subjects did you take?'

'Languages mainly. Russian and German.'

'Are your parents still alive?'

'No. My father died in a car accident and my mother died about a year later. She was very unhappy without him. They were very close.' He turned to look at her. 'Is there anything I could do to make you happy?'

She shook her head slowly. 'No. Thank you. I can manage as I am.' She looked at his face. 'You've been very kind to me. Don't think that I don't appreciate it.'

He wished that he could ask her about her parents and her life in Germany and Russia. Not just as conversation but because he would like to know. He was aware of her eyes on his face and her soft full mouth, and for a moment was tempted to

174

kiss her. He reached for the ignition key, started the car and drove back to the house.

When she had gone up to bed he sat as usual in the kitchen drinking a glass of milk as the housekeeper laid the table for breakfast.

'Is the girl settling down, do you think?'

The woman stood looking at him, hands on hips. 'She's very brave that girl. Very brave. I wouldn't say that she's settled down. She just seems able to carry on as if the bad things had never happened. She talks about her mother sometimes.'

'Is there anything I could do to make her life better?'

'Not better. Just go on caring for her. You're all that she's got. She worships you, you know.'

'She's a nice kid.'

'I've known you a long time, Mr Fisher, would you be angry if I asked you a personal question?'

Fisher smiled. 'I don't know. Try me.'

'Do you not think that she's very attractive?'

'Of course she is. She's very beautiful.'

'So why don't you sleep with her? Don't you fancy her?'

Fisher shrugged. 'I guess most men who look at her fancy her as you put it. And I'm no exception. But I wouldn't dream of sleeping with her.'

'Why not?'

'Why not? Well, first of all because she would find it almost impossible to refuse. She's dependent on me for everything. How could she say no? She'd just be agreeing as an obligation. Paying what she saw as a debt. She deserves better than that.'

'I admire you, Mr Fisher. I really do. But you're very stupid at times.'

'Tell me more.'

'I told you. She worships you. She talks about you all day long. Is she ruining your life – your career? Would it help if she just disappeared?'

'I hope you said the right things to her.'

'What are the right things?'

'That she's no problem in any way. And I enjoy having her here. To me she's my favourite daughter.'

The woman smiled. 'You're not her favourite brother – but you are her favourite man.'

'Is there something you're avoiding telling me?'

'She loves you, you silly man. Now go to bed and think about what I've said.'

There was the chill of autumn in the air and a log fire was burning in the stone fireplace. And for once they'd had wine with their dinner. Just a half-bottle between them. Both their glasses were still almost full.

When he looked across at her she looked back at him and said softly, 'Why did we have wine today?'

He shrugged. 'I thought you might like some. Why do you ask?'

'I thought you might have done it for a reason.'

'Any particular reason?'

She looked down at the glass and shook her head.

'Is something the matter, Ushi?' When she didn't reply he reached out and gently lifted her chin. And saw the tears on her cheeks. 'What is it, Ushi? Please tell me.'

She took a deep breath and her voice quavered as she said, 'It's my mother's birthday today. I was thinking of her all day.'

He tried to think of something to say. But there was nothing. He had painted too clear a picture of what would have happened to her parents to try and dilute it now. It had been the truth. And nothing would change it. But he wished desperately that there was something he could say that was both truthful and hopeful. He had not asked Lemke to see if he could find out what had happened to her parents. It would have put Lemke at risk and he already knew the answer.

He watched her stand up unsteadily and heard her sobs as she left the room. For almost an hour he stood at the window, staring out at the patches of light from the windows, casting their shapes on the thin layer of snow. For the first time in his life he was ashamed of something that he had done. It made no difference that he had been obeying orders. He could have refused to do it. But when he had kidnapped her he had had no idea of what it was all about. Nor the consequences. When he eventually had disobeyed it was too late to save anyone but the girl herself.

One thing was clear. He was responsible for everything that

happened to her after he decided to ignore London's orders. If she had been another kind of girl it would have been easier. He could have got her some sort of job, given her some cash from the Imprest Account and let her go her own way. But with Ushi that would have been like throwing out a domesticated animal to make its own way in the jungle. Like the miserable people who drove out into the countryside and abandoned the unwanted family pet.

It was nearly midnight before he went up to bed but he couldn't sleep. Finally he put on his dressing-gown and went down to the kitchen and made himself a cup of tea. His mind still gnawed at the problem like a dog at a bone but it produced no solution. Although he didn't know it, an answer to his problem, or at least a catalyst, was already lying on his desk in the radio room in the City.

Hallam had been amiable enough on the telephone. Apologising for the cryptic signal and the short notice. But they needed him back in London. Needed his experience in pulling the whole German set-up back into shape. Hallam had sounded as if he expected resistance but as Hallam chatted away Fisher knew then what he had to do about the girl. Hallam gave him two weeks to clear up in Hamburg and hand over to his replacement. They didn't know yet who his replacement would be. It would probably be Seymour who would take over from him.

After they had eaten that evening he took her upstairs to his small study. When she was settled in the only armchair he pulled up a chair and sat facing her. As he looked at her he was aware of her vulnerability, her dependence on him. When she smiled he said, 'Why are you smiling?'

'I feel like I sometimes felt in the headmistress's office, in High School, when I knew she was going to talk about my terrible marks.' She laughed softly, 'I was hopeless at school.'

Fisher shook his head, took a deep breath and said, 'What do you think I do – my work?'

She shrugged. 'I'm not sure. I always thought it must be something like the KGB, only for the British.'

Fisher smiled, wryly. 'Not quite the same, my dear. But it'll do.' He paused for the moment. 'When a person joins one of these organisations he learns that if he is caught by the other side he could be imprisoned, or tortured, or even killed, depending on who the other side happens to be. One of the differences between my organisation and the KGB is that the KGB is as ruthless with civilians outside espionage as it is with enemy agents. My outfit doesn't usually involve innocent civilians. They made an exception in your case. I think they were wrong to do that. But because of what you were doing, along with Professor Rykov, I can understand why they did it.' He paused again. 'That doesn't mean that I agree with them. What I violently disagreed with was their decision to send you back. They knew as well as I did what would happen to you. So I disobeyed my orders – and here you are.'

The girl looked scared and he reached out and touched her hand. 'Nothing bad's going to happen, Ushi. I just want to talk to you about how to make your position more secure.' He looked at her face. 'Is that OK?'

She nodded and he leaned back in his chair, smiling. 'I want to ask you a silly question.' He paused. 'Tell me what you know about me.'

'What kind of things?'

'Anything.'

'And "know" or "think"?'

'Both.'

She smiled. 'You're a very tough man, but you like éclairs and a lot of sugar in your tea and coffee. You don't like politicians so you change channels on the TV when they're on. You know more than you say – especially about people. You aren't really interested in books, or music, or any of the arts. You are very self-confident and . . .' she smiled, '. . . and I feel very safe with you.'

'How far would you trust me about you?'

She shrugged. 'A long, long way – maybe all the way.'

'Do you believe that I'm genuinely unhappy about what my people did to you?'

She smiled, her head tilted to one side. 'Of course I do.'

'Good. Now to the next item on my list.' He looked at her as he said, 'I've been ordered back to London. Permanently. And I want you to go with me. How do you feel about that?'

178

For a few moments she was silent and then she said quietly, 'Wouldn't that be illegal, with no papers and no visas?'

'It could be, but I want to suggest a safer way of doing it. Which would make it safe.'

'Tell me.'

Fisher tried to smile but it was perilously near a grimace. And he took a deep breath before he said, 'I'm going to suggest that you marry me.' He held up his hand to stop the protest that never came. 'It would be a marriage of convenience. A marriage in name only. With no obligations on your side whatsoever. And we should have to use other names, both of us.'

As she looked at him his eyes searched her face for a reaction. But he could see none. Finally she said softly, 'You are a strange man, David Fisher. A very strange man.'

'In what way do you find me strange?'

'You could have gone away to London without saying a word to me. Left the housekeeper to tell me that I had to be independent. Why should you care about what happens to me? You've given me a home for seven or eight months. Surely that pays any debts you might think you owe me?'

'That might have worked right at the start. But not now.'

'Why not?'

'Because I know you now. You're not just a name. You're a person. A good person who needs to be cared for.'

'Cared for?'

'Yes. Why not?'

'Do you care about me? Or is it just a matter of justice? Making up for false imprisonment?'

'No. It's caring.'

'Have you ever loved anyone? A woman?'

'No. There are some I have liked, but love is a big word.'

'What friends do you have?'

'Do you mean women or men?'

'Either. Both.'

He thought for several long moments and then shrugged. 'There are both men and women I quite like. But friends? I'd have to say none.'

'Has it ever entered your head that it's you who needs the caring?'

179

'I'm quite capable of looking after myself, Ushi.'

'In a fight – yes. In an argument with authority – yes. But away from your work you have nothing. No love. No caring. Nobody who cares if you are happy or unhappy. Nothing that you like doing. No interest in anything but being whatever you are. No hobbies, no sports. It isn't a life, it's an existence.'

'You must have thought all this without ever saying anything.'

'It doesn't take much thinking about, David. It's very obvious to anyone who notices what's going on.'

'Well. All this introspection doesn't answer my question to you. If you're married to me they can't touch you. Nobody can.'

'So what's the question again?'

'Would you agree to marry me? No obligations. No strings attached.'

'I'm afraid not, David.'

'OK.' He leaned back in his chair. 'I'll try and work out something else.'

'There is an alternative of course.'

He looked up hopefully. 'What is it, Ushi?'

She looked at him calmly. 'I could marry you in the usual way. *With* obligations. And with all the usual obligations from both of us.'

'Do you want that?'

'Of course I do.'

'But why?'

'Because I care about you. Almost from the beginning I cared about you. I'd count myself as very lucky to be married to you.' She smiled, but her soft lips trembled. 'I'd try very hard to make you happy. I wouldn't be a nuisance, I promise.'

He shook his head slowly. 'You won't ever be a nuisance to anybody, girl. Let me go to England for a couple of days to arrange things and then, after we have done the deed, we'll have a few days before I have to start work.' He stood up, smiling. 'You know, it's just sinking in. It's going to be wonderful.'

She sat looking up at him affectionately as he stood there. She knew that there would be no emotional response from the man. No hugs. No kisses. She didn't mind. She knew him too well to mind. And she knew that she had enough love for both of them.

He walked with her to her bedroom door and as she stood

there he put his hands on her shoulders and looked at her face, and said, 'You're far too beautiful for me, Ushi.' And then, to her surprise he kissed her chastely on the cheek before he turned and walked back to his own bedroom. She watched him walk away, opening then closing his door. No looking back.

In his room David Fisher stood at the window looking out across the wide lawns to the dark shapes of the trees. He closed his eyes to try and concentrate his thoughts, torn between the conflicting arguments in his tired mind. He had gone over it all a hundred times before without reaching a conclusion that would satisfy his fundamental question. Why was he marrying Ushi Jaeger? He had told her that it was to protect her. And that was true enough. But it wasn't the whole truth. Far from it.

When he knew that he was being withdrawn to London his first thought had been for her. When he had brought her to Hamburg he'd not looked into the future and thought about how it would all evolve. He'd taken for granted that she would always be there. But after Hallam's call he'd had to face the truth. He couldn't bear the thought of her not being with him. She was the balm that made his life tolerable. He would miss her terribly. The gentle voice, the lovely face and that lithe young body. He had felt a sudden gust of shame at acknowledging those longings to make love to her. She was in baulk. Untouchable. But Hallam's call had made the impossible possible. He despised all men who took advantage of women's vulnerability but he had rationalised that nothing would change. She would be protected and that was all. Nothing more. But her response had changed all that. She cared about him. And he cared about her.

He had always taken consolation from Kipling's dictum – "He travels the fastest who travels alone." But it seemed an empty, arid philosophy now. He turned away from the window, shaking his head as if to dismiss the turmoil in his mind. And suddenly he was at peace. What he was doing was right. Right for her and right for him.

He undressed slowly and was asleep five minutes later.

CHAPTER 25

When Ushi Jaeger came down to breakfast Fisher was already on the early-morning flight to London. At Immigration he used a Canadian passport and an hour later he had booked into a small hotel in Ebury Street.

He spent the afternoon at the General Registrar's Office in St Catherine's House in Kingsway, following the same routine that was used so often by the KGB. Checking death certificates first and then the relevant birth certificates. After a couple of hours he had two suitable candidates, both named Hunter, both the right age, and both deceased. One was Ann Hunter, the other Michelle Joanna Hunter. He paid for four copies of both birth certificates and noted the details of both death certificates.

At the Passport Office in Petty France he picked up a couple of application forms and then drove a hire-car out to the Parish Church at Putney. The grave of Michelle Joanna Hunter had a small, cheap headstone with just her name and a brief "In Memoriam 1960-1983". The grave itself had obviously been neglected. Dandelions and ragwort flourished in the thick tangle of coarse grasses that covered it. It was exactly what he wanted.

Back in Hamburg by mid-day the following day he took Ushi to the Hauptbahnhof and had four sets of photographs taken in one of the photo booths.

He filled out the application form himself and Ushi signed it as Michelle Joanna Hunter. Using the forged passport that had been employed for the flight from Berlin they were both in London the following day.

He sat with her in the waiting area at the Passport Office in Petty France and made her rehearse her story for expedited treatment. She was to say that it was her first application and she needed it for her honeymoon in Paris. It took an hour before her number was called but there had been no snags. She could pick up the passport the following day. They had booked into the Ebury Park Hotel under the names of Hunter and Dawe, the name on Fisher's Canadian passport.

Fisher sat in Ushi's room looking at a map. For no particular reason except that he knew the town well from his youth, and he had the address of an SIS safe-house just outside the town that he could give to qualify for the period of residence, he chose Tunbridge Wells as the place where they would get married. There was a slight risk in doing so but if it was ever discovered there would be no point in anyone trying to void the marriage.

It was raining as they drove down to Tunbridge Wells but he was able to park the car in the courtyard of the Registry Office. A friendly, helpful woman told them about the various licences and they asked for a Superintendent's Licence that meant they could be married two days' later. He gave the safe-house address in Broadwater Down to establish his residence and there were no problems. They arranged to be married on the Friday at 11 a.m. They booked adjoining rooms at the Spa Hotel and went shopping. He went with her to help her buy a dress at Next and a two-piece suit at Bentall's. They split up for half an hour. He'd given her money to buy anything else she might want, and he bought a simple gold wedding ring but it was too short notice to get it engraved. He drew money from Barclay's Bank on his London account and then crossed the street to Baldwin's Café where they were to meet.

As they drank their coffees he showed her the ring and she told him of the other clothing she had bought. And finally she gave him a small packet.

'That's for you, David. A wedding present from me.'

'What is it?'

She smiled. 'Nothing very much. Just a book. Look at it tonight when you go to bed.'

Fisher looked slowly around the small café. There was only an elderly couple in the far corner. He turned his head to look at the girl's face.

'There's something I've wanted to say to you, Ushi. I've tried to think how to say it, but I haven't found a satisfactory way.'

'So just say it, David.'

'This isn't the kind of wedding or marriage that I would have wished for you. I feel that I'm robbing you of what should be a very special day in your life. The cause is good. My motives are honourable and I've made it as calm and formal as I can. But it's a poor substitute for what you should be having. And . . .'

'You don't have to explain or excuse what you're doing, David. I understand. And I'm grateful.' She smiled. 'I'm pleased too.'

'I was going on to say that I shan't ever take any advantage of the situation.' He paused, hesitating. 'But I want to say that I genuinely care about you. I want you to be as happy as you can be in the circumstances. I admire so much about you.'

She smiled. 'Tell me what you admire about me.'

She realised from his quick response that his thoughts were deeper than she had imagined and his previous words were not just consolatory flattery. She watched his face as he spoke.

'You're very alive and intelligent. Very gentle and always calm. Uncomplaining and strong in a feminine sort of way.' For a moment he hesitated. 'And you're very beautiful.'

She reached out and put her hand on his as it lay on the table. 'Those were nice things that you said, they comfort me, those sorts of things, when I'm alone. There are other things – things about marriage that we have never talked about. They'll all come right for us, David. Tomorrow I'll be your wife and that pleases me. It makes up for many things that have happpened that are not the fault of either of us.' She smiled. 'Let's go back to the hotel.'

It was nearly midnight when he remembered to open the parcel. It was a paperback version of 'Palgrave' and there was a note addressed to him in her handwriting. He read it slowly.

Dear, dear David,

I know that you have been very worried on my account. So let me say that apart from what may have happened to my parents I myself am very happy with how things have turned out.

I shall be both proud and happy to be your wife. Not just

184

as protection for me but because I shall be with you. Being with you is like being with my family.

So be a little bit happy and then I can be as happy as I feel.

Your loving
Ursula

P.S. I have put slips in at the poems for you to read. One for you. One for me. Just the first and last verse of both.

Fisher opened the book at the first slip which said, 'For me. Page 73. First and last verses – "Counsel to Girls".' He smiled at the two verses.

> Gather ye rose-buds while ye may,
> Old Time is still a-flying:
> And this same flower that smiles to-day,
> To-morrow will be dying.
>
> Then be not coy, but use your time;
> And while ye may, go marry:
> For having lost but once your prime,
> You may for ever tarry.

The second slip read: 'For you. Page 65. First and last verses.'

Character of a Happy Life

> How happy is he born and taught
> That serveth not another's will;
> Whose armour is his honest thought,
> And simple truth his utmost skill!
>
> This man is free from servile bands
> Of hope to rise, or fear to fall;
> Lord of himself, though not of lands;
> And having nothing, he hath all.

At breakfast he had thanked her for the book and the quotations, smiling as he said he'd memorise the poetry. Then he said, 'D'you remember I told you I had no permanent home? Just some place where I happen to be working?'

'I do.'

'I thought after the event this morning we could visit a couple of estate agents in London and find ourselves a flat. Would you like that?'

She beamed. 'I'd love it.'

CHAPTER 26

The flat in Turnham Green was only the second property that they had looked at. Ushi wanted it the moment she saw it. Fisher thought it was small and characterless, but because he was not used to having a place he could call home, he was passively indifferent to where they lived. They had moved in four days later and spent the last few days of his leave buying furniture.

It felt strange going to Century House as if he were working for some insurance company in the City. Having to keep more or less normal office hours and playing virtually no active part in the operations he would control.

I'e had a chat with Hallam in the morning and was surprised at the size and splendour of the office he had been allocated but he was involved by the afternoon in a general briefing meeting with the SIS officers who controlled the various clandestine operations in West and East Germany. He already knew several of the members of the meeting, by name or in person. Hallam chaired the meeting and before he started the reporting he tactfully made clear that Fisher's new posting was a promotion and he was now senior to the men around the table. When he had finished his piece Fisher looked around the half dozen faces at the table and nodded to Seymour.

'OK. Mr Seymour. You start us off.'

Seymour looked down at his notes, running his fingers through his dense mop of long, blond hair. When he looked up he looked directly at Fisher.

'My sections are based on Brunswick. There are twelve full sections. Eight are deployed on line-crossing operations into the GDR and the others on intelligence-gathering operations on our side of the frontier.'

Fisher nodded. 'What kind of intelligence-gathering, Mr Seymour?'

'Mainly concerned with suspected line-crossers from the other side and to a lesser extent in topographical information covering changes in the frontier defences of both sides. There is one unit concerned solely with preliminary evaluation of accrued intelligence.'

'Who takes over after the prelims?'

'London.'

'Any particular problems?'

Seymour smiled wryly. 'No. Just the usual ones.'

'How would you define the usual ones?'

'Oh, morale, internal security, cash, and the usual bloody-minded attitude of field officers to control from London.' He shrugged. 'Or anywhere else for that matter.'

Fisher looked speculatively at Seymour for a few moments, wondering if he was trying to get at his new boss so early in the game. He decided that he wasn't.

Hallam cut in. 'Professor Clayton, how about your area?'

'Yes, sir. My remit is to keep all field units in the Federal Republic aware of current political developments in the Bundestag and the political parties.'

Fisher raised his eyebrows. 'That sounds like a monster of a job, Professor. How successful are you?'

Clayton smiled. 'Maybe I've given the wrong impression. My people are only concerned with those aspects of Federal German policy and thinking that could possibly affect coopera-tion with our people by the federal government, local author-ities and regional authorities.'

'And how successful are your people?'

'In dissemination they're very good. In accuracy I'd rate us as no better than eighty per cent.'

'Is that good enough, in your opinion?'

'No. Not by any standards. It's not much better than a good journalist would achieve.' He smiled. 'But it's eighty per cent of a much wider field than a journalist would have to cover.'

'When you're wrong, what effect has it had in, say, the last year?'

'We were wrong in our assessment of what the Bonn attitude would be when the East Germans offered to allow their citizens to cross the border in exchange for cash. We didn't think Bonn would agree to that on moral grounds. When they did, our people suspect that a lot of KGB and East German line-crossers were put through at the same time and our people had neither the time nor the resources to plan and execute a sufficiently good weeding-out process. That was a major blunder on our part.'

'What would have prevented that? More funds, more people or what?'

Clayton shook his head. 'Nothing would have prevented it. It was a judgemental decision and we were wrong. I think a lot of Bonn politicians shared our view. We were all of us wrong.'

'Who had the final judgement?'

'Me. Personally.'

Fisher said, 'Thank you, Professor,' and turned to look at Macleod.

'I think I can omit your report, Mac.' He smiled. 'I was part of your area of operation. Maybe we can talk some other time.' Fisher nodded to an older man. 'It's Mr Humphreys isn't it?'

'Yes, sir. My operations are virtually the same as Seymour's. Line-crossing operations but based on Kassel. Problems much the same but with the addition of liaising with CIC units and the CIA based on Frankfurt.'

'What problems does that give you, Mr Humphreys?'

'Well now, the Americans are very friendly but they totally ignore the operational boundaries that London and Washington agreed on. They send their people in swarms into my area. Some of them not very well trained. And those who are well trained are far too gung-ho for line-crossing operations. For example we've had a number of incidents in the frontier area where they have alerted the East German guards for miles along the border when we have been on the point of going over ourselves.'

'What have you done about it?'

'I've contacted the CIA at Langley but they don't understand. They seem to think that it's some kind of race, and we're just bad losers.'

'Have you done written reports on these incidents?'

'Yes. All of them.'

'Get hold of copies and see me tomorrow morning. OK?'

'Yes, sir.'

Fisher looked around the table. 'A couple of questions from

me. Firstly – who is responsible for liaison with SIS at the embassy in Bonn? And secondly how were these problems dealt with before this new set-up?'

Hallam said, 'Let me answer both questions. There is no direct contact between anybody we have at the embassy and people on line-crossing operations. And second question – there was no inter-connecting of information between controls before. Hence the new set-up – and you.'

The meeting went on for almost another hour and then broke up so that Fisher could start reading the files.

Chapter 27

Fisher was using Judy Miller to coordinate the arrangements in West Berlin for Lemke's defection. She didn't know the German's identity, just that it was a defection, but she had long experience of covert operations. They met in a small restaurant on the Ku'damm.

He had cleared her proposed arrangements for the few hours when Lemke would be in West Berlin and she had given him a list of the documents she would need to get him on the flight to Amsterdam, where London would take him over.

'Have you got any other questions, Judy?'

'I'd like to know what the man's temperament is like. He'll know that he's travelling on false documents. He's got to go through Immigration Control and so on. Is he going to be nervous about doing that?'

Fisher shrugged. 'Well, he's not coming under any kind of duress.' He paused. 'I guess he'll be tense but I don't see him being nervous.'

'And how soon are the KGB going to be alerting their networks on our side of the Wall? How long before he's going to be missed; and when he is missed – how soon before they suspect that he's come over to us?'

'I've allowed for a worst-case situation of six hours before they realise that he's gone. More likely to be thirty-six hours. And to answer the other point – I think they'll alert their people over here as soon as they can't find him. But they won't necessarily see him as a defector. But the sooner you get him on a flight the better.'

'They've got stooges in the airport ground staff at Tegel. They could be going through flight manifests in minutes after they were told to watch for him.'

'How bright are their stooges?'

'They don't need to be bright, David. They only need to do what they're told.'

'So what do you suggest – a diversion?'

'Yes. If he's worth it.'

'How many people would you need?'

'I don't know until I've worked something out but it would be at least fifteen to do it properly.'

'OK. You work it out and come back to me in London and I'll speak to Harris to see if he can help.' He paused. 'Anything else?'

'Only an odd piece of gossip.'

'Tell me.'

'You remember way back the girl you brought over from the other side? We covered for you at the airport.'

'What about her?'

'I heard that she'd been sent back into their zone.'

'So?'

'But in the last couple of weeks I've heard that the KGB have put top-grade agents into West Berlin. They're looking for her.'

'How sure are you of this?'

'Three of my people have been approached by them. With photographs and descriptions. And a reward for information leading them to her.'

'How much?'

'In one case they quoted thirty thousand D-Marks and in another forty thousand.'

'Are they making any headway?'

'Not so far. But they've only just started.'

He paused. 'What the hell was the girl's name?'

'Jaeger. Ursula Jaeger.'

'Maybe she decided to stay in the GDR instead of going back to the Soviet Union. If I remember rightly she was a GDR national not a Soviet.' Fisher stood up. 'Anyway, that's way back. Are you happy about this operation?'

Judy Miller smiled. 'I'm never happy until my part's over. But I've covered everything I can think of. Especially if you can arrange a diversion team for me.'

'I'll do that. You go and powder your nose and I'll get on my way.' He smiled. 'See you. And take care.'

On the plane back to Gatwick Fisher sat with his eyes closed thinking about what Judy Miller had said about Ushi. It was bad news that they were looking for her after all that time had passed. But if they were looking so intensively in West Berlin that was a good sign. They wouldn't waste skilled agents' time there if they had any idea where she really was. And she'd been in the house at Blankanese most of the time except for when they arrived and finally left. The house had been rented in the name of a Portuguese company registered in Rio de Janeiro. The news was disturbing but nothing more.

They were sitting on a bench in St James's Park watching children throwing bread from the bridge to the mallards on the lake. Penny turned to look at him.

'I like that little bridge.'

'Why?'

'I don't really know, Robbie, but it's sort of romantic.'

Thornton laughed, and she turned to look at him. 'Don't *you* think it's romantic?'

'Well, I know what you mean but it's not really romantic for me.'

'Why not?'

'Oh, for various reasons. Work reasons.'

'Work reasons? *Your* work you mean?'

'Yes.'

'Tell me. I'm intrigued.'

'In the days when our offices were at Broadway House people used to come to the park to talk when they wanted to make sure that they couldn't be overheard. The little bridge was the usual place where they talked.'

'My God. And it all looks so peaceful. Didn't it seem incongruous? The lake and the ducks and the children and you lot whispering about the KGB.'

'I don't think anybody was aware of the surroundings. It was just a safe place to talk.'

'Does that mean you don't even trust one another?'

He smiled. 'It's a funny word – trust. What does it mean exactly?'

'That you assume that people are what they seem to be. That they don't tell you lies. That they mean what they say. That they don't intend to harm you or even deceive you.'

'Why do we have to make those sorts of judgements about

people? Why not just keep to facts. *Do* they tell lies? *Are* they up to no good? *Are* they trying to deceive you? One can just be neutral.' He smiled. 'Neutral but still keep your powder dry.'

'Do you trust me, Robbie?'

'I don't think you tell lies. I'm sure you wish me well and I don't waste my time wondering if you're deceiving me in some way.'

'Why would it be a waste of time?'

'If you aren't deceiving me – then it's a waste of time. If you are – it's still a waste of time.' He paused. 'Anyway you're not part of my work and that makes it different.'

'But so far as your work is concerned, you don't trust me.'

He laughed but it was a nervous laugh. 'You don't come into my work, Penny. So the question doesn't arise.'

'Would you think it odd if I refused to tell you anything about what I'd been doing during the day?'

'Yes. But that's different.'

'In what way?'

'Nobody could lose his life from anything you told me.'

'If you told me about whatever you're doing right now, could you lose your life?'

'No.' He paused. 'Well, let's say that it's very unlikely.'

'Could somebody else lose his life?'

For several moments he closed his eyes, thinking. When he opened them he said, 'Very remotely it's possible. But *very* remotely.'

'Possible, but not probable?'

'Yes.'

'So tell me what you're doing tomorrow.'

He smiled. 'You don't need to know. And that's the rule we stick to. Even inside the business. If somebody doesn't *need* to know something, then he's not told about it.' He shrugged. 'Why burden him with the responsibility of something that doesn't concern him? It's not a reflection on the guy, it just saves him being involved unnecessarily.'

She wasn't smiling when she said, 'So tell me what you're doing tomorrow. I *need* to know.'

'Why do you need to know?'

'Because I want to find out if you trust me. Not just with the housekeeping money but with something from the part of your life that isn't mine.'

He looked at her face for a long time before he replied, and then he said quietly, 'Does it really mean all that much to you?'

She nodded. 'Yes, it does.'

He took a deep breath. 'OK. I'm looking for a man who's disappeared. One of our own men . . .'

For ten minutes he gave her the barest outline of what he had been doing. No names. No places identified. No details of Fisher's work. Just a picture of a man. She sat listening intently and when he had finished she said softly, 'You weren't making it up, were you? Just to pacify me.'

'What makes you think that?'

'Because the man you described could be you.'

He looked amazed. 'Me? In what way is he like me?'

She shrugged. 'He's tough and competent. Self-assured. But he's sympathetic to human failure. Everybody sees him differently and nobody really knows what he's like. That's why it's all so contradictory. He goes by his own standards and rules – not other people's. That's you, my boy.' She stood up. 'Let's go home.'

Back at the flat she hung up her coat.

'Cup of tea?'

Thornton nodded, and after she had switched on the kettle, she came back to the kitchen doorway and stood there, looking at him fondly.

'Thanks for telling me about that man. I'll forget all about it. I promise. And in case I didn't make it clear – I appreciate what you did. And I won't ask any more questions about your work.'

He heard the quaver in her voice and only then did he realise that she was very near to tears.

Chapter 28

Siwicki found his new work at Stanford irksome after the excitement and freedom of Operation Aeolus. He was working with a middle-aged professor of mathematics from UCLA who obviously wished he was a teenager again. He worked on his tan as if it were a condition of employment and wore grey T-shirts, jeans and trainers. His favourite entertainment was MTV and he was into heavy metal and Iron Maiden. His favourite word was 'totally', but despite everything, Siwicki realised that his collaborator was a highly creative mathematician. Their assignment was a study of 'Mathematical applications in the evaluation of ESP and pre-cognition experiments'.

It was mid-morning when the Admin Office phoned him and asked him to go over. The girl gave him a slip from a message pad. It just gave a name – 'Danahar' – and a phone number for him to ring. The word urgent was underlined three times.

He used the pay-phone in the corridor and the voice at the other end had a Texan accent.

'Where are you right now, Mr Siwicki?'

'I'm at SRI.'

'How soon can you get to the Holiday Inn?'

'I guess it would take about twenty minutes.'

'OK. I wanna see you there in half an hour. Come up to Room number . . .' There was a pause, '. . . Room number seven four zero five.'

'What is all this? I'm working . . .'

'It's an order, Siwicki.'

'Who the hell are you to give me orders?' His voice rose with indignation.

'Danahar. Tom S. Danahar. CIA. Now get your ass over here.'

And the phone was hung up at the other end.

*

The Palo Alto Holiday Inn seemed too bright and cheerful to be accommodating CIA men with rasping, commanding voices, but when Siwicki knocked at the door of Room 7405 the man who opened it looked less overbearing than he had expected. In his fifties, he was big, raw-boned and handsome in an old-fashioned Gary Cooper style.

'Come right in, boy.' He waved to a comfortable chair by the window. 'A whisky, mister?'

'No thanks.'

'Something else they can get you?'

'No, I'm OK.'

Danahar reached for a buff-coloured file and opened it, looking at it briefly before he looked back at Siwicki.

'How're you making out at SRI?'

Siwicki shrugged. 'All right I guess.'

'Interesting work?'

'A bit academic but – yes – interesting enough.'

'Not like the other stuff you were doing for the Agency?'

Siwicki smiled. 'No, I'm afraid not.'

'D'you remember being passed some material on a Soviet guy named Rykov? Professor Rykov.'

'I remember the name.' Siwicki paused. 'Wasn't he using a girl for passive telepathy or am I mixing him up with someone else?'

'No. That's the guy. What did you think of the work he was doing?'

'Interesting but I only saw the bare outlines. Looked a bit over the top to me.'

'Wasn't there some talk about you going over to England and working with the girl assistant?'

Siwicki smiled. 'There was talk of me going to England for a while but they didn't tell me what it was about.'

'It seems like that's what it was. How would you have felt about that?'

'I'd have been very interested.'

'Did you hear why the original plan went down the pike?'

'No. I just heard nothing more.'

'Well, your old friend Schaeffer went off into the wild blue yonder and got his ass kicked as a result. But the top brass have been having second thoughts.' He paused. 'If the chance came

197

up again to work with Rykov's girl – would you still be interested?'

'What about my position with SRI?'

'That would all be taken care of. No problem there.'

'In that case I'd definitely be interested.'

'OK.' Danahar paused. 'You realise that this is a very preliminary discussion? Nothing may come of it. We just wanted to make sure that if certain events took place you would be available.' He smiled and stood up, holding out his hand. 'Thanks for your time, Mr Siwicki. Maybe we'll meet again. Just remember that this chat is top security. Strictly between you and me.'

'I understand that, sir.'

As Siwicki made his way to the car park he wondered why the hell he had called the CIA man sir. At the time it had seemed appropriate. Danahar was that sort of man. But on reflection he blushed at his naivety.

During the next few months Fisher had spent most of his time in London, keeping office hours, except for the odd occasion when he had to spend a night in Germany.

He and Ushi lived a rather old-fashioned middle-class domestic life. A visit to the local cinema, a Sunday drive into the country, chess games, reading and talking seemed to content both of them. To Ushi it was not unlike her previous life in the Soviet Union and to Fisher these activities had the benefit of novelty. A novelty that he found strangely satisfying. But he was aware that there was always one grey cloud on the horizon. The need to avoid invitations from colleagues to their homes. Both Clayton and Macleod had met Ushi at the house in Berlin and, although these meetings had been brief, he had no intention of running any risk of her being recognised.

About six months passed before they came near to disaster. He had taken her to the Festival Hall to a Tchaikovsky concert. A double bill of the Piano Concerto and the Violin Concerto. They had settled in their seats after the interval on the first warning bell and he'd looked up at the second tier boxes and to his horror saw Macleod and his wife. He felt that Macleod was looking at them and then, to his relief, the Macleods were joined by another couple and he leaned forward in his seat hoping that

Ushi was hidden by his body. As the auditorium lights were being lowered before the second half of the programme began Fisher glanced briefly in Macleod's direction. He was leaning towards his wife, speaking to her, but Macleod was looking in his direction as the lights faded. He had seen Macleod twice during the following week and Macleod had made no reference to seeing him at the concert, neither did he seem to react in any way out of the normal pattern.

Hallam was filling in for two months for Ridley as CIA/SIS liaison and when the call came through in mid-afternoon it was automatically transferred to him.

'Hallam here.'

'My name's Danahar, Mr Hallam. Deputy Director Operations at Langley. I'd like to see you. When can I come over?'

'Is it urgent, Mr Danahar?'

'Yeah.'

'If you took the evening Concorde we could meet tomorrow morning.'

'Fine. Where?'

'You say.'

'How about I book in at the Hilton and we meet there for breakfast? Say eight-thirty. Would that be agreeable to you?'

'That's fine. May I ask what it's about?'

'I'd like to leave it until I see you if you don't mind.'

'Of course. I'll see you at the Hilton. Eight-thirty tomorrow morning.'

Hallam hadn't been to the Hilton since its major restructuring at street level but he checked Danahar's room number at the desk and when he rang him on the internal phone he was invited to go up.

On a trolley were the old-fashioned plated dishes covering the constituents of traditional British breakfasts. Cornflakes or porridge, fried eggs, bacon, sausage and fried tomatoes, coffee in a Cona, toast in two racks, butter and Tiptree coarse-cut marmalade.

Danahar grinned as he waved his hand.

'Let's help ourselves.'

When they were settled facing each other at the small table Danahar handed an envelope to Hallam.

'You'd better read that before we talk.'

There was an old-fashioned red wax seal on the back of the envelope and Hallam used a knife from the table to slit the top of the flap without breaking the seal. The page he took out and unfolded was on stiff cream paper.

The letter was headed – 'From the office of the Director – Central Intelligence Agency'. Above the text it said, 'Eyes only W.R. Hallam OBE'. The telephone number given was Washington DC 202 351–1100.

The text introduced Tom S. Danahar and confirmed that he was authorised to discuss, and if appropriate, negotiate all matters with the addressee on the subject which would be raised. The recipient was advised to establish the identity of Tom S. Danahar and if he deemed it necessary should phone extension 9709 to establish authenticity of the note itself. There was an obviously handwritten signature and the Director's name below it.

Hallam looked up at Danahar as he folded the letter and tucked it back in the envelope.

'OK. Go ahead, Mr Danahar.'

'Don't you want to check my identity and status before we talk?'

Hallam smiled. 'I did that while you were on the plane. Our embassy faxed me a photograph, several newspaper cuttings and your entry in our CIA file.' He smiled again. 'The photograph doesn't do you justice but it's you all right.' He paused. 'I also talked on the scrambler to our man at the embassy – Miller.'

'Ah yes – Miller. A great little poker player is your pal Miller. Probably charges his losses to your Imprest Account in the name of good relations.'

Hallam smiled, but said nothing. Danahar leaned back in his chair.

'D'you remember way back a guy named Schaeffer persuaded you people to kidnap a girl working for the Russians? Doing some kind of telepathy thing.'

'I certainly do. It caused us a lot of trouble.'

'It caused Schaeffer a lot more than that.' He paused. 'But

time moves on. The wheel comes full circle. And right now the top-brass at Langley wonder if they weren't a little – what shall we say – precipitate.'

'What's made them change their minds?'

'Several things. First of all a team looked at the intelligence that was being provided by our own operation – Operation Aeolus. It was unobtainable any other way. Secondly another group evaluated the reports on what this Professor Rykov guy seemed to be providing for the Russians. They were impressed on both counts.'

'Isn't it a bit late to change your minds?'

Danahar smiled. 'We don't think so. And we wondered if you people have been shrewder than we were.'

Hallam raised his eyebrows. 'What's that mean?'

'Our information is that that little girl was never sent back.' He smiled a knowing smile. 'We wondered what you had done with her.'

'What makes you think we didn't send her back?'

'The facts, I guess.'

'Tell me.'

'Are you still saying that she went back?'

'Yes.'

'So let me tell you what we know. We have a fairly low-grade contact in Akademgorodok. She's never been back there. Her mother's in one of the Gulag labour camps. We don't know where her father is but we do know that he was arrested in Berlin the day after your people lifted her. He's not been seen since.'

'That doesn't necessarily mean she didn't go back. They may well have seen her as a willing defector who was refused asylum. She could be in a labour camp herself.'

'In that case why are the Russians looking for her in West Berlin? They've been ferreting around for nearly six months.'

'Are you sure?'

'One hundred per cent, old friend.'

'OK. Well, let's assume that she didn't go back. Maybe she wanted to go it alone and found herself a job in East Germany.'

'With all the check-points alerted the day after she went missing? I don't think so.'

'I still don't see any problem for the CIA or us, whatever she did.'

'We'd like to get hold of her again,' Danahar said quietly.

'You mean use her?'

'Yep.'

'You're not asking us to be involved again?'

'Maybe not involved. But we'd be more than grateful for your cooperation.'

'In what respect?'

'Your guy who lifted her knows more about her than anybody else. And I understand that he knows Berlin inside out. All we ask is that you give him a couple of weeks to look for her. No action on his part. If he finds her, we'll do the rest.'

'And this is all above-board and official this time? Not some piece of private enterprise that ends in another ghastly cock-up?'

'I'd never call this type of operation "above-board" as you put it. But it's official all right. Or I wouldn't be here talking with you. And I wouldn't have been able to give you that letter.'

'And that's all you want? Our man spends some time looking around Berlin for the girl?'

'That's it.' He paused. 'And I'm authorised to tell you that in return we'll share all information we get if it works out. Your guy – the professor – Clayton is it? – can ask for throughput on your account if you wish.'

'Let's not look too far ahead at this stage. So far as our man having a look around West Berlin is concerned, yes, I can agree to that right now.'

'Thanks. When can he start?'

'How long are you here for?'

Danahar shrugged. 'As long as I can do any good.'

'Let me talk to my man and then maybe he'd like to quiz you about the information you've got so far.'

'Whatever you say.'

'I'll contact you here in about a couple of hours.'

Back at his office Hallam phoned Fisher and asked him to come and see him.

'Are you on anything complicated at the moment, David?'

'Not particularly.'

'D'you remember the girl you picked up for us in Berlin? Ursula Jaeger.'

'I certainly do.' Fisher's face was impassive.

'They say she never went back into East Berlin.'

'Who's they?'

'The CIA.'

'What the hell do they know about it?'

'There's a senior CIA officer named Tom Danahar staying at the Hilton. He'll put you in the picture. I've told him we'll cooperate with them in looking for the girl in West Berlin. I want you to give them a couple of weeks of your time seeing if you can trace her. If you find her you don't take any action. Just let me know the details and the CIA can take it from there. Danahar can fill you in on what they know already. OK?'

Fisher nodded and stood up. 'OK.'

When Hallam had first mentioned the girl's name Fisher had braced himself for a show-down. He had assumed that he was going to be confronted with what he had done. He had always borne in mind that some day it could happen, but he had been taken off guard by Hallam's words. When he realised how far they obviously were from the truth he relaxed. When the assignment was explained to him it had seemed incredible that he was being asked to look for the girl who was his wife. But it was a relief that they all still thought of her as being in West Berlin.

He had spent an hour with Danahar absorbing carefully the information that the CIA had gleaned. By any normal intelligence standards the evidence was very thin. But what was interesting was why the sudden interest in her at this time? Neither Hallam nor Danahar had offered an explanation as to why they wanted to find her.

But it still left him with a major problem. He could go through the motions of looking for the missing girl in West Berlin and come up with a nil report but if he did that it would put his original disobedience into a much more serious category. Ignoring an order that he didn't agree with about a girl who no longer had any relevance for SIS was probably just about tolerable in view of his record. Effecting a deliberate piece of deception involving both the CIA and SIS was very different. No service record would sustain that. What was worse was that it was the kind of deception that had no appeal for him. Defying desk-bound authority because what they wanted him to do was bad field work was one thing. Deception that was so easy and so bland had no such appeal. His defiance had never been for personal reasons but to ensure that his job was well done. This was just abusing his superiors' trust in him as a man. He wanted to think about all its implications before he committed himself.

Although Fisher didn't know it his dilemma was about to be resolved.

The routine description of Ursula Jaeger was sent to all field units in West Germany and West Berlin, together with a copy of the photograph of the girl on the bridge over the River Ob that SIS had passed to the CIA. Similar material was circulated inside Century House to all officers concerned with operations in the Federal Republic and West Berlin.

The half-page memo with the description and the photograph had lain in Macleod's pile of routine paperwork for two days before he decided to get rid of the backlog. It only needed a quick read before it could be initialled and passed to his secretary. He had glanced briefly at the material on Ursula Jaeger, initialled it and put it into the 'out' tray and was reading the next report when he reached back to the tray, turned over the memo and description and looked at the photograph again. The face seemed vaguely familiar. The girl was very pretty and he wondered if he wasn't mixing her up with some film star. He hesitated and then put the material back in his 'out' tray.

He was on the Northern Line that evening, on his way to his home in Edgware, when he remembered where he had seen that face before. He got off the train at Hendon Central and used a call-box to phone Hallam. The duty-officer at Century House gave him a referral number. Hallam was at a dinner party in Chelsea and was not best pleased at being asked for an urgent meeting with Macleod. But he reluctantly agreed.

*

Hallam was in evening dress when they met at the Royal Court Hotel in Sloane Square and they sat at a table in the far corner of the residents' lounge. Hallam looked at his watch.

'Can we make it brief, Mac?'

'Yes.' He paused. 'I was on the distribution list for the stuff on that girl – Ursula Jaeger. I don't know if you remember but you sent me over to Berlin to pay her off when Fisher was being bolshie.'

'I remember all right.'

'I looked at the photograph with the memo and I knew I'd actually seen that face. And when I realised where I'd seen it before, I thought I must have had in mind the few minutes I spent with her in Berlin. On the way home tonight I realised that that wasn't the last time I saw her.'

He waited for a response but Hallam just nodded. Macleod went on. 'I'm sure I've seen her recently. A few months ago.'

'You haven't been to Berlin for nearly a year, Mac.'

'I didn't see her in Berlin.'

'Where did you see her then?'

'Here in London.'

'Go on.'

'It was at a concert at the Festival Hall. We'd had a box that night and the girl was sitting with a man in the stalls just below the box.'

'You mean you recognised her face at that distance after all that time? Are you sure?'

'It wasn't her I recognised. It was the man she was with I recognised. I only saw her when I noticed the man.'

'You knew the man?'

'Yes. So do you. The man was David Fisher.'

There was a long silence and then Hallam said, 'Did he see you?'

'I'm not sure. He was looking in my direction but he didn't acknowledge me in any way. Nor me him. And I didn't place the girl until tonight.'

Hallam took a deep breath and leaned back in his chair. And to relieve the tension Macleod said, 'Have you ever met his wife?'

Hallam shook his head but didn't reply. Then he leaned forward. 'You'd better do a check, Mac. I hate doing this but it has to be done. Don't say a word to anyone. And do it yourself.' He reached in his jacket pocket and took out a slim diary. 'You'd better take down his home address.'

In twenty-four hours Macleod had confirmed his suspicions. Mrs Fisher was Ursula Jaeger.

CHAPTER 29

Hallam stood at the French windows in his dressing-gown looking out at the darkness of the garden. He could hear an owl hooting in the woods and a frog croaking in the pond. He wasn't a man who indulged in much introspection but at that moment the contrast of the peace and quiet of his house against the grim world of his work disturbed him as it had never disturbed him before. There had been times over the years when he had looked at Gabriella and the kids, and wondered what they would think of him if they knew about the things that he did or caused to be done. But they had been just passing thoughts that were gone very quickly. There was something in what men like Fisher always said, that it was easier sitting at a desk in Broadway or Century House where it was only words that you dealt with, not actual people.

He turned, closing the double doors and walking back into his study. He sat in an armchair, stretching out his long legs as he put his head back, closing his eyes. He would have to make up his mind by tomorrow how he was going to deal with it.

He had known Fisher for years, but that was only professionally. He knew very little of the man himself and his personal life. There had been no reason why he should know. Until now. From past experience he knew that all he could rely on was that Fisher would respond badly to any official threats, despite the fact that he was in the wrong in everything he had done. Not only wrong, but arrogant and defiant. On the other hand, he had done nothing for his own gain. There was no money or bribery involved. Just disobedience. But that wouldn't really wash. Disobedience was a word for kids, not intelligence officers for Christ's sake. They could throw the book at Fisher and he wouldn't have a leg to stand on. Dishonourable discharge. Pension rights withdrawn and his name on a list that would make sure he'd never get a job of any importance for the rest of his life. But who the hell benefited from all that? Not SIS for sure. And the CIA wouldn't get what they wanted. There were no prizes in this shambles for anyone.

He looked at his watch, it was 1.30 a.m. He stood up and walked through to the kitchen and made himself a cup of coffee. As he sat at the kitchen table he tried to put himself in Fisher's place. If he were Fisher what would he want? Slowly and methodically he began to sort out the pieces of the jigsaw.

Hallam decided to confront Fisher away from Century House and arranged an evening meeting at the safe-house in Ebury Street. When they were settled in the leather armchairs Hallam looked intently at Fisher's face as he said, 'Is there anything you want to tell me before we talk?'

'Tell you about what?'

'Anything. Work problems. Personal problems. You name it.'

And Fisher knew instantly that this was it. He shrugged. 'Let's just talk about whatever you had in mind when you asked me to come here today.'

Hallam nodded. 'OK. If that's how you want to play it.' He looked at Fisher unsmiling. 'Let me start by saying that at this juncture this meeting is both unofficial and off the record. Depending on how it develops I might have to change its status. But we'll wait and see.' He paused. 'Tell me about Ursula Jaeger.'

'What do you want to know about her? You've no doubt read the files.'

'Why didn't you carry out your orders and send her back?' He paused. 'And why did you marry her?'

Fisher shrugged. 'She's a very pretty girl.'

'From what I remember all your girl-friends were always very pretty. What had she got that the others hadn't?'

'The others hadn't got a death penalty or ten years in a Gulag camp hanging over their heads.'

'And hopefully they weren't employees of the KGB either.'

'What do you want, Hallam? My resignation? Or do you want my blood as well?'

'Maybe the time for resignations was way back when you chose to defy a direct order from me.'

208

Fisher nodded. 'You could be right there. But it didn't enter my mind at the time because I had no idea how things were going to turn out.'

'Why did you marry her, David?'

'When I was recalled to London it was the only way I could think of to protect her.'

'Was that the only reason why you married her?'

'That's my business, Hallam.'

'I suggest you make it mine, David. It could make a big difference as to what happens next.'

'Look, Hallam. You're not going to put me on trial because even if the hearings were *in camera*, enough would get out to shake the lot of you to the roots.'

'I think you're probably right about that. But what about the girl?'

'What about her?'

'Illegal immigrant, forgery, marriage null and void. That wouldn't be so easy to contest would it?'

'We'd both survive.'

'Do you love her?' Hallam said quietly.

And after a few moments' silence Fisher said, 'Yes. I love her.'

'So how about you stop threatening me and we talk constructively about what we do?'

'That's fine by me.'

'Right. First of all let me make clear that only your past record and my respect for you as a man holds me back from considering dealing with you in any way that the Director of Public Prosecutions might deem fit.' Hallam held up his hand to silence Fisher as he opened his mouth. 'Hear me out. You can have your say later. You know from your own experience how these things go no matter whether the man concerned is found guilty or not. So bear that in mind as we talk.' Hallam paused and then went on. 'What I want to suggest is a compromise. A creative compromise in my opinion. Let's ignore your original disobedience and come to today and the reason why we were looking for your wife.

'As you know now she has a talent that the Soviets were using successfully. The Americans want to use her talent for a short time. I've not told them anything beyond the fact that we think we might have traced her. I've pointed out that quite for-tuitously she is now a British citizen and therefore under our protection.'

Fisher interrupted. '*Is* she under our protection?'

'Oh yes. I have got no wish to disturb her or you in your relationship. But it would help me justify my attitude and some corner-cutting by me if you could both see your way clear to cooperating with us.'

'What kind of cooperation?'

'Let me tell you what I had in mind. We would regularise your wife's position. Proper citizenship and confirmation that your marriage is legal. There would be a financial inducement. A substantial one. I've insisted with the Americans that your wife would only be available in this country and for a matter of months and that you would supervise the day-to-day arrange-ments.' He paused and then went on. 'All that is asked is that your wife would cooperate with an American neurologist who would be posted over here.'

And as he stopped Hallam saw the tears at the edge of Fisher's eyes. He waited, silent.

'You surprise me, Hallam. You really do.'

'How?'

'I think what you have outlined *is* creative. And there is a streak of generosity running through it that appeals to me. It's that that surprises me. I assume that this is not the product of some committee but a personal decision by you.'

'You're right. There was no committee and nobody else will be told either the background or what is to happen. On my part, it was intended to show you that you are valued and respected by me. That I am doing what you yourself might be tempted to do if you were in my place.'

'How long have I got to decide?'

'David, the machinery is grinding away. At the moment I'm like the Dutch boy with his finger in the dyke wall trying to stop the flood pouring through. At this moment I don't need to consult anybody else. Even another day could alter that. I might get a committee to agree with my proposal,' he shrugged, 'but you know how tricky committees can be.'

'OK. We'll need to straighten out some minor details but I agree.' Fisher paused. 'And I'm grateful. I'll be glad to get it all above-board.' He paused. 'I assume that Macleod knows.'

Hallam nodded. 'Yes. You saw him too, did you?'

'Yes.'

'I've warned him that it's not for the record. He won't talk, he's not that kind of man.' Hallam stood up and held out his hand. Fisher took it and Hallam said softly, 'I'm pleased that we've settled this, David.'

Fisher nodded. 'So am I.'

'Come and meet my Gabriella next weekend. It's time we all met your girl. She must be very special.'

'She is.'

CHAPTER 30

Hallam and Fisher, together with Danahar and Siwicki, had worked out the ground rules for the new operation. A limitation of six months was put on the duration which could only be extended if the girl so wished. No pressure of any kind would be put on her if she chose to finish her cooperation at the end of the time. The experiments would take place at a house outside London of Fisher's choosing. It would be bought in his name and then purchased by SIS to show the Fishers a substantial immediate capital gain. The experimental work would be controlled by Siwicki and it was his responsibility to ensure that the girl was treated with the same consideration that she had had from Professor Rykov. If there were any problems they would be referred to Fisher and he had the final decision in resolving the problems.

Hallam had personally regularised all the legal problems that concerned Fisher and his wife in forty-eight hours.

When Fisher had told Ushi his mixture of good and bad news she had been more disturbed than he had expected. He had seen her several times standing at the window or sitting in her chair with a far-away look in her eyes, and he knew that she wasn't happy about the new arrangements. But when she had seen the house at Wadhurst she seemed to accept that there were benefits in it for them both.

Siwicki had walked with her round the garden at 'Little Croft', impressed with her knowledge of the flowers and shrubs that were growing there. He was amused that she even knew the Latin names of the weeds.

There was a white, metal garden table and chairs on the patio at the back of the house and they sat there in the sunshine and he told her of the work that he had been doing for the CIA and his recent work at Stanford Research Institute.

212

She smiled. 'I'd better explain that although I was called Professor Rykov's assistant I don't know anything about the technicalities of his work. I just looked at the pictures he showed me and told him what came into my mind.'

'How successful were the experiments?'

She shrugged. 'I've no idea. I wasn't told. Like I said, I just looked at the pictures he showed me.'

'But you must have been successful or the experiments wouldn't have gone on for so long.' He paused. 'And the KGB wouldn't have taken the set-up over if they weren't getting results.'

'I'm afraid you know more about these things than I do.'

He smiled and changed the subject, 'You've got a beautiful house here. I hope that it's not too much of an imposition me being here.'

'What are the workmen doing in the attic?'

'I wanted a room that would be quiet where we could work when you're ready. They'll be finished in a couple of days.'

Fisher had arranged for the Finn, Miss Makinen, who had acted as housekeeper in Hamburg and Berlin, to come to England to take over the housekeeping duties at 'Little Croft'.

He never asked Ushi or Siwicki how the work was going but they seemed to get on well together. The four of them were having a late supper together one evening in the kitchen and the talk had eventually drifted on to the differences between the United States and the Soviet Union.

Fisher was pouring himself another coffee as he said, 'Of course, my great fear is that they'll end up as allies and divide up the rest of us between them.'

Siwicki grinned. 'I can't see that happening in the next hundred years.'

'Why not?' Fisher said. 'They've got a lot in common.'

'What, for instance?'

'Love of children and the family. Strongly puritanical, both of them. Big countries with multi-national populations. Old-fashioned in many ways in their views on life. Almost their only tensions come from trying to control more and more countries.'

Siwicki laughed and looked at Miss Makinen. 'If you were told that you couldn't live in Finland and you were forced to choose to live in either the United States or the Soviet Union, which would you choose?'

'Nobody could force me to choose. Finland is a democratic country.'

Fisher interposed. 'It's just hypothetical. Just pretend that for some reason you *had* to choose.'

The three of them watched her intently as she sat thinking and then she said quietly, 'I'd choose the Soviet Union.'

Siwicki was shocked. 'Are you a Communist, Miss Makinen? I know a lot of Finns are Communists.'

She smiled. 'No, I'm not a Communist. I vote sometimes for the Social Democrats and sometimes for the Conservative National Collective Party. And for your information the Communists in Finland are lucky if they get ten per cent of the vote.'

'So why do you choose the Soviet Union?'

'Because the United States is an OK country for winners and the Soviet Union is an OK country for losers.'

'Don't you want to be a winner?'

'I'd love to be a winner but the price is too high.'

The American persisted. 'In what way?'

'Fear. Fear of losing one's job. Fear of becoming bankrupt paying medical bills if I became ill. Fear of losing my home if I couldn't pay the mortgage. Fear of having to conform.' She paused. 'In the Soviet Union I'm guaranteed a job. I may not like the job but that's something else. I'm guaranteed a roof over my head. It may not be a wonderful roof and it may be shared with too many others. But I'd have it. If I fell ill I'd get medical attention free of charge. These things matter to me. They matter to a lot of people.' She smiled. 'The losers. And even in the United States there are more losers than winners.'

Ushi watched Fisher's face as the Finnish woman gave her views. Expecting him to challenge them. But it was Siwicki who continued. 'What about the KGB? Could you put up with that?'

She laughed and shrugged. 'What about the CIA and the FBI? Anyway the KGB are only a threat if you do silly things.' Siwicki looked to Fisher as if appealing for his support. But Fisher just smiled and said, 'I think she's made a good case for her choice, Siwicki. Let's just hope she never has to make it.'

214

And there Siwicki left it. Uneasy that he hadn't been able to marshal a better argument for democracy and capitalism.

When Siwicki and Miss Makinen had gone to bed Ushi and Fisher remained in the kitchen, talking.

'Did you think she was right, David?'

'Well, it's much more complicated than that. She's more politically aware than Siwicki. He's totally shut off from the real world by his work so he's never really thought about these things. But on the whole I think she argued the case very well. She knows more about the Soviet Union than Siwicki does. She probably even knows more about the basics of life in the USA than he does. It wasn't a fair contest. He's never had to think about such things. Like all Americans he takes it for granted that everybody wishes they lived in the United States.'

'What are those people like who we're meeting tomorrow?'

'The Hallams? Well, I've never met her but you'll like him. He looks a bit like an overgrown schoolboy but he isn't. Far from it. He's very shrewd.'

'And he's your boss?'

'Yes. He has been for several years now. All the time I was in Germany.'

'You like him?'

'Yes.'

'You trust him?'

Fisher hesitated. 'I don't trust anyone except you. But I see him as being as trustworthy as anybody can be in my kind of world.'

'What do you think of the couple we met last week – the Macleods?'

He smiled. 'You tell me what you thought first.'

'Well, of course I remembered Macleod speaking to me in Berlin. Handing me the envelope of money and telling me how they were going to let me go back home.' She paused. 'He knew what he was sending me to but he smiled as he did it.' She took a deep breath. 'But I wouldn't like him even without that. There is something wrong with that man.'

'Tell me.'

'He is round-faced and pale like a pudding. And he sweats for no reason. His face is always shiny and he is never still. His hands are always moving. Fiddling with his glasses, fastening buttons, feeling in his pockets.'

Fisher laughed. 'OK. That's Macleod. What about his wife?'

'Whatever is wrong with him she knows about it. All the time she is watching him, ready to support him. I liked her. She is loyal to her man and that is a good thing.'

'What about the Professor. Clayton?'

'Very, very clever. Very intelligent. I was surprised that he works in intelligence.'

'Why were you surprised?'

She smiled. 'Because he likes people. He wanted to make sure that I felt at home in his big house. He took me into the library and showed me his books on natural history and botany. He asked me if I was happy and said I must be very special for you to want to marry me. He didn't avoid speaking about meeting me in Berlin. He said that it had worried him for weeks what they had done to me.'

'Did you believe him?'

She smiled, shaking her head. 'No. I've learned your instincts, David. I think he might have been concerned for an hour or two. But that's better than nothing.'

'So you didn't think too much of my colleagues?'

'Oh David. How could I? Compared with you they seem so – I don't know what – "pathetic" is maybe the word.'

Fisher smiled and reached for her hand. 'You're prejudiced.'

'And so I should be. You're special and part of the specialness is that you don't realise it.'

Danahar stood at the window of his office in the CIA headquarters at Langley. It was only the first week in December but already there was a light sprinkling of snow on the ground and there was snow coming down from the dark grey sky. Only small flurries that scattered in the wind but it looked as if the snow was going to settle.

He walked back to his desk, sat down and looked again at the three pages of text that had come from the Central Word-Processing Section. Only six lines of the sit-rep really mattered so far as he was concerned. They mattered because he wasn't sure what he should do about them. Perhaps it would be more accurate to say that he knew what he *should* do about them but wasn't sure that he would do it. He read it again despite the fact that he had read it so many times that he could have recited it.

Origin. 09/86/4071
To: C1094
Ex: CWPS-74
Subject: JAEGER URSULA see Files C1094/7/15/28/35/42

Several sources including EAGLE and ROVER continue to report evidence of continuing KGB interest in W BERLIN regarding above STOP Search in charge of BELINSKY VIKTOR – rank major – and LOTOV IGOR – rank unknown STOP Rewards offered recently increased to fifteen thousand – figs 15000 – D-marks to be paid in US dollars STOP One source claims that further searches taking place in HAMBURG and LONDON but no other corroborative material STOP KGB agent seen carrying out surveillance of private house in W BERLIN believed sometimes used as SIS safe-house STOP Your request for info regarding subject's parents – nil report STOP Comments MESSAGE ENDS.

When he had read it again his hand reached for the internal phone, hesitated and then drew back. The information that Siwicki was sending over was being used by four sections and the head of the Soviet section was amazed at the material they were getting. The wheel really had turned full circle. Poor Schaeffer's case had been reviewed but it had been decided that he should be left to rot. The fact that his instincts were right about the value of the operation couldn't absolve him from having deliberately deceived his superiors. Danahar's problem was that if he passed on this information to London, would the man Fisher see it as grounds for withdrawing his wife from the operation?

In the end Danahar flew over himself to see Hallam and showed him a copy of the CIA sit-rep from Berlin. When Hallam had read it he looked at Danahar.

'Why didn't you just radio this to us?'

217

Danahar shrugged. 'I thought if it just came over cold you might want to call off the operation.'

'And?'

'And I want to persuade you not to rush it.'

'Why?'

'If we could have another month or maybe six weeks, we could concentrate on some specific areas. Then we'd have enough for the time being and we could put the operation on the back-burner until we knew what the Soviets were up to in looking for the girl.'

'And what about security for the girl in that time?'

'You could provide protection for her at the house.'

'And not tell her or Fisher that she was in danger?'

'Not unless things hotted up.'

Hallam looked away towards the window and it was several long moments before he looked back at Danahar.

'I don't like it. I'll have to think about it. I'll let you know tomorrow.' He paused. 'I'll talk with my colleagues.'

'You've seen the information that we've been passing over to you?'

Hallam nodded. 'Not all of it, but I understand that our people see it as being vitally important.'

'Our people tell me that it's given them an insight into the KGB and the Kremlin that has shifted the whole Pentagon thinking on the Soviet Union.'

'Perhaps you could come here tomorrow. Say ten o'clock.'

'Is there anything else you need to know that would help you decide?'

Hallam opened his mouth to speak, then changed his mind and just shook his head.

Macleod was the only one available. Seymour was in Hong Kong and the Professor was interviewing potential recruits at St Antony's.

'What do you think, Mac?'

'I think you should compromise.'

'How?'

'Does Fisher see the results of Siwicki's work with the girl?'

'No. He gets a general picture from time to time. No details.'

'So you tell Fisher that what she's doing has become so

important now that the house needs security. Not only for her sake but for Siwicki's too.' He paused. 'And we make special efforts in conjunction with Five to keep track of any KGB movement in the UK.'

'We can't give details of the girl's work to Five, or to anyone else for that matter.'

'So we work out a cover story and give them that. They've got more bodies available than we have and more experience on KGB operations in the UK.'

The habits of a working life-time were too deeply implanted for Fisher to abandon and his journeys back to 'Little Croft' were changed most days on an irregular pattern. His own car, hire-cars, trains where he got off at different stations. Tonbridge, Tunbridge Wells, Frant, Robertsbridge, even Hastings and St Leonards. Taking taxis back to the end of the lane. Never going directly to the house. Even when he used his own car he left it in a small, grassy lay-by in the lane by the farm.

Fisher had protested that the security team were too conspicuous in such a small village and would draw attention to the house rather than protect it. But Hallam had persisted and had finally persuaded Fisher to accept a trial period of a month.

Siwicki was disturbed by the new arrangement but for different reasons. He had never seen himself as needing protection from anybody and the thought that someone might see him as a potential target scared him. Ushi was faintly amused by the solid-looking men who mowed the lawns and picked the dead heads off the pansies.

Chapter 31

The patrol car was on its nightly run down the LaHonda road, checking with the station at San Gregorio before heading back to Woodside. It was 2 a.m. when they turned off the road to the track that led to the villa. It was a routine that the patrol went through every night.

Chuck Powell was tearing open a packet of Marlboros when his passenger said, 'I thought I saw a light in the house. Let's go and take a look.'

'It's probably a reflection from the moon on one of the windows.'

'Not unless the moon's moving around it ain't. Come on.'

They left the car doors open as they walked towards the house and at the same moment they saw the black Volkswagen a light went on in one of the curtained downstairs windows.

They stopped. Powell's passenger, Karl Swenson, put his radio to his mouth and said softly to his partner, 'They said to notify HQ if there was anything suspicious.'

'Let's go have a look.'

'The orders were specific. Observe and report only.'

'OK. See what they say.'

Swenson pressed the speak button and reported to the duty sergeant at Woodside. There was a short delay and then they were told to keep out of sight and if anybody left the house they should tail them. Two squad cars were already on the way. Chuck Powell walked back to the patrol car, turned it and parked it in the shadow of a group of trees.

Fifteen minutes later two cars stopped at the main road and a group of five men walked quietly towards the villa. The patrol men had never seen the lieutenant or the other men before. For a few moments the lieutenant looked at the villa and then gave his men their orders and told Powell to let the air out of the tyres of the Volkswagen.

Five minutes later with his team in place the lieutenant walked to the door of the house and turned a key in the lock of the front door. The hall was in darkness and he shone his torch to find the passage to the room with the light. He had a Smith & Wesson in his right hand as he flung open the door of the room. A man in his forties was bent over looking at the controls of a Revox tape-recorder, and a girl in faded jeans and a UCLA T-shirt was sitting in an armchair watching the man. She was smoking a self-rolled cigarette, inhaling deeply and then she noticed him.

She shouted, 'Greg!' and stood up and headed for a door on the other side of the room; the lieutenant shouted, 'Don't move, girl! FBI!' The girl froze and dropped the lighted cigarette, treading it into the rug by the chair. The man stood up slowly and turned. 'What's going on? What is all this?'

'What are you doing on these premises?'

'The owner gave us permission to use it for a few days.'

'Who's the owner?'

'And who are you?'

The lieutenant reached with his left hand into his inside jacket pocket, took out his ID card and flipped it open, holding it out. 'Lieutenant Grayson. FBI. Now – who is the owner?'

The man glanced at the far door and Grayson said, 'My men are all round the house. Don't try anything silly.'

The man smiled and shrugged. 'So what's it all about, lieutenant?'

'Empty your pockets. Put everything on the white table.' He turned to the girl and pointed at the chair. 'You too. And sit down.'

Grayson sat on the arm of a chair watching the man empty his pockets while one of his officers put the contents in a plastic bag. And then he stood up and walked to the door. Two of his men were standing there and he said to the taller man, 'Check his clothes and check the girl and then take them both to Half Moon Bay.' He walked through to the hall and detailed two men to go with the man and the girl in one of the squad cars.

The mist that had rolled in from the sea during the night was beginning to lift as the sun came up and Grayson sat on the edge of the plain wooden table, his jacket thrown over a chair, his tie hanging loose. The room had one small window which had bars that looked ornamental but were sunk deep into the stone wall. The walls, ceiling and floor were all painted black. He sipped casually at a glass of fruit juice, swinging one long leg as he looked at the man who was handcuffed to the plain wooden chair. A chair that was bolted to the floor.

The Volkswagen was registered in Alameda County to a Gregory Martin. His belongings gave no clue to his identity but in his wallet were five thousand dollars in notes and two gold Krugerrands. And there was a sketch-map of the road and the path to the villa. The distances were given in metres and at the top of the sketch it had Siwicki's name in capitals. Grayson had questioned the man for half an hour but the man had refused to answer even routine questions.

He put down the glass and stood up. It was time to get rough.

Macleod read through the report from the CIA for the third time. Hallam was in transit to Singapore and he'd have to make the decision alone. There were three weeks to go before they folded Siwicki's operation. That was what had been agreed. And Fisher himself had been party to that agreement. The covering message from Danahar emphasised the importance of what Siwicki was going to do during the last few weeks of the operation. But he left the decision in SIS's hands as to what should be done in view of the new development. Twice he reached for the phone to speak to Fisher and twice he drew back his hand. He phoned MI5 liaison and they confirmed that they had no indications that the house was being watched. He slid the report and the covering note in the file. As he started to put it with the others in his 'out' tray, he hesitated again and then put it beside the files he still had to deal with.

Fisher had gone to Macleod's office two days later and found Seymour at Macleod's desk. Seymour looked up as Fisher walked in.

'I'm just trying to clear up Macleod's stuff.'

'Why? Where's Macleod?'

'He's off sick. Got the 'flu or something. Sounds like he'll be off for at least a week.'

'Do you want any help?'

'If you could just help me sort out the sheep from the goats.'
He pointed at two piles of files. 'Those can wait but these need
to go for action.' He sighed. 'If in doubt they go for a check to
Adams.'

It was nearly ten minutes later when Seymour read the
message from Danahar.

'Have you seen this message from Langley, David?' He
pointed to the red stamp. 'Looks like it came in a couple of days
ago.'

'What's it about?'

'It's about a CIA chap named Siwicki.' He looked up at
Fisher. 'Are you doing something with CIA? It mentions your
name.'

Seymour pulled out the loose pages from the file and passed
them to Fisher.

To: T. S. Danahar CIA liaison.
From: Z. P. Lennard FBI/CIA liaison.

As instructed a routine surveillance was mounted on the
vacated house off the LaHonda road. A patrol car from
PAPD noticed activity at the house and a team of FBI
agents under the command of Lieutenant Grayson investigated. A man and a woman were apprehended on the
premises and subsequently interrogated.

The man is identified as Grigor Markovich, aged 38, a
US citizen of Latvian descent. The woman is believed to
be a Sara Walker, aged 24, a drop-out from UCLA
connected to several groups of subversives. Two arrests for
dealing in marijuana. No convictions.

Markovich eventually admitted to being in the employ
of Alex Djilas, a Soviet believed to be full-time KGB with
rank of major. Djilas is employed as a clerk at the Soviet
Consulate in LA. Markovich was paid one thousand
dollars to search house used by Siwicki. He was to
establish Siwicki's present whereabouts. On being offered
a no-prosecution deal he further admitted that it was
believed that Siwicki was directing a Soviet defector
named Ursula Jaeger. He believed that the Soviets were
trying to trace this woman with orders for her to be

eliminated once her identity was established. He indicated that other teams had been posted to London, England, and West Berlin with similar instructions. The subject is being held for fourteen days and will then by arrangement be deported to Poland unless your office has any objections. Please advise.

The covering note from Danahar to Hallam was handwritten.

Dear H,

I thought you should have the enclosed as soon as possible so I am sending it in the bag tonight. You should get it tomorrow morning.

The material from Siwicki is quite unique but despite our arrangement I feel you may choose to remove the girl from any possible danger. I suspect that Fisher would be of this opinion. I must leave with you the decision as to whether or not he should be told. We will go along with whatever you decide.

There was a scrawled, illegible signature.

Fisher passed the two items back to Seymour without comment. Fifteen minutes later he left Seymour, saying that he had to attend a meeting. In his own office he phoned home and spoke to Ushi, telling her to catch the next train to Charing Cross and he would meet her at the barrier.

As they ate dinner Fisher told her about the CIA report and when he had finished she smiled and shrugged. 'Do you believe it?'

'Yes.' He paused. 'Aren't you scared, Ushi?'

'No.'

'Why not?'

She smiled. 'Because I've got you, so why should I be scared?'

He shook his head. 'We're going to get out, Ushi. I don't trust them any more.'

'Who don't you trust?'

'My people. Macleod should have warned me two days ago as soon as he read that message from the CIA. He just put it in

224

his pending file. If I hadn't gone into his office by chance today I still wouldn't know about it. He was prepared to risk your life for the sake of pleasing the CIA. He doesn't even know whether the work you are doing with Siwicki is worth taking any risk at all.' He paused. 'That's enough for me. I've had enough.'

'So what do we do?'

'When we get home tonight I want you to pack a couple of bags. Only things that really matter. I'll tell Siwicki that we're having a weekend in London. And then we'll leave the country.'

'Where shall we go?'

'I'll work that out tonight. I've got to do some basic thinking. But be ready to leave early tomorrow morning.'

They had booked into a small hotel in Bayswater by mid-day and Fisher had gone off alone. It was late in the evening before he returned. He looked tired but strangely alert and she realised that he must have dealt with similar situations dozens of times in the past.

He had a canvas travel bag secured by a small brass padlock in the ring of the zip fastener and he had Canadian passports for each of them in the name of Dawe. They checked out at 6 a.m. the next morning and took the train to Dover where Fisher bought tickets for the first ferry to Ostend. When they arrived, he hired a car and they spent the night in Bruges. Late on the Sunday evening they arrived in Amsterdam. They spent the night in a hotel on Prinzengracht and the next day Fisher rented a small furnished flat in one of the old houses on Rembrandts Plein. They moved in during the afternoon and Fisher took an evening flight to Berlin the same day.

CHAPTER 32

Fisher took a taxi to the corner of Friedrichstrasse and Kochstrasse and stood watching for a few moments as cars queued up at Check-point Charlie. Then he walked on past the Springer building to where a few houses huddled together on the Western side of the Wall in Lindenstrasse. The houses had once contained typical artisans' apartments on three floors, but with the building of the Wall they were now no more than a short row of neglected hovels that seemed to share the despair of the Wall itself.

A woman leaning out of a ground floor window told him that there were two rooms on the first floor for rent, but only for a month at a time. She told him to see Frau Kessler at the back of the house.

Frau Kessler was a cheerful blowsy woman. He could have either of the rooms for twenty D-marks a week. There was cold water only, a meter for electricity and a shared toilet. There was no bathroom but he could use the public facilities on the far side of the printing works. Blankets were extra.

Ten minutes later Fisher was alone in the dingy room. There was a tap attached to a loose pipe in the wall and a metal bowl for washing. A pair of dirty net curtains over the grimy window and a bed with a mattress and used sheets. A rack behind the door held a couple of cheap plastic hangers. A chair lay on its side by a wooden box that took the place of the missing chair leg.

He sat on the bed and opened the small canvas hold-all that was his only luggage and took out the leather-bound address-book. He checked his pockets for his passport and cash and then locked the door behind him and went down the stairs. Frau Kessler watched him from her open door at the far end of the passage.

Walking back to the Friedrichstrasse underground station he

bought a packet of cigarettes at the corner shop and got change for the telephone calls.

He met Johnny Walters in the back room of the shack in Potsdamer Platz. Walters had been a corporal in the Military Police who had opted for his discharge while still in West Berlin. In his three-year service tour in West Berlin he had got to know most of the criminals who operated in the British Sector and a few in both the French and US sectors. His main income came from running a dozen teenage girls who patrolled the Allied side of the Brandenburg Gate. Fisher had used him from time to time in the old days on small operations where Walters' contacts with petty criminals in East Berlin could be useful. The shack, which was used by the girls and their clients, had a neglected look from outside but inside it was clean and refurbished with pine and Formica that gave it a practical and clinical efficiency. Walters had a couple of rooms for his own use, but his real home was a luxury flat over one of the Ku'damm restaurants. He had a half share in several restaurants and clubs in the centre of the city.

As they sat at the table with a bottle of white wine between them Walters said, 'You still in the same old game, chief?'

Fisher smiled and shrugged. 'More or less. How are things with you?'

Walters grinned. 'Never been better.' He paused. 'What can I do for you?'

'I heard there were KGB stooges looking for an East German girl who's supposed to be here in West Berlin. Have you heard anything about them?'

Walters frowned. 'One of my chicks told me about some guy who paid her thirty Marks for round the houses but spent his time asking about some girl.'

'When was this?'

'Must be three weeks ago now. D'you want to talk to her?'

'Is she around?'

'Let me check.'

Walters reached for a modern plastic internal phone and, with the receiver to his ear, pressed two buttons.

'Yeah. It's Johnny. Is Heidi there . . ? Yeah . . . OK. Send her in.'

He replaced the receiver. 'She's just finished. She'll be in in a couple of minutes. More *vino*?'

Fisher shook his head. 'No, thanks.'

The girl who came in was a pretty mulatto teenager wearing tights, a short skirt and a tight sweater. Walters pointed to a chair. He spoke in rough but fluent German.

'Sit down, *Schatz*.'

When the girl was seated Walters said, 'Tell me about the guy who was asking about some East German girl. What happened?'

'Like I told you. He paid the asking price, no bargaining, no haggling. But when we get back here in the room all he wanted was to talk about this girl.'

Fisher said softly, 'Did he say who she was and why he was looking for her?'

The girl smiled. 'He said he was in love with her. Wanted to find her so they could get married.' She grinned. 'I didn't believe him.'

Fisher said quietly, 'Why not?'

'He was making it all up. He hadn't got a photograph of her. He couldn't say where he'd last seen her or why she walked out on him. He was just fishing. The only thing he'd got was her name. And he wasn't the kind who'd love anybody but himself.'

'What sort of accent did he have?'

'Typical Berlin accent.'

'What was the girl's name?'

'I don't remember.'

'Think about it,' Walters said. 'Now, was it a foreign name?'

The girl shook her head slowly. 'No . . . I think it was Ursula something . . . or it could have been . . . no, I'm sure now it was Ursula.'

'Where did this guy pick you up?'

'In the Platz. He was pretending to look at the paintings on the Wall.'

Fisher said, 'Was the other name Jaeger? Was it Ursula Jaeger?'

'I honestly can't remember. It could have been. Do you want me to check on it?'

'How?'

'I've seen the guy several times in the past couple of weeks.

He hangs around Check-point Charlie, afternoons and evenings.'

Walters said, 'OK, kid. Have a drink in the bar. Tell Berni it's on the house. I'll talk to you later.' When she hesitated Walters said, 'It's OK. I'll pay you trick money. Just hang around.'

When the girl had left Walters looked at Fisher. 'Do you want to talk to this guy?'

'Yes.'

'D'you want to screw one of the girls while you're waiting?'

Fisher smiled and shook his head. 'You know me, Johnny. I never mix business with pleasure.'

'OK. Hang on here. I'll talk to Heidi. Tell her what to do.' He stopped at the door and turned to look at Fisher. 'Are you OK?'

'Yes. Why?'

'You look kind of tense. You sure you don't want a chick?'

Fisher shook his head. 'I'm OK. But thanks.'

The man had looked scared when Walters brought him into the back-room and he saw Fisher sitting there. He turned to go to the door but Johnny Walters stood with his back to the door.

'What is this?' the man said. 'What's going on?'

Walters looked back at the man. 'You told Heidi you were looking for your girl-friend.'

'So what?'

'So this gentleman . . .' Walters pointed to Fisher, '. . . might be able to help you.' Walters half-smiled at Fisher. 'I'll wait outside so you can have your chat, chief.'

Fisher pointed to a chair. 'Why don't you sit down?'

The man sat slowly. 'Why were you speaking English to that guy?'

'You told one of the girls you were looking for a girl. A girl from the other side. From the Democratic Republic.'

'That's what she says. All these little whores are born liars.'

'Is your girl's name Ursula?'

Fisher watched caution battle with interest on the man's face. 'What's it got to do with you?'

Fisher shrugged. 'Maybe I could help you find her.' He paused. 'Provided we're both talking about the same girl.'

There was a long silence before the man spoke again.

'Who are you?'

Fisher smiled. 'It doesn't matter who I am. It doesn't matter to me who *you* are.' He paused. 'But your boss in Karlshorst would be very angry if he knew you'd missed a chance of finding the girl.'

The man shifted uneasily on the chair. 'Who said anything about anyone at Karlshorst?'

'You're wasting time, mister. If you're not interested I'll talk to one of the others. Maybe they're brighter than you are.'

'What is it you want? Some sort of deal?'

'No. I just want to talk with the man who sent you over to find the girl.'

'Do you know where she is?'

'I'll talk to your boss. Nobody else. He'll understand. He'll want it that way.'

'Who are you?'

'You just contact him.'

'How can he get in touch with you?'

'I'll give you a note for him.'

'When?'

'Now.'

'OK.'

'When will he get it?'

'About one hour after I leave here.'

As he got into the street the man looked at the address on the envelope. It just said, 'C.O. Directorate 4. KGB Karlshorst.'

Just before midnight the call came through to Johnny Walters' office. The voice at the other end spoke good German but with a strong Russian accent.

'I got the note, my friend. When can we meet?'

'You tell me.'

'We meet this side of the Wall so let's not play games . . . you agree?'

'What guarantees do I get?'

'Have you heard of Colonel Levchenko?'

'Yes.'

'I'm Levchenko. I give you my word that you will go back freely . . . we talk off the record like you asked until we agree to talk officially.'

'OK. When?'

'Come through the Check-point in half an hour. I'll be waiting for you.'

'The Check-point is closed already. I'll be checked on this side. I don't want that.'

'Good. OK. Nine tomorrow morning but we meet away from the Check-point.'

'Where?'

'Do you know Waisenstrasse?'

'No. But I'll find it.'

'Opposite the corner of Waisenstrasse and Parochialstrasse there is an inn called Zur Letzten Instanz. I'll be waiting for you inside. OK?'

'OK.'

The phone clicked at the other end and Fisher replaced the receiver slowly as his mind went over what had been said. It had been a crude, rushed approach but he had no time for checking and cross-checking. It was the only chance they had, and there was no going back now.

CHAPTER 33

There had been no hold-up at the Check-point and Fisher had walked to Leipzigerstrasse and turned right. It took him twenty minutes to reach Molkenmarkt and another ten minutes to find the inn. There were tables and chairs laid out on a small patio area and a young woman was serving coffee to two men at one of the tables.

The door of the inn was open but the shutters were closed and when he walked inside it was so dark that he stumbled against a table before his eyes accommodated the dim light. There was nobody in the room, but he could hear a radio playing somewhere at the back. After a few moments he turned and walked back slowly towards the outer door. As he stood looking down the street there was a tap on his shoulder and when he turned quickly he recognised from the file photographs the face of Levchenko. He looked younger than in the rather grainy record shot and he smiled as he said, 'There's a room upstairs where we can talk.'

The room upstairs was comfortably furnished with old-fashioned, typically German furniture. It was obviously part of somebody's house. There were flowers in vases, books on shelves and a violin case propped up in the corner of a sofa. And there were coffee and cups on the low table. Levchenko pointed to the tray.

'Help yourself.'

When Fisher had fixed his coffee the Russian said, 'Are you the Fisher who was operating out of Hamburg at one time?'

Fisher smiled. 'I'm sure you checked my file before you came here.'

Levchenko shrugged and smiled. 'Your note said that you wanted to discuss the girl's status.' He paused. 'I'm not quite sure what you mean by that.'

232

'It was a form of words that I hoped might tempt you to a discussion that could save your people wasting time and help me at the same time.'

Levchenko smiled wryly. 'It doesn't sound a likely outcome to me. We have our interests, you people have yours.'

'I'm not talking on behalf of my people. I speak solely for myself. But unless we can both talk without prejudice we should be wasting our time.'

Levchenko shook his head. 'You've lost me, my friend. You're talking in riddles.'

'Before I explain I'd like to ask for an honest answer to one question.'

'OK. Ask the question.'

'If I was able to persuade you that it would benefit the KGB to call off your operations concerning the girl, do you have enough authority to agree to that?'

Levchenko was silent for a moment. 'Let's say that I have enough authority to persuade people above me to agree.' He paused. 'But I can't think how it could possibly benefit the KGB.'

'Do you have all the background on the girl?'

'I do until the time when she defected.'

'She didn't defect. She was kidnapped.'

'How do you know that?'

'Because I kidnapped her myself from the airport. And I took her over to the other side by deception.'

'Why?'

'Because that's what London wanted. They didn't tell me why. But I know now.'

Levchenko said quietly, 'So tell me why.'

'Because of the work she was doing for Professor Rykov. The CIA wanted to use her.'

'Go on.'

'The CIA pulled out and I was told to put her back on your side of the Wall. But I didn't do it.'

'Why not?'

'Because I knew she'd go into the Lubyanka and end up in some Gulag camp. You wouldn't believe her story. You'd think we had turned her.'

'Why should you care what happens to her?'

'Because she was innocent. She didn't deserve what had happened to her.'

'And then?'

'I let her stay with me but I didn't tell London.'

'So she became your mistress?'

'No, she didn't.'

'So what did you get out of it?'

'A slightly easier conscience.'

Levchenko: 'A new phenomenon, an SIS man with a conscience.'

'That's rubbish and you know it. That's how outsiders think. Not people who are in the business.'

'Do you think there are KGB men with such a conscience?'

'I know there are.'

'Name me one.'

Fisher shook his head. 'I could name two or three but I won't. It could be used against them by the wrong people.'

'You mean people like me?'

'I don't know you so I've no opinion. I had to take the risk.'

'I still haven't heard your proposition.'

'Did you know that the girl was being used by the CIA?'

'We heard rumours that she was and there were reports from our intelligence evaluation teams that somebody was using her. But you said the CIA pulled out of the operation.'

'She was drawn back in later.'

'There's something you're not telling me, my friend. What is it?'

'There's a lot I haven't told you but I want some reaction from you first.'

'About what?'

'Are you worried about her working for the CIA?'

'Not only worried, but angry. And we are determined to stop it.'

'Are you interested in stopping it or in taking some sort of revenge on her? I heard that there was a reward for finding her, dead or alive.'

'Maybe there is. But our main concern is to stop her cooperation with the West.'

'So if she stopped working for the West she'd be safe?'

'You're still holding something back, Mr Fisher. I thought this was to be a frank discussion.'

'If I could stop her, would she be left alone?'

'Why should your people agree to that? They are getting invaluable information from her every day.'

'I didn't say that they would agree.'

'How could you stop her without their agreement?'

For a moment Fisher hesitated, then he said, 'Because Ursula Jaeger is my wife. I've already taken her away from the operation.'

The Russian couldn't hide his surprise and it was several moments before he replied.

'Why did you do that? Surely you'll be arrested?'

'They don't know where I am. And my wife is with me.'

'You mean you've resigned?'

'No. I just walked out and took my wife with me.'

'But why?'

'I saw it as an abuse of her mind. And an abuse of me too. I was not officially told that she was a target of the KGB. I found out by chance. That's why I walked out.'

Levchenko stood up slowly and walked to the window where he stood, hands in pockets, looking out without seeing as he digested the strange facts of Fisher's story.

It was several minutes before the Russian turned back to look at Fisher.

'I'd like to make a phone call. Will you wait? I could be twenty minutes or so.'

'Yes. Of course I'll wait.'

'What exactly do you want us to do?'

'I want you to leave us in peace.'

'What if your own people won't do the same?'

'They will.'

'How can you be so sure?'

'They won't know where we are and more important they're well aware that I know too much about too many things. I could expose them.'

'Would you go that far?'

'If necessary. I'll go however far it takes.'

'I'll make my call.'

'Is it to Karlshorst or Moscow?'

For a moment Levchenko hesitated then he smiled. 'To Moscow.'

An hour later and Levchenko had still not come back. Fisher had moved to the sofa, leaning back with his eyes closed but his mind working furiously. It was like working out two moves ahead in a chess game. Levchenko could be taking longer because they wouldn't agree with his analysis and he was arguing with them. But would he have risked putting his judgement on the line by phoning Moscow if he felt they would disagree? He had remembered so little from Levchenko's file and it had been years since he had read it. But he remembered that both the Russian's parents had been killed in the war. A lot of Russians still hated the Germans no matter which side of the border they were on. And Ushi was a German.

But what had influenced him most to trust the Russian was the only other thing that he remembered from Levchenko's file. There was a note in the file of a conversation about Levchenko between one of the embassy staff and an American woman journalist. She had wanted to do a piece about him because his wife was paralysed from the waist down. It was nothing to do with the war, she hadn't even been born then. And it wasn't something that happened after they had married. She had contracted multiple sclerosis when she was twenty years old and was paralysed and confined to a wheelchair when he married her. A friend of the journalist had told her that if she wrote anything about his wife Levchenko would certainly make sure she lost her Moscow accreditation.

Fisher was going over his contingency plans if the Russians wouldn't cooperate. He knew what to do and it was unlikely that they would ever be discovered. But agreement would mean real security.

Then the door opened and Levchenko half-entered, talking to someone in Russian who was outside the room. Then he closed the door and pulled out one of the chairs and sat facing Fisher.

'It took longer than I expected. One of the people I wanted to contact had to be traced. He was on leave.' The Russian looked at him in silence for a moment. 'There are some rituals that I have to go through first. OK?'

'Yes.'

'Before I give you their views I have a counter-proposition to make.' The Russian paused. 'If you would come over to us you would be guaranteed a high status and a high standard of living. We would not ask that your wife cooperates in any way. In addition her parents would be released and reinstated with compensation.'

'And all I would have to do is betray my networks and my colleagues. Yes?'

'You didn't sound very pleased with your colleagues' attitude to your wife's security.'

'I've already squared that account by walking out.'

'As a matter of fact the proposal was that you would give us an appreciation of recruiting and training methods of SIS and MI5 and after that you would not be concerned with any matters connected with your people.'

'What would I be concerned with?'

'We should like you to be a consultant on our operations in the USA.'

Fisher shook his head. 'I've had enough of playing those games. I want out. Completely.'

'What are you going to do then?'

'I'm going to relax for at least a year. Maybe fish or play some sport. I don't really know.'

'Have you enough money to live on?'

'Enough for our needs.'

'That's your final answer? Is there anything else we could offer to make you change your mind?'

Fisher smiled. 'I'm flattered at the offer. In the circumstances it's generous. But the answer is – no thank you.'

'So where do we go from here?'

Fisher shrugged. 'Maybe you tell me what Moscow's response was.'

'There are problems, but I'm sure you expected that.'

'Tell me.'

'How do we know that you will keep your side of the bargain?'

'I'll come to that later. What are the other problems?'

'How do we know that your old friends won't do a deal with you? No harassment in exchange for just a tiny bit of cooperation?'

'You'll have to make your own judgement on that. I'm not

likely to cooperate with people who were prepared to risk my wife's life without even telling me. And they won't try harassing me, only your people are likely to do that.'

'Why not your people?'

'Because I could expose so many scandals that they'd be blown sky-high.'

'Can I ask you something personal?'

Fisher smiled. 'Try me.'

'Tell me about the girl. What attracted you to her?'

'She's very pretty but I wasn't attracted to her at first. I was angry that our people used her so badly and callously. I wanted to protect her.' He paused. 'And as time went by I got to know her and like her. And when I was posted back to London I think I rationalised the situation and asked her to marry me so that I could still protect her.'

'What was the rationalisation?'

Fisher sighed. 'In my heart I knew that I would miss her terribly if I left her in Germany. I loved her too much in my own peculiar way to be without her.' Fisher shrugged. 'That's about it.'

'You said you had a solution to us not knowing what you are doing or where you are.'

'It's not foolproof but it's the best I can do.' He paused. 'Can I ask you another question for an honest answer?'

Levchenko nodded. 'Go ahead.'

Fisher took a deep breath. 'Do you believe what I've told you? Do you trust me at all?'

Levchenko smiled. 'I'm a KGB officer, Fisher. I'm trained not to trust anybody. And experience has taught me that my training was correct.' He paused. 'But these are strange circumstances. I'm not in uniform. We're sitting in this small room in East Berlin discussing two people's lives. Yours and your wife's. Senior colleagues in Moscow asked me if I thought you were genuine – they didn't ask if I trusted you – and I told them that in my opinion you were genuine. Does that answer your question?'

'It's enough. What I had in mind was to write down our address and put it in a sealed envelope and place it in the care of Wartski. You would only open it if you had genuine doubts or suspicions about what I was doing.'

'Who's Wartski?'

'He's the West Berlin lawyer who Moscow uses to negotiate the exchange of prisoners with the West.'

'Of course.' He paused. 'What if you needed to move for some quite sensible reason?'

'Then I would write out our new address and give a new sealed envelope to Wartski.'

'It's a bit amateurish, isn't it?'

'If you can think of anything better I'd be glad to consider it.'

Levchenko smiled and shook his head. 'It will do. Do you know why?'

'No. Tell me.'

'There are two reasons. First of all Moscow were influenced that you came across to this side just on my word.'

'And secondly?'

'And secondly something more down to earth. We have had somebody to replace your wife for the last four months. Somebody who shares your wife's talent. All we are concerned about is that your people should not be able to use your wife.'

'I'm very grateful and very relieved.'

'I could trade you one more thing if you want.'

'Tell me.'

'Your wife's parents are both in labour camps. Gulag camps. We would be prepared to release them both immediately if we could cut out the sealed letter and you tell us where you will be living. Just the country would be sufficient.'

'And then you'll be tempted to put a search team out to find out exactly where we are. And our peace of mind would be gone.'

'Say you told *me*. Just me. And I gave you my word that I would not pass it on. We'll keep appearances with the sealed letter held by the lawyer.'

'Can I have time to think about it?'

'Twenty-four hours.'

'You're turning our arrangement into a test of whether I trust you personally.'

'Maybe.'

Fisher stood up. 'If I say no, the other arrangement still goes ahead?'

'Of course.'

'How shall I contact you tomorrow?'

'Leave a note for me at the check-point at Friedrichstrasse.'

'OK.'

Levchenko put out his hand and Fisher took it and then headed for the door. At the door he turned and looked back at Levchenko. 'The deal about Ushi's parents, is it still available?'

'Yes. Of course.'

'We're going to live in Ireland. The Republic.'

Fisher saw the surprise on Levchenko's face and then the Russian said, 'You don't *have* to tell me, but why there?'

'Because they are not too fond of the British and they don't like you people much either. And they don't have an extradition treaty with the UK. And they don't have an intelligence organisation that kills people.'

Levchenko half-smiled. 'I'll see that the arrangements are made about her parents.'

'How are they?'

Levchenko shook his head. He wasn't going to answer, so Fisher closed the door behind him and walked down the stairs to the street. With the tension over, all he wanted to do was sleep. He phoned Ushi and gave her the news as soon as he was through the check-point. And then he went back to the sleazy room and slept.

CHAPTER 34

Thornton and Smallwood were sitting in the cafeteria at Century House. It was late at night and Thornton said, 'Can you think of any files we haven't checked?'

'Only the withdrawn files at the top-security place in Wales.'

'Hallam swore that the only withdrawn files were high-security operational files and not relevant.'

'D'you believe him?'

'No.'

'So?'

'I think I'll demand to see them.'

'And he'll just say no again.'

'If he does I'll ask to be taken off the case.'

'He won't like that.'

'Too bad. I'll say that there's nothing more I can do.' He paused. 'Is there anything else we *can* do? Anything we haven't checked that we could check?'

Smallwood shrugged. 'The thing about his wife has always bugged me.'

'You mean that his "P" file shows that she's dead but the old lady at their flat said she'd seen her not too far back?'

'Yeah. How about we have another talk with the old lady?'

Thornton leaned forward knocking over his half-empty coffee cup in his eagerness.

'We haven't looked at Fisher's pay slips.'

'No. What will they tell us?'

'If he's still getting his married allowance then she isn't dead. It'll prove it one way or another.' Thornton looked at his watch. 'The Pay Office will be closed by now.'

'There'll be a duty clerk, there always is. He issues cash that's wanted urgently.'

'See what you can find, Tom, but don't press too hard.'

In fifteen minutes Smallwood came back. A buff file in his

hand. He leaned over the table and said quietly, 'We'd better go to your office. I've got to return it in an hour.'

In Thornton's small office Smallwood said, 'We were right, skipper. Those bastards have been playing games all along.' He opened the file and spread the pages, flattening them with his hand. 'It's not just the payments. But he *is* still drawing full marriage allowance. It's a lot more than that.' He pointed to three pages clipped together. 'Look at that.'

The first page was a photostat copy of a birth certificate and a death certificate, one below the other. They were both in the name of Michelle Joanna Hunter born in February 1960, died in June 1983. Cause of death – pneumonia.

Thornton turned to the second page which showed photostat copies of two marriage certificates and an A5 letter from the Immigration and Nationality Department at Lunar House, confirming to W. Hallam that his instructions regarding Ursula Jaeger had been carried out, and a certificate was enclosed for forwarding with the application to the Passport Office at Petty France. The first marriage certificate recorded the marriage at Tunbridge Wells Registrar's Office between David Dawe and Michelle Joanna Hunter. A large cancelled stamp ran across its centre. The second marriage certificate recorded the marriage of Ursula Jaeger – British national – to David Beauclerc Fisher. The date of the two marriages was the same.

The third page was a photostat copy of a page of notes in Hallam's handwriting listing various instructions including the issuing of a British passport to Mrs Fisher and the issue of a new marriage certificate. The instructions went on to cover the purchase of 'Little Croft', a property in Wadhurst, East Sussex and the issuing of a work permit for a USA citizen, Dr Siwicki, valid for one year only.

Thornton leaned back in his chair until it creaked as he turned to look at Smallwood.

'They probably didn't realise that this stuff had gone into a routine admin file.'

'You got the point of the woman's name?'

'You mean Jaeger being the German for Hunter?'

Smallwood nodded. 'What do you think it's all about?'

Thornton shrugged. 'Haven't a clue. But whatever it is I'll

find out when I throw this lot at Hallam.' He paused. 'Will you photostat it before you return it?'

'I'll have to record what I'm statting.'

Thornton smiled. 'Record it as "Instruction from Mr Hallam concerning Mr Fisher's marriage". They'll have a fit when they see that.'

Hallam wasn't available until mid-afternoon and his secretary had said that he could only give him fifteen minutes or so. When Hallam waved him to a chair he pushed aside the files on his desk.

'Any progress to report, Mr Thornton?'

'Yes, sir.'

Hallam looked surprised. 'Tell me.'

'Can I ask you a question, sir?'

'By all means. Go ahead.'

'Who is Ursula Jaeger?'

Hallam pursed his lips and looked away. When he looked back at Thornton he said quietly, 'How did you come across the name?'

'It's in Fisher's file in the Pay Office with copies of various documents and a handwritten list of admin instructions from you. And there's a visa clearance for an American named Dr Siwicki who seems to be connected in some way with the Fisher business.'

'How long have you known about this?'

'Since about eleven-thirty last night. You weren't available earlier today.'

Hallam spoke slowly as if he was choosing his words very carefully. 'Ursula Jaeger became Mrs Fisher. She had a certain skill – talent. She worked for us for a short time.'

'And Siwicki?'

'She worked alongside Siwicki.'

'Was he CIA?'

'Let's say he had CIA connections.'

'Was Fisher involved in the work?'

'Not directly.'

'Was this work any reason for him disappearing?'

Hallam sighed. 'Yes. I think it could have been.'

'Why?'

243

'There was an element of danger that could affect his wife.'
He paused. 'Somebody here handled the situation rather
clumsily. I think that Fisher might have thought it was
deliberate.'

'Was it deliberate?'

'Possibly. There's no way of knowing.'

'Was Fisher angry about it? Did he complain?'

'When Fisher discovered the . . .' he shrugged, '. . . the
carelessness, he just disappeared the next day with his wife.'

'Have you any idea where he went?'

'None at all. By the time we knew that he had gone it was too
late to stop him. And we were inhibited anyway as we didn't
want to raise any undue alarm.'

'Mrs Fisher was originally German, wasn't she? I saw that in
the instructions.'

'Yes.'

'Was that where the danger came from?'

'No. The KGB were looking for her.'

'Because of her work?'

'Yes.'

'What was her work?'

'I'm going to give you clearance to read all the relevant files,
including those that were withdrawn. From now on there will
be nothing kept back from you for the sake of security. But you
must treat it as "eyes only". You understand?'

'Of course.' He paused. 'And you and the others have no idea
where he is?'

'Not the faintest idea. Fisher's an experienced field officer
and he knows how to cover his tracks. It won't be easy.'

'It would have been easier if people had been frank with me
from the start.'

There was a strange mixture of annoyance and relief on
Hallam's face as he stood up dismissively.

'My girl will give you a list of the files and a clearance note.'
He stood up. 'Keep me in touch.'

CHAPTER 35

Thornton and Smallwood sat for two days in one of the Security Reading Rooms, making notes as they read the files. As Hallam had originally said, they were not really relevant but there was always the hope that there may be some revelation of where Fisher might have gone to.

By the end of the second day they had very few notes between them of any apparent significance.

Thornton looked through both sets of notes and then stood, stretching his arms and yawning.

'We'd better decide what we're looking for.' He wiped his hands over his face to loosen the muscles. 'I'd say that at this stage we're looking for only one thing. Which country would he head for?'

'Maybe he found some remote place in the UK. Scotland or Wales. Some place that's miles from anywhere.'

'I don't think so. The more secluded a place is the more the locals are suspicious. And he wouldn't feel out of our clutches in this country. He'd know that we'd hear of him sooner or later and he'd be pulled in. He'd want to be in some country where extradition isn't that easy.'

'You mean somewhere where he knows the ropes?'

'Yes.'

'Most of his time he's been in Germany. Berlin and Hamburg.'

'Too many people know him in those cities. Why should he take the risk of being spotted? No. If it was Germany it would be somewhere else. Maybe down south. Munich maybe.'

'At least he'd have no language problem there.'

'Nor would his wife.'

'Could be Austria. Vienna perhaps.'

'Or Switzerland?'

Thornton shook his head. 'No way. Who the hell would want to live in Switzerland? Not Fisher, for sure.'

Smallwood put on his jacket and tightened his tie. 'D'you think Macleod deliberately held back that warning?'

Thornton shrugged. 'He's not a man I'd trust and he'd left the message just lying around without taking immediate action to protect Fisher's wife. And the CIA man for that matter.'

'Do you think the KGB have grabbed the Fishers?'

'No. Fisher's too experienced for that.' Thornton smiled wryly. 'Maybe we should have a word with the KGB team looking for them. Let's sleep on what we've learned and meet again tomorrow morning.'

'You fancy a drink, skipper?'

'Thanks. But I'd like to get home. Penny will be asleep already.'

When Thornton got to the flat there was a note on the table.

Dear Robbie,
   Am staying overnight with Julie (plays Rosie when adult) and spending Sunday with Aunt Jennie at Didcot. Tried to phone you but they didn't know where you were. See you Monday after show. This was your weekend with Jamie. Did you forget or did you let him know?
                    Love,
                    Penny

He felt depressed as he made himself a cup of tea with a tea-bag. He had not only not contacted Jamie or his mother but he hadn't even realised that it *was* the weekend. It was already Sunday morning. He remembered something that Penny had once said. She'd asked him if he got any real enjoyment out of seeing Jamie, or was it just a piece of ritual. A duty. He'd said he did enjoy it, but Penny had looked as if she didn't really believe him. And he knew that she was right. He loved the boy but in practical terms of being a father he was a total failure. And he wasn't all that good an intelligence officer either.

That thought triggered another thing that Penny had said. She'd listened to his bare-bones description of Fisher and said that it sounded like him. He had thought at the time that she was wide of the mark, but she was a very perceptive young woman. So if she were right, what would he do in Fisher's place? Where would he go?

Thornton fell asleep in a chair, the tea untouched; moving only when the pain in his neck made him stir as he tried in vain to find a more comfortable position.

Back in Amsterdam Fisher had made a series of telephone calls and the next day he and Ushi took a plane to Paris. They had an hour to wait at de Gaulle for the PanAm flight to New York that stopped at Shannon to pick up freight and passengers.

From Shannon they took a train to Dublin and checked in at Blooms. Fisher had never been to Ireland before but as they walked around the Dublin squares that night he felt strangely at home.

They had visited two or three estate agents' offices and had looked at two or three apartments. But it was a week before Fisher found what satisfied his criteria and also pleased Ushi. He wanted a place that was too high to be overlooked by windows of other buildings, with no garden, and only one entrance. And expensive enough to have a porter permanently on duty. The old three-storey house had been professionally converted and the top floor was for rental, fully furnished.

The apartment had been vacant since the conversion and they would be the first occupants. It was expensive by Dublin standards but with the rate of exchange between sterling and the Irish punt it was less rent than they had paid for the small flat at Turnham Green.

Fisher signed a three-year lease in the name of Dawe and paid a quarter's rental in advance. They moved in the same day and Fisher knew instinctively that he had chosen the right place for at least their next few years.

The phone calls had moved his money from various banks to one bank in Basle. The small interest and the income from his investments would allow them to live modestly but comfortably for the rest of their lives. The following week he bought a small second-hand car.

CHAPTER 36

The trio had sung every verse of 'The West's Awake' and then, by popular demand, had started over again. It was a Saturday night and to an outsider it might look as if a riot was in progress, but in The Wishing Stone it was just a typical Saturday night. Everybody happy, and Guinness flowing faster than the Liffey.

When the dark-haired lad walked over and sat on the bench beside Old Charlie the old man recognised him. He said, 'And how's your father now?'

'Much the same. They say he's not got more than two or three weeks left.'

'God bless his soul, Lonnie. He's a lovely man and far too young to be . . .' he shrugged, '. . . is there anything I could be doing for him or your ma?'

'He's beyond helping.'

'And how's your Mairaed and the little girl?'

'They're fine.'

The old man smiled. 'She's a little dote that Mary. She'll be the lucky one all her life. You mark my words. You can see it in her face.'

'I hear you've got a new tenant on the top floor.'

'And so we have. A nice couple. Quiet and no bother to nobody. He's a Canadian. Retired.'

'He don't talk with a Canadian accent.'

'Who says so?'

'Aisling, the little girl who does the cleaning for them. And he keeps the spare bedroom locked. Special security locks.'

The old man shrugged. 'So what? Why shouldn't he?'

'Why should he? That's what I'd like to know.'

'You just mind your own bloody business, Lonnie. And keep your games the other side of the border.'

'What's his name?'

248

The old man looked at the younger man. 'What's it to you? He's not the kind that'll be of interest to your people.'

Lonnie smiled, but there was no smile in his eyes and the old man noticed that. 'So what's his name?'

'Dawe. David Dawe. And there's no cause for you to be takin' notice of him.'

The man called Lonnie stood up and pushed his way into the crowd around the bar.

It was three days later when Lonnie Ryan parked his car by the sweetshop and walked past the row of houses in the back streets of Dundalk. He slipped down the passage at the side and knocked on the door and waited. It was a couple of minutes before the door was opened by a young girl who pointed to the flight of uncarpeted stairs.

In the bedroom the tobacco smoke and stale air caught at his throat as the man sitting upright wrapped in a grey blanket pointed to a chair beside him.

The man's hair was laced with grey and his face had the raw redness of a man who had spent a lifetime working in the open air. His hand trembled as he reached out to tap his cigarette ash into a plastic bowl. His whole body was trembling for a moment and then he turned to look at his visitor.

'Did he turn up? The Arab?' He pronounced Arab the way Americans say it.

'Yeah. He turned up.'

'Who else was there?'

'Just him, me and Kenny.'

'And what did he say?'

'He said the shipment was on its way.'

'Where from?'

'Amsterdam.'

'Did he give you the name of the boat?'

'Yes. Declan checked on it. It's due in Cork tomorrow night. They'll be lying outside national waters about eight.'

'And Declan can deal with it?'

'He says he can.'

'You sound like you got doubts.'

'Maybe.'

The old man looked intently at the younger man's face and

his body shook again for several moments. When he was still he reached under the blanket and pulled out and unfolded a slip of paper. He read it, his lips moving silently, before he folded it and tucked it back below the blanket.

'The man at the place in Lansdowne Road. Dawe. The one we got the tip-off about.'

'Yeah.'

'I got Kevin to do some checking for us on the name they give us. His real name's David Beauclerc Fisher.'

'How'd he find this out?'

Lonnie smiled. 'He's got a contact. One of ours. He's a clerk at Century House. The passport in the name of Dawe was an official SIS forgery issued to a David Fisher.'

'Go on.'

'He's listed as a major in the Intelligence Corps on secondment to the Foreign Office.'

'Jesus God,' he said softly. 'And he sits there right in the middle of Dublin. Calm as you bloody like.' He sucked his teeth. 'Well, we'll shake that bastard up, that's for sure.'

'You'll do nothing of the sort, Lonnie. You'll carry out the orders I give you.' He nodded his head in time with his words. 'And you won't go anywhere near that man, nor his house. And you won't talk again to Old Charlie. Do you understand?' When Lonnie remained silent the old man said again, 'Do you understand, boy? Those are my orders.'

Lonnie nodded and stood up. At the door he turned and said angrily, 'Why are you letting him get away with it?'

'Maybe I'm not letting anyone get away with anything. There's more ways than one of skinning a cat.' He paused. 'Remember, if we hadn't got a friend in London we would never have spotted him.'

'So what?'

'So we got friends. Friends we can use.'

Thornton had read the two short paragraphs in the list of minor news items on page two of the *Evening Standard* and had passed on before he realised who they were about. It was quite brief. Arthur Padstow had been awarded a *decree nisi* that day on the grounds of what the judge had described as outrageous behaviour on the part of his wife Elaine Patricia Padstow. They had been married for only two years. There was a grainy picture of them standing on the steps of the Chelsea Registrar's Office on the day of their wedding.

The old man's hand was shaking violently as he let the phone fall back, clattering, onto its base. He closed his eyes as the trembling took over his whole body. The phone rang as he sat there, his body huddled under the blanket, then it stopped. As slowly the spasms subsided, the phone started ringing again. He lifted the receiver to his ear; only his hand was shaking now.

'Why d'you hang up, Michael, you got some problem?'

'Just one of my turns. It's gone now.' He sighed. 'Tell me what they said.'

'I spoke to the contact at their embassy . . .'

'Which one?'

'The Russkis.'

'Go on. What'd he say?'

'Dead cool. I had the feeling he knew about him already.'

'Did you tell him what we had in mind?'

'Just an outline. Sat there po-faced. Said they weren't interested. But I think he was. Took it all in anyway.'

'And the others?'

'Well, you know the Brits. You can't tell what those bastards are thinking. Like the other fella, said they weren't interested. But they was. And I think they weren't surprised.'

'How do you know?'

The other man laughed harshly. 'They left the S & W at the place we said. By the telephone kiosk.'

'Anything else?'

'No.'

'When you gonna do it?'

'Sunday.'

'Good luck.'

'Keep takin' the pills, old 'un. We need that crafty mind of yours.'

While he was giving his report to Hallam Thornton sensed that something had changed. He had a feeling that Hallam's interest was feigned. He wasn't listening to the dates and places, he was only listening because it was his duty. When

Thornton had finished he waited for Hallam's comments. But Hallam looked back at him as if he was waiting for more.

'That's all I have to report, sir.'

'What? Oh yes. Right,' Hallam said, as he moved his pipe nearer the tobacco tin. He looked across at Thornton, his lips pursed. 'You know, I've got a hunch that we're flogging a dead horse, Thornton. Wasting the valuable time of an experienced man.' He searched his pockets for something that he appeared not to find. 'What do you think?'

'Whose time are we wasting?'

'Yours. And Smallwood's of course. I've got the feeling that we might as well call it a day. If he was going to cause any trouble he'd have been at it by now.'

'You mean you want to call off the search for him?'

'Yes.'

'But why?'

'Look. Because of a piece of carelessness by Macleod, Fisher walked out. Angry that he hadn't been warned. Who can blame him? If he'd raised hell with me I could have put things right, maybe. But even if I'd put a full team on the house Fisher would never have forgotten that his wife was left in danger for over forty-eight hours. To him that would be unforgivable. So he walks out.

'It wasn't premeditated. They left their car, furniture and household goods. But now he'll have cooled down.' Hallam shrugged. 'OK. He doesn't like us. He's washed his hands of us. But that's all. If he was going to cause trouble he'd have contacted us before now. There's no hard evidence he could provide. Everything's been tidied up and destroyed. Nobody'd believe him if he decided to make a song and dance about what we'd been up to.' Hallam half-smiled. 'There's times when I don't believe it myself.'

Hallam stood up. 'Have you heard of a group that calls itself The Levellers?'

'Only what I've seen in the press and on the radio.'

'I think it's time we gave them the once-over and I had in mind you and Smallwood. You seem to work well together . . . it would be a step up in grade for both of you.'

They had closed the lane to traffic and two soldiers with sub-machine guns stood guarding the tapes that marked off the area. An RUC Land-rover and a camouflaged half-track were parked by two civilian cars. The Land-rover's engine was running and a cable from the battery led to a light over the group of men by the ditch. A green canvas sheet had been stretched across two iron staves to protect the two bodies from the thin drizzle.

An army captain was holding a torch for the doctor. When the doctor stood up he cleaned his hands with a tissue as he collected his thoughts. Then he looked at the captain. 'How long did you leave them in case they were booby-trapped?'

'Nearly an hour.'

'You're sure it wasn't longer?'

'Quite sure.'

'OK. There's massive lividity on both bodies. I'd say they were killed somewhere else and dumped here later. They've been dead at least eight hours.'

'Enough time for them to have been brought over the border.'

The doctor sighed and nodded. 'Another thing. They were shot in the head after they were already dead. Two shots in each head. There are a lot of bruises on the man so he must have put up quite a struggle. The shot that actually killed him made scorch marks on his clothing. The woman the same. No signs of sexual assault.' He shrugged. 'Have you taken photographs?'

'Yes.'

'OK. I understand your people want an immediate autopsy, is that right?'

'Yes.'

'I'll warn Dr Simmonds when I get back. You take them to our own lab not the mortuary. OK?'

'OK, sir.'

Major Richards, SAS, had been roused from his sleep by Lieutenant Phillips, accompanied by the pathologist. He sat on his bunk in his dressing-gown and listened attentively to the pathologist's comments. When he had finished, Richards said quietly, 'What you're saying is that both the man and the woman were killed by gunshots. That they died instantly. But the man had put up a struggle. And that some hours later they had both been shot in the head. Despite the fact that they were both already dead. Is that it?'

'That's roughly the evidence, sir,' the pathologist said.

Richards looked at his junior officer. 'And ballistics say that the fatal wounds were in both cases made by 9 mm bullets almost certainly fired from a pistol and that the head wounds were definitely caused by .38s from a revolver. Almost certainly a Smith & Wesson.'

'Yes, sir.'

'Have you informed Special Branch?'

'Not until I'd spoken to you, sir.'

'OK. I'll speak to them myself.'

'Right, sir.'

Thornton had been in the flat for ten minutes before he noticed the envelope propped up on the mantelpiece over the gas fire. It had his name on it and he tore it open slowly and unfolded the note inside.

Dear, dear Robbie,

I hate having to write this note but it has to be done. It's been ages since I've seen you to talk to.

I've been thinking things over these last few weeks because I've been torn between two choices. You might remember Joey Rose who was our ASM at the start of the run. (He's now SM.) He's asked me to marry him. I like him a lot and I think I would have said 'yes' on the spot if it hadn't been for you.

But in thinking about us I had doubts on that score too. I've come to the conclusion that you're not the marrying kind. It may be because of your job but I've got the feeling that it's more than that. As you know, I was concerned that you didn't do more to get custody of Jamie and I'd hoped that if you had him you might feel that I'd make a good step-mum and wife. But I don't think that was ever in your mind. Not for him nor for me.

So I decided to say 'yes' to Joey and we're getting married when the show goes to Birmingham. As you can guess, I've shed some tears over all this and there's a lot I'm going to miss, especially you and your funny ways.

I hope you'll understand and I hope all goes well with you and Jamie.

Love,
Penny

P.S. The small parcel is for you – with love.

Thornton unwrapped the oblong parcel that had been placed behind the note on the mantelpiece.

It was a Hornby Dublo locomotive – 'Duchess of Athol'.

The news of the double murder on the Northern Ireland border was the third item on *News at Ten* and although it didn't give the victims' names Hallam switched off the TV as soon as it started.

Smallwood also saw it on TV and Thornton read it in the following day's newspaper but neither of them saw any significance in the item.

Thornton sat on the bench in the September sunshine watching them looking at the sea-lions being fed. It didn't remind him of when Penny had sat there and it had been he who was standing by the rails with Jamie.

Elaine was wearing a wide-brimmed straw hat with a cluster of daisies caught by a white ribbon, and she was laughing as she pointed something out to Jamie. The white cotton dress made her look young and vulnerable. As they turned to walk back to him her hand went to her hat against a sudden breeze and he was aware of the dress clinging to her long, elegant legs.

They had tea at Lyons at Charing Cross and had gone back to her friend's flat and played Monopoly until it was time for Jamie to go to bed.

She made coffee for herself and Thornton when she came back and as they sat there she said, 'What's Penny doing? Is she still in the show?'

He nodded. 'Yes, they're opening on tour next week.'

As he put his cup on the low table she got up and sat on his lap, one slim arm around his shoulder. She looked at his face for a moment and then said, 'Thanks for not trying to take Jamie away from me.'

She kissed him gently on the mouth and from old habits and instincts his hand closed over one of her big breasts. For long moments her mouth responded and then she drew back her head and smiled at him as she said softly, 'Do you want to do it to me?'

It was past midnight when she reached over to the bedside table for a cigarette and before she lit it she said, 'Do you want to stay the night?'

'Thanks,' he said. 'But I'd better get back.'